I0593410

The Dragonfly

The Rohendra Complex, Book 1

Georgina Makalani

Cover Design by Deranged Doctor Designs

Paperback ISBN: 978-0-6453956-6-2

Also by Georgina Makalani

The Dragon Skin Chronicles
The Legend of Iski Flare
The Magics of Rei-Een
The Mark of Oldra
The Raven Crown

The Rohendra Complex:
The Dragonfly
Sparrow Song
Shimmering Bear
Rohendra Queen

One

I sla flinched as the young, dark-haired man kicked the side of his racer. The sun-bleached paintwork had been sandblasted smooth from racing across the desert planet's course. If he continued to treat the machine that way, he wasn't going to last the race. But then, he rarely did, and taking his frustration out on the racer wouldn't make his chances of winning any better this time.

Isla placed her hand on the warm metal of her own racer and closed her eyes. She walked alongside it, her fingers moving over the smooth surface as she breathed in the bitter scent of the metal. She patted it gently, as though it were alive.

The alarm sounded. She stepped nimbly up onto the single, rickety step and leapt into the cockpit. She clicked her seat belts into place in the same motion as the tinted cover closed above her. Taking a deep breath, Isla held her hands above the panel before her. Her sole focus was the race ahead. Despite the excitement and her certainty that she had a good chance to win this time, she was calm. Her red curls were restrained in a long braid down her back, any fly-aways tucked under the helmet—not that she needed one. But she liked the idea of the old racers from the histories, and she'd found it in a junk shop when she'd first arrived on Urgway.

She often came close to winning, but this time it was her turn. She knew it. Maybe the other racers had felt it too, for one of them had stared at her a little too long in the pit that morning. She hadn't seen him before, or if she had, she hadn't noticed him. With his blond hair falling across his face, she had wondered how he would see to race.

She grinned at the idea that he might have heard about her racing and considered her a strong contender. Her heart rate increased as she waited for the starting buzzer. He might have recognised her from somewhere else. But that was a long time ago, and she hadn't wanted to be remembered. That was why she was out here on Urgway racing under the blistering sun.

The sound of the second alarm drew her from her thoughts, and she focused ahead of her as she started her engine. The vibration of the machine moved through her as the hum of engines matched her heartbeat. The announcer's voice filled the cockpit with the single word "Go." She moved her fingers slowly downward as the racer shot forward and past the racer that had been kicked, sure something dropped off it as she passed.

Isla moved quickly into the lead. She glanced around her through the tinted cover and then down at the small monitor hovering above the instruments, and both actions confirmed the same. She was in front. She grinned, pushed her racer faster and stretched out the lead. A mountain loomed ahead of her and she banked easily to the left, following the course. It was more like a simulation than a race. With no one else around her, she could focus on the course.

She banked right, gliding through a narrow pass. As she watched the world rush towards her, she ran her hand over the sensor to ensure she hadn't damaged her ship. A ping sounded, and she groaned. They were catching up to her, although there were fewer racers following only partway into the race.

She banked again, following the edge of the ravine around as it curved sharply to the right, and then there was nothing but desert before her. She pushed forward. The sudden lack of landmarks might have put her off, but she had raced the course many times before and the course was clearly marked on the monitor just below her line of sight. Any deviation from the set course would mean disqualification. Each vehicle started out as a standard racer, and yet it was theirs to maintain and upgrade as they had the means to, or the inclination. Isla didn't have the funds, but she had the know-how. She had spent a lot of hours tinkering with all manner of vessels in her past, and her racer had been no different. Her control panel was all her own work. She had spent the time working on it that she would have wanted to spend on her own ship, the only thing of value she did own. She'd left that with an old friend to watch over. For the moment, racing and this racer was all she needed.

Few tried to install systems that would give them an unnatural advantage. Although the racing industry wasn't well regulated, the authorities came down hard on cheating. It was a risk she wasn't willing to take. They might only start with confiscating her racer, but the few she knew had been caught cheating had never been seen again. She could only guess what might have happened to them.

Isla needed to race. It was the only freedom she had—it was all she had. Even if she was just entertainment for others, others with power and wealth. She would race until she could race no more.

A racer appeared in front of her, and she cursed as she tried to manoeuvre around it. Where had it come from? It certainly wasn't part of the race. It wasn't a racer she recognised, and after five years, she knew every ship. It pulled out ahead of her. She pushed her hands down into the controls, racing after it. She was going to win this one. She had to win this one.

She glanced at her monitor, and the ship ahead of her wasn't showing on her map. Heavy uncertainty settled in her gut.

"Control," she said, moving her hand to activate the communicator.

There was only static. She must have been too far out on the course, although they should have had deflectors up in case something happened and a racer needed to make contact. There were enough crashes during the average race to warrant that.

"Control," she tried again. "Unauthorised vehicle on the course."

More static. The other racer was pulling away, and she couldn't let it win. But as she glanced at the map, she realised it was leaving the course. She turned left sharply to ensure she stayed within the markers, cursed herself for getting distracted and flicked her hand angrily over the panel. "Control!" she screamed.

Someone was trying to put her off. Someone saw her as a threat, and she couldn't let that interfere with her winning. "OK," she murmured.

The rest of the pack were catching up to her. Four racers were close behind and then one pulled alongside her, the new guy with the hair. His wings were too close to hers. Alarms sounded around the cabin as she cursed again.

She couldn't increase the distance between them despite accelerating as much as possible, and she cursed loudly as something bumped her from beneath.

"What is it with people not following the rules today?" she growled.

She had heard of some racers doing odd things to spice it up for the crowd. *Watching small fast craft should be enough.* Isla rose up as another bump hit her hull. A bridge spanned across the cavern before her, and she rose up and over it before she realised she had missed the course. She thumped her hand on the panel as a voice filled the cockpit.

"Disqualified."

"Damn it," she grumbled.

She hadn't left the course, just didn't complete a task.

"Return to the stables," the same voice instructed.

Isla slowed down and hovered above the race. This was supposed to be her race. There was no sign of the impostor. As she watched the racers fly into the distance, the new guy who had nearly touched her wing blew up. The whole world went into slow motion as the smoke filled the course and the remains of the ship dropped like a stone from the sky. She didn't wish for anyone's race to end like that.

Deflated, she was about to turn for the stables when she caught sight of something bright on the sand beneath. She ran a hand over the control panel. A small blip lit up on the screen. "Damn it," she grumbled again and took the racer down towards the ground.

Isla slowly flew towards the base of the cliffs, looking around and searching her sensors at the same time. The blip might not be the racer. There were people who lived out here, although how they survived, she had no idea. She didn't know what they might do to scrounge a wreck even if they found someone in it.

A sick feeling filled her chest. "Damn it!" The ship touched down on the soft sand. The sunlight could melt a man on the surface. Isla had enough protection in the ship to not notice the heat while racing, but willingly heading out onto the surface was something very different.

Tucked into the narrow pocket at the back of her seat was a cloak. As her fingers found it and pulled it from its hiding spot, she knew she was making a mistake. The cloak held too many memories, but she pushed those aside as she unbuckled herself and held it over her head. She hit the release, and the tinted cover slid open.

"Don't look up," she muttered to herself as she stood in the well and looked out at the distant wreck of the other racer.

It was a jump down into the sand, and she wasn't quite sure what she would do when she got out there, or if she managed to find this guy alive. A thin line of black smoke wove into the sky. She glanced back at the monitor and the lone red flashing dot. How he had survived, she had no idea. She only hoped she didn't die trying to help him as she leapt out into the sand and pulled the cloak around her.

She heard the roar of the racers as they flew somewhere above her. She didn't look after them. She didn't want to know who was winning her race. She just trudged forward through the soft, hot sand towards the black line of smoke and the racer it indicated. Another ship zipped above her, and she was reminded of her childhood, listening to them fly past and imagining the freedom she'd thought racing would bring.

It was only when she was halfway between the racer and the wreck that she worried it might be a trap. No one could have survived such an explosion, let alone the fall. But she continued on, then tried to run through the sand when she saw him sprawled out on it. His blond hair had fallen back, and his pale skin was already burning in the sun or had burnt from the explosion. Either way, she couldn't leave him out here.

Isla nudged his still body with her foot, and he groaned. "Damn it," she muttered. "This is a bad idea," she told herself as she hooked an arm under his back. He groaned again. She lifted him to his feet with a groan of her own and then wondered why she hadn't called for help. She tucked her cloak around him and started towards the racer, but his feet or legs weren't working. He slipped from her grasp and into the exposed hot sand at her feet.

She held the cloak out over him as best she could and looked back to the racer. There was no way they would make it together, and she couldn't leave him here. Something blinked in the sand behind the racer, something reflecting the light. She heard the quiet hum of a machine, and then a larger ship came into view. It was sand coloured, flying low, and very nearly took out her racer as it flew past it to land just before her.

Before she had a chance to determine if it was there to help, a ramp opened in the side and three men rushed forward. They were dressed in the same sand-coloured material, wound loosely around their bodies and around their heads, their faces covered.

Two picked up the man at her feet and carried him without hesitation back onto the ship; the third reached for her arm as he indicated the ship. She didn't think she had a choice here, but she couldn't seem to move.

"Please." His voice was polite, but he had a Urgway accent. Isla hesitated before she nodded once and allowed him to lead her onto the ship. The door closed immediately behind her and the ship lifted into the air. She looked back through the small porthole towards her racer to see someone else climbing into its cockpit.

"Hey!"

"You don't want it left out there, do you?"

She shook her head, but she wasn't sure where they were taking her.

The blond man rolled over and groaned, then tried to climb to his knees.

"Do you want to explain exactly what you were doing?" Isla asked, aiming all her frustrations at him.

He raised his bright blue eyes to hers, and she tried to maintain his stare as he smiled and blew out softly, trying to lift the hair from his face. "You're welcome," he murmured.

"Excuse me? You very nearly took me out."

"And then someone took him out," said the man who had directed her into the ship, his arms crossed and a disappointed look on his face. She reached for a handhold as the ship shuddered and the blond man slipped back to the floor.

"I think you should be thanking me," she said, looking between them. "You would have burnt to a crisp."

"That is a nice cloak, Ms Tarle," the blond man wheezed, his eyes closing against obvious pain.

She gritted her teeth. The other man gave a small smile. "Reilly," he said, tapping his chest, "and this is..."

"I don't care who you are," she snapped. "And my name is Isla Dee."

"Of course, it is," Reilly said, the smirk growing wider.

"And I was helping," the man on the floor murmured. She almost missed it over the hum of the engines.

"Helping who?"

"You," Reilly offered.

"He's a racer who tried to knock me out. He was trying to win. Did Boss set you up for this?"

"Ms Tarle," he whispered hoarsely, then coughed. Reilly rested a hand on his shoulder.

"You haven't been racing very long, have you?" she continued as though he hadn't used that name again.

"Everyone in the Complex knows who you are," Reilly said. She glared at him, and he looked down at the man he was squatted over.

"Are you spying? Did someone send you in?"

"We were watching, sure that something was going on that shouldn't be. Didn't expect to come across you, but I think someone else recognised you."

She glared again. "No one cares who I am. And what could be going on that you would need to be watching some racers?"

"Why are you on Urgway?"

"I'm a racer. I've been a racer for five years," she said.

"How have you been racing for five years with no one working out who you are?"

Isla looked around. "What does it matter? I'm just a racer."

"No one here is just a racer. Everyone is hiding from something, but they aren't as anonymous as you think."

She shook her head then. "What do you think you are learning from this? What would Boss know other than the occasional rigged race?" Not that she had been asked to throw or win a race herself. There were times she'd been asked to help others win, but that was different. And she just wanted to be out there, racing free and fast. The risk, she thought. That was the draw. The risk wasn't as great as she had faced before, but it helped her make it through the day.

"So, you want to tell us what you're doing here?" the man asked. The bright light around them disappeared as they flew under low hanging rocks. She stepped around him and over the pilot's shoulder to look at the cave they were angling towards.

They seemed to be maintaining their current speed, and she wondered if the ship would fit through the rough narrow entrance. The sensors lit up, outlining the tunnel ahead despite nothing visible but black. Isla clutched at the back of the pilot's seat. She could feel the purr of the engines, and they were travelling far too fast. But then, they might have come this way before.

The dark continued for too long. She closed her eyes against it, her grip tightening. When she took a deep breath and opened them again, there was a faint light in the distance. She looked between it and the panel. The ship slowed, and the door opened without hesitation. The young man who had piloted the ship unbuckled, stood and then looked at her as though surprised to find her right behind him. He looked over her shoulder, then back, and indicated the door. She turned slowly, prised her fingers from the seat and followed Reilly, who was supporting the other man down from the ship.

She followed slowly behind. She wouldn't like to try and fly out of here on her own. Several others rushed forward to take the other man from Reilly and help him inside the building that had been built into whatever rock structure they were under. Isla stepped forward into the light, and those moving around barely stopped to take her in.

The space was large. She walked to the nearest wall and put her hands to the cool metal.

"How did you build this here?" she asked.

"We didn't," Reilly answered as they helped the blond man onto a narrow bed. The wall behind him came to life with images and lights, she hadn't seen technology of this level for some time. "We found it."

"And those who built it?" she asked, stepping forward.

Reilly shrugged and turned to the blond man, who was trying to sit up. An older woman stepped forward and put her hand to his chest. "Give it a minute," she said, but she was looking at the indicators on the wall and not the patient.

Isla leaned against the cool metal and watched as the woman put some information into a panel. Then a thin blue light moved out from the wall and formed a shield around the man.

"You're a hummer," someone whispered.

Isla laughed, and turned back to the room. "Hummers don't exist."

"Maybe," Reilly said.

"Where is my racer?" Isla pushed her helmet back and ran her hands over her wayward hair, sure that the curls were sticking up all over. "And what were you doing, pushing me out of the race? I was winning."

"You were never winning," the blond man murmured from within his blue cocoon. The older woman shushed him.

Isla hadn't been in a place like this in more than five years. The blue light winked out, and the man sat up and swung his legs off the bed. He waited while the woman ran a scanner over his skin. Then she nodded, and he sat up. His skin was pink, but clear of the burns from his exposure to the harsh Urgway sunlight.

"You haven't answered any of my questions," Isla said, crossing her arms.

"You didn't have to come back for me."

"I couldn't leave you to die," she murmured. "How long have you been here?" she asked the older woman, who glanced over her shoulder at Isla but said nothing. Instead, she looked to Reilly and then left the room.

"So, who is trying to kill you, little hummer?" the man asked.

"I'm not a hummer, and no one."

"You were lucky he took the hit for you," Reilly said while the blond man just grinned.

"The hit?"

"Sniper in the rocks, and then there was the racer that wasn't a racer."

"Maybe they were trying to disrupt the race," Isla said softly, remembering the race continuing above her. Although she had been sent back to the stables, there hadn't been an emergency vehicle racing out to help the damaged ship.

"Were you even in the race?" she asked.

"He wouldn't have made it as far as the starting gates if he wasn't," Reilly answered.

The blond man held out his hand. "I'm..."

"I don't want to know," Isla interrupted. "The less I know, the better. I won't tell anyone where you are, and I'm grateful you helped him, even if he caused all the mess." The man's hand dropped back into his lap, and he gave her a look she couldn't read. "Now take me back to my racer."

"Where do you think you can go?" Reilly asked.

"The stables, for a start. They'll be mighty pissed that I didn't return when directed. If I have to sit out a race for this, you'll be the one paying." She pointed a finger at him. "I was going to win this one."

He shook his head and looked down at his hands. "Surviving is winning," he mumbled.

"Don't care," she returned, then walked back out into the main space and through the people working on various screens. A few people looked up as she drew closer, but she wasn't interested in what they were doing. She only wanted her racer back. She tried not to see the weapons, but it was too late. As she turned slowly to the man who had led them here, he crossed his arms, and she wondered if she was ever going to get out.

"Don't care," she repeated. He sighed and indicated down a tunnel with his chin. She nodded her thanks and headed that way. It was wide and dark, and she felt along the wall as she stomped along it. Her heart rate was far too fast. Although the cool metal was somewhat comforting, she needed light. It was almost as she thought it that the dim light ahead of her brightened. She smiled as she stepped out into another large space. This one was filled with vehicles and ships, her racer in the middle of it. She walked straight to it and put her hand against the worn paintwork. "Did they hurt you?" she whispered.

"It's a fine ship," a young man said, appearing around the edge of it. His hair hung in his face and he wiped it back with greasy hands, which he then wiped on the rag hanging from his overalls. He looked like one of the mechanics from the race pit, but she would never let any of them close to her ship.

"What did you do to her?" she demanded, her hand still on the metal.

He raised his hands in defence. "Not a thing. Just looked her over."

"Did he hurt you?" she asked the racer, and he looked at her as though she were odd. Which wouldn't be the first time. But this little racer had done her well.

"Impressive wingspan," he said. "I'm surprised you made it through the pass."

Isla stared at the boy. He fidgeted, clearly waiting for some sort of response.

"I have to go," she said, looking for a way to clamber into the racer. Usually, she was leaping in or out of it against the starter blocks. And it suddenly seemed too hard. She unclipped the cape from around her chin and rolled it into a tight ball.

"That looks military." He nodded at the wad of material in her hand.

"Picked it up at some junk shop," she muttered, looking around for some steps.

"They are worth thousands."

She turned on him then, and he looked at her seriously. Then he nodded, skipped away, and returned promptly with an old set of steps.

"You were lucky to have survived all that," he said, standing too close behind her as she climbed up and into the racer.

"They both were," Reilly said, appearing in the door. "You can get back to work now, Johnny."

Johnny nodded and looked around again, then disappeared.

"I need to leave," Isla said firmly.

"I think you need to stay."

"Lucky for me, you don't get a say. But I do have to report back." She ran a hand over the panel. The controls lit up, and she knew no one had tampered with anything.

"And where did you get a panel that sophisticated?"

"I made it," she muttered without looking up. "Control."

"You won't get a signal in here."

"I can get a signal anywhere," she said. "Control."

There was no response, and she could find nothing on her sensors. "Damn it," she murmured, then started the engines. She felt their hum, the slight rise from the deck, the loud swearing of someone too close to the ship. She grinned as Reilly scampered away.

"I won't say anything," she called out and lifted higher into the space.

Isla glanced at the controls and ran her hand above where her race map usually was. A map appeared, showing her the tunnel ahead and the open space beyond. The race would be over now—she just had to hope they weren't going to shoot her out of the sky as she approached the stables.

Two

Isla touched down without incident in the pit, only to be greeted by the stable master—an overweight, grubby frangar who was too friendly, stood too close and, if she wasn't paying attention, would take the opportunity to grab whatever he could reach. She wasn't alone; other racers, no matter their species or gender, all endured the same.

"Twiggy," she murmured, hovering in the racer.

Frangars were native to Oric, as widespread across the Complex as humans, and not usually as round as Twiggy. He was all pink skin, which she was sure would burn at the idea of heading outside in the Urgway daylight. He barely covered it, and it exuded a pungent odour. His face was similar to a man's, but with a flatter nose, and instead of ears he had two large tentacle-like protrusions that grew from the top of his head. They were usually short, hanging to his chin, and at times they could extend down his back. Isla was sure they did much of the grabbing.

"You didn't win then." He smirked and spat out whatever he had been chewing. She had been trying to guess what the substance might be for as long as she had known him, and she was still trying.

"Fell out of the sky," she murmured, climbing down from the racer and trying not to turn her back on him.

"Racer looks ok. You want me to run an eye over her?"

"Nah, all good." She made to walk away when a woman, tall and too thin, stepped out from behind another racer into her path. It took everything she had not to jump. "Boss."

"You were recalled."

"Had some trouble getting back."

"That is not like you, Isla." She was too sweet. "You seem to be able to fix anything on your racer with just a look."

Isla gave her a shrug. "So, who won?"

"Cruzer," the woman said, her grin too tight across her face. Isla forced a smile across her own.

"I should go say well done." She made her way around the woman, only to be stopped by a slender hand on her arm and too-sharp nails pressed into her skin. Isla looked at the hand pointedly, then back to the woman when she didn't let go. "Problem, Boss?"

"You tell me." The tone was dangerous. Isla wondered just what Boss knew.

She shook her head quickly and made to walk away again.

"How long have you been with us, Isla?" Boss asked.

"Feels like forever," she said casually. If pressed, Isla could have told her down to the minute.

"Five years."

"Really, that long? Well, what do you know? I should catch Cruzer."

"Leave him," Boss growled, and Isla stopped.

"I got knocked out," she said matter-of-factly. "I got knocked about. It took a bit to fix it. I tried to call it in, but got no response."

Boss cocked her head to the side. Isla knew she didn't believe her, but she wondered what else she knew that she wasn't telling. Isla waited. She didn't want to provoke Boss, but she also didn't want to stand there all day trying to make conversation. Isla glanced over her shoulder at the racer, wondering what secrets it might hold and possibly tell.

"You've done wonders with this machine," Boss muttered, her gaze lifting from Isla for the first time as her hand rested on the side of the racer. Isla had the same feeling she got when Twiggy tried to grab her.

She waited, unsure what Boss wanted to hear.

"Maybe it is time we helped you win a few more."

"Really?" Isla asked. She was fairly sure the races she'd won had been with her own skill alone.

Boss grinned, and Isla nodded. She wondered about the men she had met out in the desert. They knew there was more going on, although she wasn't sure she believed them. Would Boss want her dead, or was it someone else?

"A ship exploded during the race," she blurted, and the look on Boss's face didn't change. "Was someone hurt?"

Boss shook her head slowly. "I think you made a mistake," she said softly.

"It happened right in front of me," Isla continued. She had heard the danger in Boss's voice, but was unable to heed the warning inside her head.

"No explosion. No one lost."

"That's a relief," Isla said, turning away again. Was she insane?

"What are you doing, Isla?" This time, the tone of Boss's voice made every hair on her body stand to attention. Although she had her back to the woman, it took everything she had not to look up at her hair and see if that too was standing up.

"Change rooms," Isla muttered, taking a slow step forward, half expecting the woman to stop her again. But when the silence continued, so did she. She almost ran the last part of the hallway and into the open space. There was no one there; there never was. No one used the change rooms anymore. Everyone had their own small room with facilities above the stables. In many ways, it was like being back in the corps.

Isla ran her hand over the old-style lockers. As her finger brushed across one, it opened with a gentle click. She glanced over her shoulder before opening it wider and looking at the small package inside. She wasn't willing to give up the weapon, but she couldn't carry it with her. It was against regulations. She wasn't going to leave it in her room because she doubted it was the private space they were guaranteed. Twiggy would likely rummage through her things the moment she was out on the track.

She tucked it inside her belt and cursed the fitted flying outfit. She withdrew the weapon and put it inside her helmet, tucked it all under an arm and hoped no one stopped her. She wasn't sure what she would have done out on the planet's surface if she had been armed.

"Damn it," she murmured as she headed back out into the corridor. She looked both ways to ensure there was no one around and then headed towards the lift to take her up to her quarters.

"You heard the news?" a cocky voice called out behind her as she waited for the door to open.

She tried not to groan, turning with a grin she was sure matched the man's marching towards her. "Well done," she said, trying to sound like she meant it.

"I was sure you had it in the bag this time. You were so far out!" He slapped her hard on the shoulder as they stepped into the lift, and she nearly dropped her helmet.

"Bloody fault took me out."

"With that machine?"

She tried not to look around.

"You have that thing running better than the military cruisers—even The Hendra's own guard would kill for a ship that ran like yours."

"And yet I win so few races."

"Three in a row for me," he said, as though it was nothing but everything at the same time.

"Mmm," she grumbled.

"Talk to Boss. Maybe she could fix things."

Isla turned and looked him over as he grinned. Why was she always so surprised that the racers accepted it was fixed? Isla was sure it depended on who had money against them. Her odds were certainly pretty good now. When she'd first started, she was winning nearly every race, and then Boss wouldn't put her up.

"How far behind me were you when I fell out of the race?" she asked as the door opened and she stepped out onto her floor. The racers from the same division tended to be housed together, so Cruzer wasn't too far from her room.

"Didn't see you," he said, turning down the nearest corridor.

"Cruzer?"

He stopped and turned around, giving her a shrug. "You were so far out in front I thought you had already won. It wasn't until Control called in that I knew I was winning."

"Don't you have a map? Trackers?"

He shrugged again and walked off. She wondered what else he had gained by winning, or what he might have been offered. She was tempted to call after him again and tell him Boss had offered her another chance at winning, but she was standing in the middle of the hall with a military-issue weapon. Better not to be caught.

She entered her room to find the bedding crinkled. Someone had sat on it. Her hand closed around the handle of the Starduster in her helmet, and she waited. For a small weapon, it was surprisingly effective, usually referred to as a duster. The nickname belied the power within. There was no sound and nowhere for anyone to hide in the small room. But it gave her theory bones that Twiggy had been in here. She sniffed but couldn't detect his pungent body odour. Maybe it had been Boss, or they had sent in a lacky.

She smoothed over the blanket, making it crisp. The sarge would have been proud, if he'd had the chance to see. Although a well-made bed was really all she had to boast about, and that would disappoint the sarge more than she would like to guess at.

She pulled the band from her braid and ran her fingers through her hair, getting them snagged several times as she tried to pull the braid free. After she had thrown the helmet and duster on the perfect bed, she put her pin code into the door and hoped it held while she stripped off her racing uniform, glanced again at the handgun and stepped into the shower bay. Hot water streamed over her skin, and she flinched. She must have burnt her arm after all in the heat of the desert.

She had tried to shield herself, but it had been hard to do that and pick up the guy who had been blasted out of the sky. She wasn't sure how he had survived. First the blast, which had destroyed his ship completely, and then the fall.

She suspected that he might have faked it all. He wanted her attention, wanted to get her out in the desert. She could see him sitting on the edge of the bed, his skin damaged, keen to introduce himself. But no, she wouldn't think of him again.

The water stopped too soon. Isla allowed the hot air to dry her off, sure her hair was frizzier than when she'd gotten in. She walked out into her room naked, catching glimpses of her scarred body in the mirror she tried to avoid before she threw on an old oversized t-shirt and a pair of shorts. She breathed in the scent of the cloth, disappointed that it now only smelt of laundry soap, and then returned to the washroom to gather two small tubs of cream.

The contents of the first one smelt of the forest. The relief was immediate as she rubbed it carefully over her burnt arm. It would be healed by morning. The other she smothered over her hands and then raked through her hair. Soft curls bounced around her shoulders and down her back. She rarely wore it out now, let alone out of the room, and she pulled it back into a loose, messy bun. Tomorrow she would tame it into a tight braid, which would again have worked its way free by the afternoon.

She lay back on the bed, the duster across her chest, and closed her eyes. Another man came to mind, one she didn't allow herself to think of very often. But the sandy-haired man she had tried to drag from the heat of the surface had reminded her somewhat of him, if only in the blue eyes they shared, and possibly his height and broad shoulders. Not that she was looking. She rolled towards the door, the duster still tight in her hand.

"Dim," she murmured. The lighting of the room reduced but did not go out. She couldn't sleep in the dark, even with that kind of firepower at hand.

Standing at the gate the next morning, Isla found that she wasn't as enthusiastic for the race as she wanted to be. She knew it was hers. Boss had made that clear, and even Twiggy had winked at her when she'd gone to warm up the ship. But she hadn't slept well, plagued by dreams she'd thought long gone. She rested her hand against the ship, hoping the familiar feel of the metal would help draw out some enthusiasm. But she was still standing there when the first buzzer sounded.

She walked too slowly and climbed in. The starter sounded before she had even buckled herself in. She waved her hand over the panels and started the engine. She pushed her fingers through the controls, and the ship lurched forward. She growled something about Twiggy, wondering if anything was every truly hers as she tried to focus on the racers pulling away from her.

"Too many ghosts," she muttered as Cruzer took the lead.

He was not going to beat her this time.

"Come on," she growled, pulling a belt around her middle while pushing her hand forward over the controls. This was her turn.

Isla moved easily through the field of ships around her, but she couldn't quite get around Cruzer. She cursed and grumbled as she watched the race map, doing everything she could to overtake him. When she moved up, so did he. When she tried to slip underneath him, he suddenly dropped from the sky before she could manoeuvre past him.

"It's like he knows what I'll do before I even do it," she muttered, looking over the control and trying to work out what the others were doing. The field was tight. Although she was at the front with Cruzer, it would only take a small mistake for someone else to take that lead from them. She shook her head. She didn't like this. "Has Twiggy done something to you?" she asked the ship.

"Did you call in, lovely girl?" the slimy voice came over her headset.

"No, Control."

"Sure?"

They were midrace—what was he playing at? They never talked to Control unless there was a problem. Or they were getting specific information or instructions. Isla ran her hand over the communication panel. Although the lights dimmed, she knew they weren't out.

"What you playing at, Twiggy?" she muttered.

"Could ask you the same," he returned too quickly.

Before she could reply, another racer pulled too close beside her, nearly clipping her wing. She cursed.

"Problem?" Twiggy asked, his voice too chirpy.

She wasn't going to be winning this one either. Maybe the guy in the desert was right. But why would they want to take her out? She was good, she knew that, but it wasn't like she was dominating the race wins. Despite the Boss's talk of helping her out, she knew it would never happen. Isla was entertainment, one of the few female racers, one of the few ex-military. Although, she hoped no one remembered her anymore. She'd served long ago, and people didn't remember war heroes like they used to.

Not that she would ever describe herself as such, but back then they had honoured her in such a way. That had been far from here, this little dry planet they raced around. They would spend several weeks or months racing in an area and then move the whole thing to the next city or region. Buildings, stables, crew. Sometimes accidents happened; sometimes people were hurt, but they rarely died. And none at her hands. She worked her fingers across the panel, slowing down enough that she was still in the race, but not near the front of it. The panel glowed green and the communication light went out. She grinned. That would fix Twiggy and his floppy ears.

"Control. I have a problem. Control."

Nothing. She ran her hand over another part of the panel and made sure all communication and microphones within the cockpit were disabled.

Another racer skimmed past her. Isla banked, taking the corner with them, but they were closer than they needed to be. She sucked in a breath and, moving her hands slowly through the panel, she flew forward, leaving them behind. Something caught the corner of her eye, and a rock face started to crumble. At first, she couldn't believe it was happening. Pebbles, followed by rocks, and then the top of the cliff all tumbled down into the raceway.

She pulled up just as a rock hit the side of the racer who had touched her, and they were thrown out of the race line. They wobbled back and forth, a stream of black smoke trailing behind as she watched them land.

Isla's sensors showed someone on the ridge, but she kept racing forward. She overtook the two racers in front of her with little effort, although they tried to make it difficult. They nearly took themselves out in the process. This was turning into the race from hell. Someone else shot in beside her, dropping out of the sky, and her sensors couldn't identify them. Not a racer, although they looked like one—likely the same ship that had tried to take her out the day before.

The bang to the side of her ship made her curse. This was quickly turning from a race to a fight for her life. It bumped against her again.

"I'm sorry," she murmured to the racer. It was being beaten up for a second day in a row.

Isla rose up above the race, and the other racer followed. She flew down between two other racers, just missing them, and one spun off with the surprise. The mystery racer was not far behind. She growled her frustrations, overtook the ship in front of her and dipped down to the lower level of the track. Her hull nearly skimmed the ground. Rock and debris exploded out in front of her, and she turned to miss as much as she could. The racer was a tough one; a few rocks wouldn't do too much damage, but something much stronger had hit the rock to cause it to explode that way. Isla wondered what weapons they had managed to get onto a racer, then reminded herself that it wasn't a racer chasing her down.

The serious look of the men she had met the day before made her curse again. They were right. Someone was trying to kill her, and she was sure it had nothing to do with racing, although now she was fairly certain the racers were involved.

Isla glanced through the tinted panel above her to see the race apparently slowing down as they moved through tall rocky formations. She would finish this if it killed her. As she had that very thought, the stone archway ahead of her started to disintegrate, coming down onto the track and those flying under it. Isla pushed her fingers through the panel before her, accelerating past those who had been ahead of her and sending a silent prayer to whomever might be listening as she willed her ship forward. The crash of stone was overwhelming as she steered her racer through the remaining racers and tried to outrun the falling rubble. Then she was tumbling out of the sky, alarms ringing around her as she was thrown around. She was thankful she had managed to secure one belt, but she should have had more on.

She winced as she was twisted sideways. The dust and debris made it hard to see what was happening around her as she slammed into the ground, and she withdrew the wings as she spun across the dry rocky surface. When she came to a stop, she rested her head back and hoped there wasn't too much damage to the racer. But the panel was dead, and a light flickered somewhere behind her.

She was almost disappointed she had disabled the communications patch; she would need that now. As the dust started to settle around her, she undid the belt, wincing at the pain in her left side and the bruise she knew would cross her stomach where she had been thrown against it. She climbed slowly onto the seat to peer out of the cover and wished she had found a way to keep her duster on the racer.

Through the dust starting to settle around the ship, a man walked towards her. Tall, broad and yet unfamiliar. He wore the same cloak she usually had tucked away behind her seat. She turned, wincing again as she slipped her hand behind the seat. It was still there.

It was only issued by the military, so this man walking towards her could only have gotten it from someone else or the military itself. Isla felt her heart quicken. She leaned back against the seat as the man walked slowly forward. Then he stopped, and she wondered if he could see her through the tinted glass.

He raised a duster very similar to her own, but he holstered it instead of firing it. Then he pulled from beneath the cape a much longer hand-held rocket launcher.

"You can't be serious," Isla murmured. She had played with the idea of shields, but couldn't justify the tech in a racer. She wouldn't need it, she'd thought. Who would be interested in her?

As the rocket left the launcher, the whole world seemed to slow. She grabbed at the seat with one hand as the recoil made the man's shoulder jump back. The sun lit up his face for a moment, just long enough that Isla thought she recognised him. And then smoke billowed out from the rocket and she closed her eyes, waiting for the inevitable. She should have died six years ago. Now she would.

The bang was loud, but it wasn't quite right. She opened her eyes to smoke, but not even the glass was scratched. She collapsed into the seat, her legs finally giving way, and cried out as she sat heavily against the firm surface. That seatbelt had done far more damage than help. She held her hand to her side before she lay back.

Reaching out to the cool metal of the racer, she sighed. "I'm sorry," she murmured, sure she could feel the distant hum of engines that were no longer working. As she closed her eyes, she remembered the man with the blond hair in his face, his skin blistered as he looked at her from the edge of a bed. She squeezed her eyes closed tighter. It was his fault. He had pulled her out of a race, drawn the Boss's attention to all that was wrong and reminded her of a life she had wanted so desperately to forget.

And then someone was pounding on the cover of her racer. She groaned, but that was about all she had. She couldn't get up; she couldn't give instructions. This was likely the man trying to kill her, although she wasn't sure why. The glimpse of his face she had seen in the sun returned, but she was sure she was mistaken. It was not him.

The banging continued. She stretched out her fingers across the metal, willing the door to open and for it all to be over, when the banging stopped. She thought she heard shouting and then nothing.

Who would have thought she would die in the silence? The seal broke on the cover, and she waited for the hot sun to cook her inside the racer.

Three

Isla opened her eyes to a flash of pain and groaned despite her best efforts. She was being lifted over a shoulder. The person shushed her as a woman Isla could only see part of draped a cloak over the two of them. She wanted to protest, but she couldn't find the words needed to stop them, and any chance she had to see what was going on vanished in the dim light beneath the cloak.

"Don't leave her," the woman whispered.

"She'll be fine," the man carrying her responded, and Isla recognised the voice. The same man she had dragged from the sand. The man who had started all of this. She tried to move, but the pain took her breath away and his hold around her legs increased. In the dim light beneath the cloak, Isla could just make out the shape of something against his side. She reached out slowly, trying not to make a sound at the pain that flashed through her body. She closed her hand around the handle of the duster and pulled it slowly from the holster. He didn't give any indication that he knew what she had done, but she held it tight as they moved quickly over the sandy terrain. The movement made her cry out in pain.

She didn't want to risk anything in the sun, or she might fall and lie exposed. Only moments ago, she'd thought she might already be dying, but something always seemed to prevent it. Maybe it was her need for answers.

Listening carefully to the surroundings, she heard no indication of anyone else around. No racing overhead, no shouts or calls for help. No hint of the man who had tried to take her down. Maybe she was losing her mind. Maybe it had all been in her head. The echo of an energy bolt hitting the metal of what she thought was the racer bounced around her, and then they were running. She tried to cling to the weapon as the movement nearly caused her to black out with the pain. And then she was being lowered onto the floor of a larger ship as the door slid shut and the engines hummed to life.

Despite the pain, she held tight to the weapon and stretched her other hand across the cool metal. She felt a familiarity with the vessel. The engines roared as the ship lifted from the sand, and she loathed leaving her racer behind. From the tilt of the ship and the white knuckles of the man holding tight to the controls, Isla knew they were not flying along the ground but directly up into the sky.

The engines were working hard. Although the ship could make the flight, it wasn't what it was used to. Isla took a deep breath that hitched in her throat. "You can do it," she whispered, her hand on the metal. The other hand dropped, the weapon banging on the grate floor as she lay out flat.

As they levelled out, someone tried to prise the weapon from her hand, but she couldn't find the strength to open her eyes. "Please," she whispered, and they left her with it. Isla focused on the ship around her and the hum of the engines beneath her. She breathed slowly, ignoring the pain in her side and the whispered conversation of the men at the controls. She knew one; she could guess at the other.

But all she could see was the man in the cloak standing in front of her racer trying to destroy her. He nearly had once—she wasn't sure she could survive it a second time.

"Where are you?" she wondered.

"Ms Tarle," a voice said too close, but she couldn't open her eyes.

"You have me mistaken for someone else," she whispered.

"I don't think so," he said, too confident and still too close.

"Isla Dee," she wheezed, her hand finding her side. She thought it was wet, but she wasn't quite sure of anything at the moment.

"It is nice to meet you, but I think it might be best if I take that back." His hand closed around hers, and she fought back tears as he pulled the duster from her hold. She could only nod, her earlier fight evaporating.

"Did you send him?" she asked, her eyes still closed.

"Who?"

"The man who knocked me out of this race. Becoming a pattern." She wasn't sure if her last words were spoken or thought.

"Stay with me, Isla," he said, his hand around hers even though the duster had been retrieved. She tried to pull away from him, but any strength she had was slipping away.

"E'anah!" the other voice called, and he was gone. She was alone in the dark.

Isla rolled over, stretched and blinked into the dim light. It wasn't her room. It wasn't anywhere she thought she knew. She sat up slowly, touching her hand to her side. It wasn't as painful as it had been. She looked over her clothing, then sighed and swung around to put her feet to the floor. It was stone and cool. Her head ached as she tried to piece together what had happened and when.

The door opened, and she squinted into the bright light beyond. A woman stood in the doorway, a tray in her hands. She was stern as she looked Isla over.

"I have water and broth." She sat them down on a small table, and Isla took the chance to look over the small room. It wasn't a table; it was a desk. It could have been a child's room at one stage.

"Where does the water come from?" Isla asked.

"Thank you would have done," the woman muttered as she turned and left the room. The door closed, returning her to the same dim light.

"Thank you," Isla said quietly to the door. She stood slowly and lifted the loose-fitting, lightweight, sand-coloured top to look over her side. There was some bruising, but it didn't appear too damaged. The skin wasn't marked any more than before. Isla wondered what the woman had thought when she'd changed her clothes, what she might have guessed or invented of her past to explain what she saw.

Isla pulled her hair behind her ears and wondered at it being loose and wayward. Just what had these people done to her while she'd been unconscious? She looked over the tray and lifted the metal cup to smell the water before taking a tentative sip. She could taste the stone it had been filtered through, but it was fresh—better than any water she'd had at the stables, which had been synthetically filtered.

Her stomach growled at the scent of the broth. She dipped the spoon in and tasted a small amount, but her stomach protested. She set the spoon down and sat back on the edge of the bed, taking the time to look over her new clothing and the body within it. The burn on her arm was almost healed, and there were no signs of further sun exposure. She glanced around for her cloak but couldn't see it. They hadn't left her with the duster either. Isla had slept, and she didn't remember any dreams; yet as she brushed her hair back from her face again, as it had sprung out from behind her ears, his face appeared again from the shadows of her memories.

She shook them away as the door opened. The blond man entered, closed the door behind him and sat down at the desk. She glared at him. Although it was on the tip of her tongue to thank him, she couldn't.

"Ms Tarle," he said again, and she scowled all the more. "Isla," he said with a bow of his head. "Are you prepared to listen now?"

"To more stories? For all I know, you were behind the attack on the race—you were behind the attack on my racer." She swallowed down her regret at the small vessel out there somewhere without her.

"Your racer is fine," he said as though he understood her. But she doubted very much he did.

Anger bubbled to the surface as he continued to sit and watch her, an annoying smile on his too handsome face. "You cause this trouble, get me patched up, steal my things, and now you want my thanks?"

"Patching is something you seem very familiar with." He didn't take his eyes from hers, but there was something in his voice—was it pity? It was as though he was trying not to look at her. She wondered just how much he had seen.

She waited.

He sighed, running his hand through his hair. Then he sat up straighter, and it fell across his face again. Isla would have found it something to smile about—someone with the kind of hair she had always wanted, and it was as troublesome as her own. But she couldn't smile for him. She couldn't trust him.

"E'anah," she said. He cocked his head to the side. "I won't thank you for any of this. I would like to leave."

He shook his head slowly. "Just to run into more trouble. I don't think I could save you a third day in a row."

"Your wife does not want me here," she said.

He raised his eyebrows, then turned to the door and smiled. "She is not my wife."

"People rarely formalise the agreement nowadays," Isla said, shrugging.

He scowled. "She is Reilly's wife. And it's Gray E'anah. Most people call me Gray."

"Gray," she repeated. "I don't really care who you people are. I want to leave." She chewed on her lip for a moment, wondering if she had really seen what she thought she had, and how close they might be. "Did you see him?"

"Who?" he asked, leaning forward.

She opened her mouth and then closed it. Was she asking about the man who had tried to kill her, or someone else?

"We saw you slide out, and we landed not long after. There was a lot of debris and dust about. Did you see someone?"

"I'm not sure," she admitted.

The door slid open again, and a boy stood silhouetted in the sunlight. "Did you tell her she's a fug—a fug-a—" He scowled as he stepped into the room.

"Fugitive?" she asked.

He nodded. "You made a mess with that race."

"I did not!" She stood up, swayed, and sat heavily again on the bed.

The boy sat beside her, unperturbed by her outburst. "They say you killed those racers, and that you were jealous."

"Of what?"

"When did you last win a race?" Gray asked.

She looked from the boy to him. How would anyone think she had been behind this? She was at the back of the pack; they were trying to take her out. Permanently. "Boss," she murmured.

"Who?" the little one asked, looking up at her with bright eyes. Isla had to blink herself back to the present. It wasn't doing her any good being around these people.

"Who wants you dead?" Gray asked. She wondered at his candour in front of the boy, but when she glanced at the boy, he was looking at her expectantly.

"No one," she said, taking a moment to stand slowly.

"Someone appears to," he said quickly, standing with her. She swayed a little as her head spun, and he offered her a hand. She smacked it away.

"Are you someone important?" the boy asked.

She shook her head. "Where are my clothes?"

"Ruined," Gray said. "You can keep those. Where are you going?"

She stopped by the door. "I left some things at the stables."

"You're wanted for the destruction at the race—you can't go in there. And if they are behind the attack, you certainly can't."

"I've managed to look after myself this long," she said, pushing her way out into the house, where the woman looked at her with worry. "I won't hurt you," Isla said, more from an old habit than any fear the woman might have had. "Thank you," she added, bowing her head a little with respect she hadn't shown anyone in too long. She headed out towards the main door and then stopped. When she turned back, Gray held out her cloak.

"It is too far," he said.

"Where is she?"

He nodded towards the door. She headed out, pulling on the cloak and wincing at the pain in her side. She just needed to get back to her racer and then consider the stables. She didn't have much there, and if the news could be believed, Twiggy or the security had already been through those meagre belongings. She paused just out of the house; it was suddenly too far to go. But she wasn't sure who might be out there looking for her and what they might do if they found her here.

"I could run you out there, but I'm not sure it will do you any good. And you certainly don't seem prepared to listen to me." Gray stood in the shade on the porch, a weathered canteen in his hand.

"Let her go," Reilly called from the house.

Gray held out the canteen. She stepped back to take it, but he held it tight as her hand closed around it.

"It is a long walk."

She raised her gaze from the canteen to his very blue eyes, and he let it go.

"Go straight out," he said, indicating beyond her with his chin. "When you reach the long ridge, follow it around to the west and you'll find it tucked under the rim."

"You moved her?"

"Not really. You landed close enough to it; we went back and gave it a bit of a nudge."

She nodded and turned back to the expanse of sand that stretched out before her.

"It is a good couple of days' walk."

"I could do with the quiet time," she murmured as she headed off. There were no landmarks in the direction he had indicated. It was going to be some time before she found it, and she had no idea whether or not it would be a way for her to get back to the stables. It wasn't like she was going to be able to fly in there.

She tucked the canteen in her clothing, amazed by the pockets in the roomy top. And it might be that the loose bit at the back of her neck was a hood. She was covered by her cape, and although she could feel the heat of the sun, it wasn't as intense as it might have been without it.

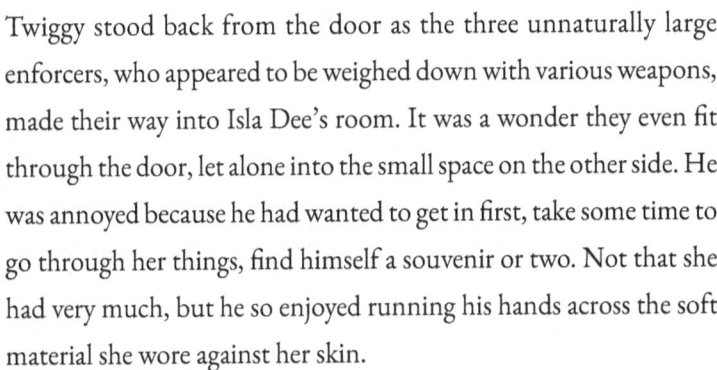

Twiggy stood back from the door as the three unnaturally large enforcers, who appeared to be weighed down with various weapons, made their way into Isla Dee's room. It was a wonder they even fit through the door, let alone into the small space on the other side. He was annoyed because he had wanted to get in first, take some time to go through her things, find himself a souvenir or two. Not that she had very much, but he so enjoyed running his hands across the soft material she wore against her skin.

Boss had insisted that the enforcers were to go in first. He didn't mind that she knew he visited some of the rooms during the day when the racers were busy with training or maintenance or racing. She didn't know which rooms, although it wouldn't surprise him if she had cameras or detectors in each space.

He hadn't been in Isla's room for some time, though. Boss had hinted that she didn't want him anywhere near, and he'd thought she might be planning something.

One of the large enforcers reappeared in the doorway, glaring. Twiggy gave him his best grin and sauntered back down the hallway. It wasn't like he could stop them taking anything. He headed back to the pit. Pacing the large space, he looked over the remains of the ships that had been dragged back in. They knew what they had signed up for, but it was hard to explain when someone died during a race—and half the field had died or been seriously injured during this one.

Isla was a pretty thing. He had tried to get her attention, but she would never let Twiggy get as close as he would like. Some of the others would, but they weren't as pretty. She had always joked she was going to the locker rooms after a race. No one had used the locker rooms in more than twenty years, but she'd made the same comment every time.

He walked in to find Boss standing in front of a locker, the door open, her brow creased. He paused mid-step, but she glanced his way. He had never worked out how she seemed to know he was coming.

"Where do you think this came from?" she asked, unmoving.

Twiggy stepped up beside her, reluctant because she was scary even if they had worked together for most of his life. He glimpsed the old, beaten hand-held weapon, a Starduster, in the base of the locker. "How long has that been there?" he asked.

She shook her head.

"Who?" he asked.

"Isla Dee," she whispered, the venom palpable. He ran his tongue over his lips, sure he could taste it.

"She was military," he murmured, as though that answered the riddle of the prohibited weapon.

"We don't ask." Boss turned a hard glare at him that made him step back. "But they know the rules. We could lose our licence."

Twiggy gulped down the fear rising in his gut.

"Get rid of it."

"Me?" he asked, his voice rising oddly into a squeak. There had just been a major incident mid-race. The enforcers were covering the building. "If they test it and find her prints, more blame on the rogue loser."

Boss made a low growling noise as she closed the locker door, a gentle click indicating it had locked.

"I'll go find someone. Make sure they search everywhere," he said. "Almost everywhere," he added under his breath as he ran from the room in search of one of the enforcers he hoped would clear out his stables, sooner rather than later. And allow them to keep racing after they had gone.

Four

"How many times have you saved her already?" Reilly asked as they stood at the window, looking out across the sandy expanse that stretched away from the dwelling. Reilly's son raced in circles around the room, making sounds as though he were a racer.

Gray had watched Isla cross sand the day before. He could have helped her, could have taken her closer to her racer. He had hoped the long walk would give her time to think about what had happened and clarify for her that someone was seriously trying to kill her. But as he had watched the empty expanse until the sky had turned to inky blue and the stars had filled the void, he knew she would be going exactly where she said and right back into the middle of all the trouble.

A long time ago, he had made a promise to a friend, and that meant something. Even if there was little he could do to keep it.

"He's gone," Reilly said, pulling him from his thoughts. Gray nodded slowly. "But I can't let you head off on your own. You won't last a minute without me to pull you out of trouble."

"No," Suo, Reilly's wife, said from behind them. "Don't go chasing trouble. Stay. Please." Gray could see the worry etched into her frown. "You know the risk if you are caught. Don't let some girl who doesn't even want your help get you caught."

"She's right," Gray admitted, turning back to the sand. "You shouldn't come."

Reilly intercepted the boy's path, lifted him easily into the air and kissed his cheek. The boy squealed, and Reilly put him down to continue his crazy run. Reilly stepped up to Suo as Gray left the dwelling to stand in the shade of the porch. He didn't need to be party to that conversation to know how it would go and that he would wear any blame if anything happened to the man.

"Where do you think she is headed?" Reilly asked, coming to stand beside him.

"Straight back to the stables."

"She's insane. You know that, don't you? And we are just as crazy to follow."

"You don't have to come," Gray repeated.

Reilly lifted an eyebrow, as though there was no question as to whether he would come.

"It's a hike," Gray said, looking across where Isla had headed the day before.

"We have one of our own." Reilly pushed a bag into his hands.

Gray slung it over his shoulder, lifting the cloth up over his head and across his face in the hope it would go some way to protect them from the heat of the sun. They had a small vehicle close to the dwelling, but it was a long trek out from there to the ship they had hidden in the mountains, and in the opposite direction to Isla's racer.

"You aren't leaving us without an escape," Suo said as they stepped out into the sun.

Gray stopped and looked back; she was similarly covered, following them into the bright light.

"We are walking," Gray said, as though it was a given.

"Then you won't reach her before she gets to where she is going." She was right, of course. Reilly sighed loudly.

"I can run you out. The boy knows to keep low and quiet."

They climbed into the small vehicle without a word, and it lifted from the sand with a rumbling noise. How they thought they could sneak anywhere in it was impossible. But then, no one lived out here; or if they did, they were like Reilly's family, looking for a quiet life out of the spotlight. They wouldn't be reporting anything to the enforcers or anyone else who might be asking.

"I don't know why you insist on this," Suo murmured as she slowed the vehicle down and they flew in under a rocky overhang. They landed with a thump in a large cave, worn into the side of the mountain by the millennia of sandstorms. It was close to the ground, but not close enough to see unless someone was looking.

"I made a promise," Gray said as he unbuckled and leant forward, resting his hand on Suo's shoulder. He gave her a peck on the cheek. "Thank you."

"You and your chivalrous ways." She had said that before, joking about how good and helpful he was, but her voice lacked the playfulness that usually accompanied the words. She clutched at his hand that had rested on her shoulder. "You bring him back." Her voice was low, and he understood the threat behind it.

He nodded slowly without saying the words. It wasn't a promise he could keep. Just like the last one he had made. At least he had found a way to fulfil it.

They moved quickly through the dark, cool cave towards the ship that was tucked towards the back. They had managed to hide it here for some time, but Gray worried as the smaller vehicle hummed to life and headed out into the sunshine. Suo might be in danger on her own. He wondered at someone seeing her leave the cave, but it wasn't something they had worried about for themselves and the much larger vessel.

The door squealed open, echoing around the cavern, and for a moment Gray was sure he saw something else in there as the light from the doorway spilled into the darkness. As Reilly started aboard, he waited, searching the surrounding darkness—which now seemed even darker in the shadow of the ship—for movement or a hint of what he might have seen.

"Gray," Reilly prompted.

Gray took one last look around and started for the doorway.

"What now? You see a ghost?"

"Maybe," he murmured, wondering at what had caught his attention. He wasn't even sure what he had seen, if anything, but something had made him look.

"What are we going to do when we find this girl?" Reilly asked as he strapped himself in and the engines roared to life. For the first time, Gray was sure others would hear the mountain rumble.

How did they think they could have lasted this long without getting caught? And why was he so worried about it now that he was chasing after ghosts and some woman who didn't even want to be saved?

No matter how beautiful she was.

"Are we headed for the racer in the hope we catch her first, or back into the city?"

"The racer," Gray said, buckling himself in and pushing his hair back from his face. They had a better chance of getting out of this unscathed if they found her before they had to head into the population. Once they were out there and seen, it would be difficult to reach Isla, even if they could find her amongst the population.

Isla chewed on her lip. She was desperate to get back to the stables, but Gray was right. And that was more frustrating than the things she had left behind. It wasn't very much, and the place would be crawling with enforcers. But she had little choice. All that was left of what she wanted to remember of her previous life was in that little room. She wasn't leaving it behind.

And that wasn't all she had left in the little city that the stables had spent so many years jutted up against. Her dragonfly was in safe hands, but no matter what it represented, she couldn't bring herself to leave it behind. Too much work had gone into it already.

Despite the conflicting feelings and her desire to both run away from and into the mess that was now the stables, she urged her racer across the sand towards the distant buildings and hum of ships and vessels moving between them. Whatever it was she wanted, it certainly didn't include that man with the blond hair and blue eyes and too firm chest. She grinned and ran her hand over her hair.

"Damn it!" she muttered. She had even lost her helmet. That had been a lucky find. It was starting to look like her luck was running out. For half a heartbeat, she wondered if she could claim to be the victim she was. But she knew they wouldn't believe her. How anyone could believe her capable of such a thing was beyond her. Such a thing was not beyond Boss, though, and Isla wondered what was in it for her. Why would Boss want her dead, and during a race? It was too risky.

Isla needed to get in there, risk or not. She landed the racer outside the city limits, at the edge of the desert, on the opposite side of the city from the stables and nowhere near where she had hidden her dragonfly. She moved quickly, leaping down and towards the buildings, but there was no one around to see her. She stopped in the middle of what would usually be a thoroughfare leading into the city.

Dressed like anyone else who lived in the desert, she hoped she wouldn't stand out. Despite the shade the buildings provided from the sunlight, Isla pulled the hood up over her hair. Either her crazy mane of red curls was going to draw a lot of attention, or she would be nearly unrecognisable with her hair free.

It had been far too long since she had allowed herself to walk about like this. To take in the quiet streets. Although she was trying her best not to be seen, it was almost like life used to be, when she had walked and laughed with others, allowing a strong hand to pull her along and into all sorts of trouble.

For five years she had managed to make it through this world, on this dry little planet, with hardly a thought for what had gone before, or so she had let herself believe. At the sound of a vehicle, she ducked into a doorway, hidden in the shadows. It moved by quickly, but the shiny, jet-black vehicle made her heart skip. Enforcers.

The sun was climbing higher, the temperature rising, and even the city cover wasn't enough. She pulled the cover further over her forehead and cursed leaving the cape behind. Although that would have given her away.

She clung close to the buildings as she made her way carefully towards the stables. The streets were too quiet, she thought again as she got closer, and yet there were more enforcers than necessary to find a rogue racer. Did they really think she would have been capable of bringing down not only that many racers, but half the course as well?

A newsstand flickered across the road. Isla stepped up behind the small crowd watching the screen. There was far more damage than she'd realised. At the sight of Cruzer's damaged ship, she wanted to turn away, but she focused on the screen as her race image flashed up, her face looking left and right. She held her breath. She was dressed in her racing suit, her hair neatly braided close to her scalp. She was surprised they had managed to capture such an image with her hair as it was.

"How could such a pretty little thing be responsible for that?" a man closer to the screen asked. Isla couldn't see him through the crowd.

"Maybe she isn't," a woman on the other side of the small group offered.

Footage of the race filled the screen, her moving through the field although she hadn't really; she had been pushed back. Then she banged into another racer, pushing them out of the line of the race. But she hadn't hit anyone—they had hit her.

"Hey," someone mumbled, and she realised she was pushing her way through the group towards the screen.

"Sorry," she murmured. This wasn't right.

And then there was gunfire, and Cruzer was blown off course, hitting the cliff as the rock came tumbling down on the others.

"That is not what happened," she whispered.

"Were you there?" a man beside her asked.

She shook her head without looking up. "They can't have weapons."

"Maybe she snuck them on. Just because it's law doesn't mean it doesn't happen," the man offered.

"The race officials check them," she insisted.

"Looks real to me," someone further back said.

"When did you ever see a news flash that was accurate? We see what they want us to see," someone snarled behind her. "Leave the girl alone. She's right, this is faked."

"I..." Isla wasn't sure what she could say. She didn't want to get into a conversation with these people; someone would recognise her. Loose hair and baggy clothing couldn't hide enough of who she was.

A reward message flashed up on the screen.

"Someone wants her dead," the man behind her muttered as the crowd dispersed, leaving her to stare at the screen and the insanely large number.

"I suppose people died," someone else said as they were walking away. "But a price like that you'd see for someone threatening the Hendra, not taking out some racers."

The conversation continued as people disappeared, but Isla couldn't make out what they were saying. She turned slowly and took in the empty street, then hurried along towards the other side of the city and the stables. Just who did they think she was?

She stopped and looked over her clothes, cursing her own stupidity. Gray and his friend knew who she was. They had called her Tarle. "Bastards," she said under her breath. But then, that in itself wouldn't be enough to warrant her death. Why had they been so sure someone wanted her dead? Now they would see to it her image shone around the city—and for that price, the old woman who had watched the screen with her was likely to turn her in if she could.

Isla glanced over her shoulder towards the news stand. "They didn't say armed and dangerous," she murmured. But with that price and the number of enforcers around the city, it gave that idea. No one carried a weapon unless they had to or could manage to get away with it. Enforcers here didn't look kindly on anyone who did. A threat to their threatening behaviour. Not that Isla had a problem with the law—she had once been a part of it, after all. She kept a low profile, raced and stayed put.

She rounded a corner and stopped. A couple of enforcers stood by a vehicle, blocking the street. The stables were just beyond. Isla was getting hotter. She just wanted her things, and she'd be gone.

"What ya doin'?" one of them said, standing up from the vehicle and walking towards her.

Isla's mind whirred. "Visiting my gran," she said quickly. "She's all alone."

"My gran always expects a treat," the other enforcer said, sauntering up to stand beside the other. She might have been able to take one of them. Two, in this heat and with her aching side, she doubted she had the energy for.

"They are funny like that, grandmothers," Isla said, trying to smile, then looked down at her empty hands. "She won't remember." She leaned in close as she spoke conspiratorially. "She doesn't appreciate my baking, and I didn't have enough for the baker today."

The two looked at each other and then back to her.

"Her mind is going," Isla said, trying to give her story more credibility. "She'll complain about the biscuits I took her yesterday, even though I took a cake, and then she'll say that today's baking was so bland she can't remember eating it."

One of the men began to laugh, but the other scowled. "That's sad," he said, turning on her.

"Very," Isla agreed. "But what can I do? I'm all she has, really. My uncle doesn't care for her as he should."

"You want us to come along and remind him of his familial duty?" the sad enforcer asked.

"Thank you for the kind offer." She gave him her prettiest smile. "She's not good with strangers, and she struggles enough with family. Will you be here for a while if I change my mind?"

He nodded solemnly.

She smiled again, nodded her thanks and hurried past them. She only hoped they weren't watching her back as she passed down the street and around a corner towards the back of the stables. She glanced around. She knew there were cameras around, but not all of them worked. Boss liked to keep tabs on her racers, but a lot of it was hot air. She hoped.

Isla secured the scarf around her neck and lifted the long pants, which she instantly regretted in the heat of the sun. Then she hooked her fingers into the stonework of the wall. It was slippery, and hot from the sun. It was also the only way she could be sure she was out of view of the residences and anyone else when she landed on the other side. But getting over took her longer than she liked, and she was even more drained when she reached the top.

As much as she wanted to lie across the narrow edge, she rolled over and landed on her feet on the other side. It was thankfully cool, but as she looked up at the wall behind her, she wasn't sure how she was going to make it out. It would have to be a different route. She was in a small gap behind a building, used by Twiggy for storage for things he thought made the ships go faster. Those things he didn't always want Boss knowing he suggested or sold at too high a price to the racers.

Isla had been in the space only a couple of times, and he certainly had some good bits and bobs that she would love to build into her racer. He also used it as an excuse to get close to the racers, and close to Twiggy in any sense was not something Isla wanted.

It was crammed with precarious piles of machinery. The deeper into the space she moved, the more nervous she was of knocking something down and alerting someone to her presence. Likely enforcers—but worse, Boss. Isla stopped. A duster sat on top of a barrel of maybe oil, although Twiggy rarely kept anything in a container that described what it actually was. A duster very much like hers. She stepped closer, then looked round the shadowy space and hoped it wasn't a trap. Maybe someone had found hers in the locker—but then why would they leave it out here? She lifted it slowly, the metal cold against her hand, and sighed with relief when she turned it over and discovered there were no marks. It had been well used, but it wasn't hers.

At the sound of something being knocked against the building wall, she raised the duster. It hummed to life, her finger hovering over the trigger. A grinning blond man stepped out of the shadows.

"Are you going to lower that?" Gray asked, his hand on his own weapon in a holster at his hip.

"No," she said, the weapon still trained on him. "What are you doing here?"

"Getting ready to save you again."

"Don't need it," Isla muttered, creeping around the side of the building and then lowering the weapon and tucking it into her waist band beneath the layers of cloth. She only hoped she could reach it in a hurry if needed. Heading out into the stables with a gun wouldn't do her any favours if the enforcers were here. "How do you know who I am?" she asked, pausing to look out around the building. It was too quiet, just like the street. It made her even more nervous, and he was too close behind.

"Mutual friend," he said.

She stopped and turned around, her hand reaching for the duster, but he gave a slight shake of his head as though he guessed what she was doing.

"I don't have any friends."

"Old friend," he said.

"They're all dead." She turned back, and before he could do anything stupid like stop her, she was around the side of the building and racing inside.

The relief from the change in temperature was instant, although she made no move to change her appearance. The pit, as Twiggy called it, was abandoned. There were some remains of racers that had been out in the race, but no sign of any people. There was always someone in this space, tinkering, building, or testing. They were waiting. Isla felt an odd calm cover her body. One she hadn't felt for some time, even going into a race.

She could play games, she thought as she raced across the room. She tried hard to keep her feet light, but there was a slight echo. She made it to the door and into the corridor beyond with no incident. She paused by the locker room door, but she wouldn't go in. They had found her weapon; she was sure of it. All she had to do was enter the space, and there would be no leaving it. Instead, she headed for the lift.

That was also a risk; she was sure the cameras there were working and they would be watching. The fifteenth floor would be too high to jump from, but she was committed to reaching her room and what she needed from it. She left the lift without incident, and the duster remained hidden. There was a moment when she wondered what Gray might be up to. But she was certain he was here for his own reasons. Instead of heading towards her room, she turned left and headed to Cruzer's room. She hit the panel at the same moment she kicked the bottom right-hand side of the door, and it slid open silently. She stepped inside and closed it.

Lucky for her, Boss didn't move quickly on getting anything fixed around here. Cruzer had been breaking into his own room for the better part of two years. She looked over the messy space and stopped. Had someone been through his things? Was that why he had died, or had he just been collateral damage in their efforts to take her out? She wasn't sure where to even start. She was starting to feel claustrophobic with the mess even though she could handle small spaces. Her whole life had been small spaces. When she raced out in the open plains of Urgway, she did it from within a small space.

She was tempted to start picking things up, but stopped herself. She opened drawers to find them just the same as the piles on the floor. She rummaged through the piles and then back to the door before spotting what she'd hoped to find on the edge of a shelf. The very edge of it was poking over. She reached up on tiptoes, closed her hand around the small device and pocketed it.

Lucky that man never kept his mouth shut. Over a couple of drinks early in her racing days, when she'd tried to interact with others—just sometimes so she looked like one of them—he had bragged about his thieving days. She wondered briefly if he had been the one in her room. But she doubted it. There would be nothing of interest for him there.

She hit the panel and was down the hallway without waiting for the door to close, around the corner and racing towards her room. She expected half a battalion of enforcers to appear at any point. So far, the whole place appeared to be abandoned, and yet she was sure her luck was about to run out.

She opened her door using his small device held against the panel. At least they wouldn't think she had been here. The door opened, her room in a similar state to Cruzer's. Although she doubted some-one else had done that to his space, she knew very well that someone, or several someones, had been through hers.

The bed had been stripped, the blankets on the floor covered in the few clothes she had that had been pulled from the drawers, most of which were still open.

She pulled the bottom drawer right out and turned it over on the bed. Her heart was thumping when she found the envelope intact. Hard plastic, taped to the bottom of the drawer. *Who is the mutual friend?* she wondered as she hid it inside her clothing. She was starting to appreciate this outfit.

The t-shirt she often wore to bed lay half covered by other cloth-ing. She stepped over it and into the bathroom, where she pulled her lotions out of the cabinet and into the small bag that had sat on the counter since she'd arrived. As she turned to leave, something caught her eye, and she stopped and turned back to the shower bay. A poorly made bomb sat awkwardly on the floor of the shower bay. When she stepped closer, a click sounded and it started to beep.

"Damn it!" she shouted, racing for the door and along the hallway. She wasn't headed towards the lift but the narrow, too strong window at the far end of the hall. She had half suspected long ago that it wasn't really a window to the outside, but she was willing to risk it now. One hand closed around the bag while the other pulled her weapon from the folds of her clothes, and she shot at the would-be window as she ran.

Five

It may have shattered, but the glass still cut into her skin as she leapt out over nothing. The whoosh of air behind her pushed her further out from the building while she held her breath and closed her eyes. The ground was still a long way beneath her, and she didn't want to see just how far she was falling. She hit something hard, the impact jarring her, then slid across the shiny metal and fell again to land on the hard deck of a familiar ship. Winded, she struggled to gain her breath, then closed her eyes against the pain in her skin and lungs and pressed her hand to the cool humming metal beneath her.

"Is this really important?" Gray said, leaning over her. She groaned, trying to reach for the bag he lifted out of her reach. Instead, she raised the duster, still tight in her other hand. "Not nice when I just saved you. Again."

Her head thumped back against the floor; her hand still tight around the weapon aimed at him. It wouldn't matter if she missed; it would be enough to scare him. Not that she would miss.

"Give it back," she murmured as the zip opened loudly and the bottles clinked inside.

"Hair product?" He didn't hide the laughter in his voice, and as she sat up, she was even more grateful she had taken the time to collect her things.

Fighting against the overwhelming stinging in her skin, Isla leapt to her feet, snatched the bag from his hand and pushed the duster into his chest.

He released his hold on her belongings, raised both hands and stepped back. "Not very trusting," he murmured.

"Someone is trying to kill me," she said. "I'm starting to think it might be you."

"Saved you," he said, wearing the same grin he'd worn earlier. She looked away from his sparkling eyes. She wasn't getting drawn into that.

A violent shift in the ship and the accompanying explosion threw her against him. She didn't think the bomb had looked that well put together, and it had taken some time to damage the building. But there might not have been just one.

"Hang on!" Reilly called from the controls as they righted. The engines hummed as they strained against the effort, and Isla wondered just how old this ship was. She tried to right herself but staggered back into Gray, his arms closing around her. She cried out involuntarily as the splinters of glass pushed deeper into her skin.

He released her, genuine remorse etched across his handsome features. She reluctantly dropped the weapon and reached for a hand hold as they banked. The stables were gone. What had been eighteen stories of pale, reflective tower was a pile of rubble almost indistinguishable from the desert it bordered.

"There was no one there," she said, scooping up the weapon and moving quickly towards the cockpit.

"Maybe we should do something about the glass," Gray suggested.

"It can wait," she said, looking over Reilly's shoulder.

"Morning," he said politely.

Isla nodded once, but she wasn't giving him anything more than she already had. "Enforcers around the perimeter. No one inside. They were waiting."

"You appear to be predictable," Gray commented. She turned slowly, raising the blaster with the movement.

"I don't like you," she said. "Even with your smiles and promises of secrets."

"Now, Ms Tarle—or should I call you Sergeant?"

"You should call me Ms Dee, as it is my name. I think you are somewhat confused."

He shook his head and reached into his pocket. The duster in her hand hummed to life, power building, and he opened his hands again.

"You want to bring us all down?" Reilly asked.

"Tell me why I shouldn't," she said, never taking her eyes off Gray.

The handheld monitor he produced was battered. She stepped forward and took it from his hand without thinking about keeping her weapon trained on him. The image was almost as faded as the case. A uniformed group grinned back at her. Arms linked around each other, they looked fit and keen. Happy. Her eyes settled on the tall broad man in the centre of the group. His blond hair was close cropped, blue eyes twinkling with trouble, arms around the woman in front of him. It was clear there was more there than friendship.

Her hair looked so neat, so professional. She remembered that morning like it was the only day in her life that mattered, because by the end of it her life had been very different.

"Isla," Gray's soft voice broke through her foggy reminiscence, and she blinked as though just realising where she was.

"It's not me," she lied, handing the image back to him, although it took everything she had left to release it. She could have studied those faces, but she didn't need to. Every one of them was burned into her memory, although they'd all looked very different that last time.

She cleared her throat, ran her fingers through her hair and winced. She pulled her hand from her hair to find it covered in blood. She wasn't sure if that was due to her cut hands or her head.

"Let me..."

She shook her head, looking around the ship properly. It was bigger than her own dragonfly, and older. Much older. It could once have been used for military ops. It appeared to be an early class Pelican, as chunky as the name implied. The space was open, designed for supplies, the cockpit simple and part of the open space. But there was more beyond what she could see, such as bathrooms and a bunkhouse. It was designed for long-haul flights. She closed her eyes against the memories. "Drop me in the sand."

"No." Gray crossed his arms.

"It wasn't a request."

"Will you jump if we don't land?" Reilly asked.

Isla rolled her shoulders and tried not to wince again. She was hurting more than she would admit to these two. "You got a shower in this bucket?"

"Hey!" Reilly objected.

Gray pointed to a hatch, and she looped her bag around her finger before following where he pointed.

Isla entered the small space and came face to face with a hideous sight. It took her a moment to realise it was her own reflection. A very different picture from the one she had just held in her hand. Her clothes were torn, her face scratched, her hands bloody along with the trail of blood that dribbled down her forehead. She'd seen worse, she reminded herself.

She wished she'd blown a hole in the man on the other side of the door. Taking that monitor with him. She had wanted to live, she was sure, that was why she had survived that day. That and sheer luck. She wouldn't have survived the fall when she'd leapt from the stables—but then, she might have. She didn't need Gray thinking he was saving her all the time. She didn't need that, and she didn't need him.

As Isla carefully pulled the ruined cloth away from her skin, a hiss of pain escaped before she could stop it. Other than a couple larger pieces of glass in her arms, the damage was made up of more scratches than glass shards. Either way, her skin stung when she stepped under the hot water. She almost cried out as she pushed her head back under the stream. As the water stopped and the air started, she slumped down into the base of the shower and pressed her back into the wet surround. She could feel the hum of the engines, and although she couldn't say why, that feeling was the only thing to offer any comfort.

She had spent too long with the racer, but her dragonfly was still hidden away. She hoped not enough people knew about it to keep a watch on it or damage it before she could reach it. And then what was her plan? Part of her wanted to cry for the loss of a ship she wasn't sure she had lost yet; but there were other losses she was yet to cry for, and she wouldn't be letting these men, whoever they were, see her vulnerabilities. She stood and, although damp from sitting in the shower, stepped out into the small space, lifted what was left of the clothing and shook it out. Some more fragments of glass fell to the smooth floor at her feet. She sat them on the small bench and rummaged through her bag for the lotion. She dabbed it on carefully, grimacing with pain. It would help. She hadn't used it in so long, and now it was starting to feel like she was using it almost every day.

She held the jar up to the light. There was enough left for another serious run in with someone, but then she would need to work up some more. It had been some time since she'd made this batch, and she couldn't get what she needed to make it on this dry rock. No matter what food they thought they grew here, it was nothing like her home planet.

The door slid open. Gray stood in the doorway with his eyes closed, a pile of clothes held out in his hands.

"I thought you might need something else," he said.

She took the clothes silently from his hands. He opened his eyes and looked her over. He didn't seem to be interested in her, just looking.

"Do you need help?"

"No," she said, turning from the door. He followed her into the small room. As she reached for the weapon on the counter, he rushed forward and grabbed at it. She would have been impressed by the move, except he was now pressed against her. He stepped back quickly.

"Rather not be shot," he murmured, his focus on her back. "You missed a bit."

She wasn't sure what to say, trying not to imagine what he thought as he looked over the crisscross of scars that covered her body. He had made reference to them before when he'd called her patched.

She held up the jar. He scooped a small amount of the lotion out, and then she sucked in a breath as he pulled a shard of glass from near her shoulder blade. Odd that she hadn't felt it before. He wiped the lotion over her skin, his touch soft and gentle.

"How do you have that?" she asked, watching his reflection in the mirror.

"Mutual friend," he murmured, focused on her skin, not raising his eyes to meet hers as she expected.

"You're lying," she said, wondering what he was up to. Then his fingers traced over one of the scars that ran across her back. "Enough." She turned in the small space, the armful of clothing held against her chest.

"How?" he asked, his face serious for the first time as he looked at her.

"It doesn't matter," she murmured. She pushed at him, finding the space too small and Gray too close.

He nodded slowly and left the room. She watched the door for a moment before she started to pull on the clothes. They were very similar to what she had been wearing before, and she wondered what else they carried with them. All the while trying not to look at herself in the mirror. When she was dressed, she realised he'd left the weapon. She tried not to sigh as she tucked it inside the folds of her clothing.

Gray stood against the door and tried to breathe. She was a mess, a bigger mess than he'd expected. He knew it had taken her months to heal, and yet he was surprised by the damage that still marked her skin.

He walked back towards the cockpit.

"Still trying to save her?" Reilly asked without looking around.

He didn't say anything. There wasn't anything he could say. He shook his head once.

Reilly remained focused ahead of them. Within minutes, Isla was standing beside him, dressed in fresh clothes and looking over the cockpit.

"Where are we going?" she asked.

"Away from where they can find you."

"Who do you think is looking?" she asked, but the question didn't contain the same anger she had shown earlier, nor the disbelief that someone was trying to kill her.

Gray shook his head.

"But you know," she said, turning to him, her green eyes intense. He looked away, back towards the world rushing beneath them.

"We have an idea, but we don't know why."

After too long a pause, he could sense her tense stance and anger. "Are you going to tell me anything? Or just hide me away?"

"Hendra," he murmured, unsure how he could express his concerns.

"Hendra?" she repeated. "Why would Hendra want me dead?"

"I think you know." He turned to take her in. She crossed her arms savagely, but he could see her trying not to grimace as she uncrossed them and let them fall by her side. "I know who you are, who you are hiding from, although I don't know how you thought you could hide. The entire solar system knows you. And not because of what happened in that race—there was more to that day, and it might be that now someone wants you dead."

"If they did, they've had plenty of opportunity in the last six years..." she offered, taking a step back from him.

"Maybe you learnt something and they tried to destroy you all then."

Isla shook her head, her hair smooth and buoyant. Gray wondered absently at the lack of flyaway curls.

"You survived," he continued, "and they have decided they need to finish the job."

"The mine is coming up," Reilly said.

"I'm still not sure how I survived," Isla said softly, turning to the view. "But we worked for Hendra. There is no way they would kill their own. And we knew nothing that would have warranted an attack."

"Someone might have—someone above you?"

She turned an angry glare on him. "No." There was no argument.

He looked back out over the desert and the tall, narrow buildings pushing out of the sand in the distance. "Put it down here," he said.

"What is happening at the mines?" she asked. "I thought you wanted to hide me away."

"Maybe you can help with the knowledge you don't know you have. There is a whisper that Hendra is involved with continued illegal mining. That might be connected to Hendra wanting you dead."

"You made that connection on your own, did you?" He could hear the scepticism in her voice.

He shrugged. "We've helped you out a few times. Maybe you could give us a hand."

"Is there a plan, or are we going in blind?"

"I can plan. You and I check it out. Reilly waits with the ship."

"You don't trust me." It was a simple statement. He couldn't look around to see if she was disappointed, because he knew she wouldn't be.

"I don't trust you with my ship, and you might leave us here to find your own way off this planet," Reilly said.

Gray turned to see her smile as she placed a hand on Reilly's shoulder. "You wouldn't be wrong."

"Don't feel you have to bring her back," Reilly muttered as he landed the ship behind a rocky ridge.

Without a word, they raced out in the same instant as the side door opened. Isla kept up easily, and he wondered if she did need saving. She'd just survived a bomb blast, after all, and he was dragging her closer to those who wanted her dead. Somewhere at the back of his mind, he felt as though he had let his old friend down.

They lay down in unison at the top of a dune and looked over into the mine complex. There were small huts grouped together on one side, likely accommodation for the miners, then some larger buildings that would have been the offices, dining hall, or more accommodations. A large framework stood over the desert, long spires reaching up from it containing wide pipes billowing smoke and gasses into the atmosphere. There was a metallic taste to the air.

"What did Reilly say they are mining for?" The scarf wrapped around Isla's face muffled her words a little.

"Rohen."

She rolled to her side and stared at Gray. "Are you serious?"

He nodded once, looking back towards the mine. At the sound of engines, he rolled onto his back and looked up at the belly of a sleek silver ship, the reflection burning his eyes.

"Hendra," Isla whispered.

"At an illegal rohen mine, who would have thought it possible?"

She glared at him and turned her attention back to the mine as the silver ship landed. Two large men leapt out, carrying long Barilla rifles that glinted in the sun. They wore the sand-coloured, high-tech uniform of the Elite. One scanned the surrounding area as men came out of the larger building to meet them. The other stood stock still, his weapon at the ready. Isla crept forward.

"No," Gray whispered hoarsely, grabbing at her clothing and pulling her back. She gave him a look that made him lift his hand, but she worked her way back. "You can't just race in there. Can't you see the Barillas?"

"I wasn't racing," she murmured. "Everyone can see a Barilla; it doesn't mean it'll get you. I think that big one was the one who tried to shoot me after I crashed."

He pulled out a small pair of old and trusty binoculars. He tried to get a look at the stationary soldier, but the man wouldn't turn around. Then another man stepped out of the ship, this one wearing a suit as though he were sitting in some office in Hendra Central on Rennet. The stationary soldier erected a cover that protected the man from the sun.

Gray couldn't quite see the soldier's face, but he had close-cropped blond hair.

"Why would a Hendra official be visiting a rohen mine?" Isla asked.

"Good question."

"Got an answer?"

"I do," he said. "But you didn't like it earlier, and now wouldn't be any different. And we won't get the chance to get close with those two."

"You won't," she murmured, rising quickly to her feet. Then she was over the lip of the dune and away.

Gray growled his frustration under his breath and followed. It was turning out to be much harder than he thought keeping her safe. Particularly when she kept leaping into trouble. But she wanted answers, and he was doing nothing but giving her the chance to get them. Only he was fairly sure she wasn't going to walk out of this one.

She made a direct line for the office block, and Gray wondered exactly who was behind this. If it was money related, the offices would be more modern, with the opportunity to land inside.

These men would be used to Rennet and a kinder climate. Urgway was dry and desolate; its people either learnt to survive under the sun or were burnt by it. Urgway might be part of the Rohendra Complex, but it didn't rate high on the needs list, or the receiving list when it came to it. It did have one thing in the Complex that was wanted—rohen. Although now highly illegal, it kept the planet alive.

Isla pressed against the building and moved silently. Gray could only hope to keep up. Then she slipped around a corner, and by the time he made the edge of the building, she was gone. He would have sworn out loud but for the soldier standing just out from the wall, looking everywhere but behind him. Gray sucked in a breath and moved forward. He hoped he could find her before he was discovered because, by the shine of the Barilla the soldier held, he thought the man would shoot first and not bother asking questions.

Gray slid along the side of the building and then through the door to find Isla standing there, her finger to her lips. She motioned down the hallway, and he nodded mutely before he followed her. She paused at the far end and peeked around a corner, then pulled back and walked towards him.

He tried to ask what was going on with his eyes, but she walked past him and stopped at a door partway along. She held a small device to the hand panel, and the door opened. She secreted it away somewhere in her clothing, and he followed her into the room before the door closed after them.

"What are you doing?" he whispered.

"Elite," she said, looking around the office.

It was small. Maps of the area covered one wall, and a narrow desk sat in the middle of the room with a simple chair tucked beneath it. Gray stepped forward to look at it. Isla was looking at him, but when he looked up, he realised she was looking behind him. He turned slowly and noticed another map of the mine in detail. It could have been any mine, but it did show that much of the storage of the metal occurred underground.

"What does Hendra want with rohen? And what makes you think it has something to do with me?"

Gray shook his head. They had been watching the mines for some time. He knew where they were. Many of the locals did on this planet; they just weren't talked about. But Hendra should have been shutting them down. He had seen them visit before—officials and soldiers.

"What does this official want?" Isla asked.

He shrugged again. "The whole system is corrupt. Bribes, money?"

"They are not that corrupt," she said. "Many are good men, doing the bidding of The Hendra, keeping the peace, keeping the Complex together."

"You sound like an Elite," he muttered, still looking over the map.

She pulled out a drawer in the desk and moved some papers around. He turned around to look when she didn't answer, but she was focused on the drawer. "This is low tech," she whispered, more to herself.

"Urgway isn't known for tech," he said.

"But this isn't even low tech—it's no tech. Who uses this?" She held up a pile of white papers. "Where do you even get this from?"

"Made from sand and rock dust. We used to make it in school for art."

"Art," she muttered, pulling out more pages. "This is a list," she whispered. Something on her face changed, but her eyes never left the page. Then she folded it carefully and slipped it inside her clothing.

"It is time we left," he murmured.

"We haven't even found out why they're here."

His eyes moved to where she had secreted the page. Someone didn't want a record of this, or at least a digital signature. "It was never made clear why rohen was declared dangerous and illegal in the first place," he muttered, looking up as she lifted the duster from her belt.

"We can always ask," she said, heading for the door.

He grabbed her arm and she glared at him, but there was something else. He realised she would still be sore from the glass cuts, although she didn't indicate she was in pain.

"I can take him," she whispered fiercely.

He shook his head, his hold still tight. "There are two of them. And we need to get an idea of who is coming to collect the store."

"What store?"

He pointed to the map.

"The rohen is liquid and highly unstable. No one is going to just fly in and pick it up."

"Someone is," he assured her. "Maybe they found a way to stabilise it."

"There is a way to find out."

"No." His grip tightened around her arm.

"You dragged me here," she hissed, leaning in close.

"It isn't safe."

"Nowhere is with you. If I'm the person you're so sure I am, I can look after myself."

"You're doing a great job so far."

She growled, pulling from his hold, and opened the door to a large Elite soldier staring in at them. He raised his Barilla, and Isla froze. Gray pulled her away while banging the mechanism to close the door. The soldier pushed the long muzzle of the Barilla into the gap, blocking the door, then pushed his way in too easily.

"Well look what we have here." His voice was low and gravelly, and his smirk make Gray shiver. He wondered just what they could do to get around the man. The Barilla shone even indoors. Gray was sure he could hear a hum in the air when the soldier suddenly flew back against the wall and slumped down.

"You killed an Elite," he stammered.

"Stunned," Isla murmured, stepping forward and lifting the long weapon from his unconscious hands. "Come on."

He followed as she paused in the hallway for a moment and ran the small device over the hand pad.

Isla dragged him by the arm, back out and into the hot sun.

Six

It wasn't him. He was just some random soldier—built in the same way, but it wasn't him. The relief was almost overwhelming as they made their way around the building. Isla knew in her bones that Gray wanted to head into the mine. But if they managed to find their way down there, they wouldn't be the only ones to die. The whole situation was insane.

Rohen had been the centre of trading for the Rohendra Complex since the five planets had come together under the rule of the first Hendra. The liquid metal had been used in a number of applications and had provided advances previously only dreamed of in communication, travel and other technology. But it had never been stable, and the mining of the metal itself was dangerous. The liquid metal caused damage to anything it came into contact with and produced fumes that could kill the miners.

When the Hendra had replaced her father as the new head of the Rohendra Complex, one of the first decrees she had made was to ban the mining and use of rohen. What was already in circulation could continue, or it could be reused in some instances. But the mining ceased immediately. The whole idea that Hendra, or the Hendra herself, was involved with the mining of rohen was unthinkable.

The Elite was a special military force that protected the Hendra and her interests. As the Hendra was head of the Rohendra Complex, her interests were everyone's interests. The Hendra, the head, and the government wore the same name. All those officials ensured the planets of the Rohendra Complex were functioning to help the others.

"This is insane," Isla murmured aloud.

"Insane? You just shot an Elite soldier."

She stopped as they crossed the ridge and sat down. Gray looked back at her, the shiny Barilla cradled in her arms. It was familiar, comfortable. "I stunned him."

"Those dusters have various settings. They don't have stun."

"He was wearing armour."

An alarm sounded through the mine, and she was on her feet running after Gray through the hot sand towards the ship. As soon as they were through the door, Reilly lifted its bulk from the ground and they were away.

"What is that?" Reilly asked once they had been in the air for a while. Isla was still standing where she'd been when they'd lifted from the ground.

"Elite Barilla Rifle," Gray said, but he didn't take his eyes from her.

She breathed slowly, trying to clarify in her head what was going on and what she had seen. And who she hadn't. The cold metal appeared to shine even in the dimly lit interior of the ship. She might have thought it was glowing. Reilly grumbled something as Gray backed up.

"They are coded," Gray said.

"Are they?" Isla looked at the weapon in her hand. "Maybe they just tell you that."

"I've seen it. I've held one." He motioned for her to hand over the rifle, and she reluctantly did. It seemed to die in his hands. The shine dulled, and the gentle hum she had felt through her body disappeared.

"I told you she was a hummer," Reilly murmured loudly.

"There is no such thing," Isla said. "Now take me back to my dragonfly."

"The whole area will be crawling with enforcers."

"They'll be sifting through the remains of the stables, trying to prove I'm gone. You think I need to understand what is going on here. And..." She wasn't sure she wanted to share anything with these men. They wanted to use her, not save her. "My ship can get me to Rennet, and this rust bucket can't."

"Rust bucket!" Reilly cried.

"You wanted me in this," she said again, looking at Gray.

"I thought if you understood, you might help us."

"Yeah, Sergeant—you and your magic," Reilly said.

The ship tilted slightly as Isla pressed the duster against his temple. "Don't call me that. Or anything close to it. I'm not who you think I am."

He nodded slowly, righting the ship, and then cleared his throat. "They'll see you coming."

"It is a risk I'm willing to take. Because it is my risk, and it is my name on the list."

"What list?" he asked, trying not to move.

She slipped the page from her pocket and held it out in front of Reilly. He reached up and took it from her, scanning it, maybe looking for his own name.

"Some impressive people on that list," he said softly. "How well do you know them?"

"I don't." But in many ways, she did. They were names she knew, names she was familiar with, only she didn't mix in those circles. She might have looked out for one or two at different times, might have met them after they had patched her back together. But she didn't remember any with clarity, and she didn't know why she would be on a list with them. A list someone had written down. The hand was neat and perfect. She pushed the list back into her pocket and turned to Gray, who was still standing with the lifeless weapon in his hand.

"Explain the stun."

She sighed. "Elite armour, thin but high quality. Takes a lot to get through it." She rubbed absently at her collarbone as she remembered the feel of the bolt that had torn through her chest. "That old duster didn't have the power to get through anything."

Gray opened his mouth and then closed it.

"Anything else you want to tell us?" Reilly asked.

She shook her head.

"Was he the one you thought you saw?" Gray asked.

Isla reached out and took the Barilla back. It hummed to life in her hands. "No." She didn't want to talk about this anymore. She walked quickly through one of the doors leading from the main space of the ship and into a narrow room with bunks lining the walls.

Isla needed sleep, but it wouldn't do her any good. She lay down on the nearest bunk, laid her head back and, with the rifle still humming in her arms, she closed her eyes.

The man smirked in the doorway. The look was familiar—but then, so many of them wore that look. That *I have more power than you can imagine* smirk. Isla might have worn one herself once. The soldier's build was similar, as was his hair, but it wasn't him. In many ways, it was harder to believe it might have been him than it was to imagine him being sent to kill her. At least she would have had the chance to see him again.

She woke with a start to a hand resting on hers. The Barilla hummed to life, making the person lift their hand. She had dreamt of them again. All of them lost, dying slowly, the world a bloody mess. She sucked in a deep breath and sat up slowly. She could still taste the blood that had splattered the world that night.

"Bad dream?" Gray asked, sitting beside her.

"Are we any closer to you dropping me where I asked?"

He nodded and stood up. "We can help each other."

"What do you get out of it?"

"A chance to help others. You once did that, Isla—worked to help."

"I'll help my way."

"By going to Rennet and finding the Hendra men who are doing what exactly? Working illegally with the mines? Or are they buying the metal, and if so, what for? Are you going in Barilla glowing?"

"I have contacts. I used to have contacts. I might be able to learn more. You are the one who's determined these men are corrupt. That something illegal is occurring. If mining were so taboo, they wouldn't be able to do it so openly."

"Depends what they use it for."

"And that might be to help the Complex." She jumped up from the bunk, rearranging her loose clothing and ensuring the duster was still secured amongst the folds of fabric.

"Why did you run?" he asked. She stopped and turned back, the Barilla pointing towards him. He maintained his serious pose, unfazed by the weapon in her hands.

"I didn't. I started over."

"As a racer, and an average one at that."

She walked away. She didn't have to explain anything to this man. To any of them.

Reilly reluctantly put the ship down in the desert out from the city limit, but it was closer to her dragonfly than she had been for some time.

She could walk; it wouldn't be hard, and although Gray had tried to talk her out of the Barilla, she'd managed to hide it beneath her clothing. The day was drawing to a close. It was still light, but the heat had eased, if only a little. Isla moved quickly, glancing over her shoulder, half expecting Gray to follow. He seemed so determined they should work together, that she should help them. And in doing so, help her. But she didn't need to get involved. She just needed to find out who exactly was trying to kill her and why.

She passed a couple of newsstands as she made her way inside the city, but she didn't stop to look at the images flashing across the screen. She was fairly sure they were the same as she had seen earlier. There was no news about visiting officials. She stopped when she saw an image at one stand about the stables—the ruin left behind, the Boss distressed. That woman had to have something better underway if she'd allowed her livelihood to be destroyed. No sign of Twiggy. And then Isla's racing image flashed up again. They still thought she was out there, then. Blaming her for the explosion.

The bottles inside her bag clinked together. If she was to go all the way to Rennet, could she take some time to visit what had once been home? She ducked into an alley as enforcers cruised by. People in the street put their heads down, and those around the screen at the newsstand disappeared.

Then another person flashed up on the screen, blond hair over his face, one blue eye sparkling with mischief, a duster in hand and dressed in sand-coloured clothes similar to what everyone else wore.

A red message flashed across the base of the screen. What had he done that had him almost as wanted as she was? So far, all she had managed to do was survive.

"The Sparrow" flashed across the screen. Isla pulled the list from her pocket and scanned the list again. Sparrow.

One of the most wanted criminals in the Rohendra Complex. He had been blamed with all sorts of misdeeds against the Hendra. Isla had thought he was only an idea. Something to gather people to a cause. Not that she could guess at what that might be, other than antiestablishment. The Sparrow hadn't been around when she'd been Elite, but there had been plenty of groups with similar ideals. And she had no idea how deep Gray and Reilly were in whatever Sparrow was.

What did he want her help with? What did he think the Hendra were doing with the metal?

She shook her head. It didn't matter. She had her own worries, her own name on a list, and one she now shared with him. Was that the name Reilly was looking for? Or could Reilly be the Sparrow? His wife certainly didn't want them involved with her.

Isla looked up as the screen went blank, disappearing against the darkening city around it before the royal blue covered the screen.

"It is with great joy," a voice hummed sweetly through the streets. It was loud and it echoed, overlapping a little with the other screens along the street, all a little out of sync. "The Hendra would like to announce her pregnancy. The line continues."

I wonder what her wife thinks of such a proclamation? The Hendra was the first in the long line of leaders to marry the same sex, and there had been whispers at the time as to how the line might legitimately continue. Isla was sure they had the money to access the technology to make it happen. An image of the happy couple appeared on screen. The Hendra, in her formal uniform, smiled and waved. Her wife, dressed perfectly in the fashions of the day, was slight and blonde compared with the strength of the Hendra. Her eyes never landed on the Hendra, despite the smiles, and they stood a little too far apart. The Hendra reached for her, and there was a delay before she took the offered hand. It was brief and could be construed as her not noticing the hand immediately. Isla saw it for something else. She wondered just what the Hendra would do to secure her future—and what her wife might put up with to secure her own.

Isla disappeared deeper into the alley. When she thought she heard something or someone following, she put her hand on the Barilla, still hidden in her clothes. The touch made it hum to life, and the noise behind her disappeared. She wasn't far now. She slipped out of the other end of the alleyway, a short distance from the garage. She moved slowly, as though she wasn't worried about a thing, and then ducked into the shop.

"I don't like this," an older man greeted her with as she stepped into the space.

"Sorry, Mac."

"No, you're not. If you cared at all, you would have left it elsewhere."

"There is no safer place for her, and she's stayed here as long as I've been on planet."

He sighed and crossed his arms, then looked her over. "You ok?"

She nodded once. "How's my girl?"

"Just like you left her. I'm not stupid enough to touch her," he snapped. When she opened her mouth to apologise again, he shook his head. "You could have asked me."

"And drag you into I'm not sure what?"

"But you do know, don't you?"

"I'm getting an idea. You see the happy news?" She moved around him and out into the yard that stretched beyond the shop front, towards her ship.

"Odd news. But she's got all the money in the Complex; she can do what she wants."

Isla ran her hand over the ship, despite the cover stretched across the yard, the metal was warm from the sun. The Barilla was now in her hand.

"Where did you get that?" Mac asked.

"Borrowed it." Isla tried to smile for him, but it was harder than she remembered.

"I thought you left this behind."

"Me too," she said as she placed a hand on the panel and the door opened. She climbed aboard, and the old mechanic followed. "You can't come, Mac."

"Who said I'm coming? I just want to check my girl over."

"My girl," she said, the smile coming more easily.

"I meant you." He pulled her into his arms with no warning and, despite the scratches and cuts still covering her body, she allowed him to hold her close to his large, soft frame. "Missed you," he murmured into her hair.

She nodded against him. Mac was one of the few she really trusted. There had once been so many, but it was hard to trust. She tried not to groan at the stiffness in her body. "Seems to be a lot of ghosts around at the moment."

"You can't blame yourself for surviving," he said, holding her out at arms-length. As little as she was keen on human contact, inside his arms was a very safe place to be. She nodded as he gave her that fatherly stare.

"Easier said than done," she said, looking away. "Mac, have you heard of the Sparrow?"

"Are they that random group of vigilantes doing what they think will help the Complex when really they are just helping themselves? No. Why?"

"Just saw an image of a man I might have met recently flashed on a news stand, naming him the Sparrow."

"It's a group, innit? Why do they think this one man is involved?" She shook her head.

"You met him? He the one trying to hurt you?" Mac's gruff exterior grew gruffer.

"Claims he saved me, and maybe he did. Mentioned a mutual friend."

"You haven't got any friends."

"That's what I said." Isla turned away to look at the panel, and the lights flickered to life as she ran her hand over the controls. "Twiggy played with my racer communications."

"You disabled that, I assume."

She nodded, keeping her focus on the panel. "Do you think anyone else survived that day?"

"Island, even you didn't survive that day."

She let out half a sob, and he closed his arms around her again. "I thought I saw him," she whispered.

"Who?" he asked kindy.

"Bear."

"Not possible." Mac's voice was soft and consoling. She wished he was wrong, like she had wished so many times before. "That boy did all he could that day; you heard the recordings. But he was lost, just like all the rest."

She nodded again. "He knew me," she whispered.

"I know."

"No, the Sparrow. He knows who I am. He knew it when he first met me. No one out here knows."

"You were big news once."

"Years ago," she murmured. "Mac, what do you know about ro-hen?"

"That you don't go anywhere near the stuff."

She nodded again. He sighed and looked her over. "How bad?"

"Not too bad—just some cuts. I managed to retrieve my goodie bag," she said, holding up the bag she still held tight in her hand.

"You and your potions. Can I feed you before you disappear? You are going to do that, aren't you?"

She nodded slowly. "My name is on a list of people someone thought important enough to get rid of. I need to know why."

Seven

"Don't you think you should have waited?" Alice asked, the frustration evident in her voice.

"For what?" Hendra replied, looking up at the woman standing in the doorway. Alice looked perfect, and she had done just as required. As Hendra had known she would. The woman always did what was needed; it was one of the reasons Hendra had married her. Being in such a position required a partner who stood by and smiled and waved at the crowd, no matter what was going on around them.

"There is a precedence. What if something happens?"

"Then I blame it on someone appropriate," Hendra said, allowing the anger to be heard in her voice.

"You need to be careful. I'm assuming you are still in the early stages of this pregnancy," Alice continued, ignoring the possible danger by questioning her, although Hendra wasn't sure that she had sensed it.

"The people need to know that the line will continue."

"They don't doubt," Alice said, something warning in her tone.

Hendra stood and came around the desk, taking the woman in her arms and holding her tight to her chest. "There is always doubt.

There has always been doubt in the line. Those who think they can oppose us or replace us. This solar system would die without us."

"I wish you had told me you were doing this. It isn't unheard of. It might have been nice to do it together. When did you take my DNA?"

Hendra patted the woman comfortingly on the back. There was a lie, a well-rehearsed lie ready to tell her. "It isn't yours."

The woman stiffened and pushed away. "What?"

"You will raise the child, of course. You are perfect for that. But I needed someone stronger—someone I knew would breed a leader."

Alice's jaw dropped open. As Hendra reached out to push it back into place, Alice wrenched herself out of reach. "You weren't going to tell me," she said. Hendra could see the sadness, but Alice didn't cry. She was too strong to cry. Hendra shook her head.

"I suppose you want thanks. You won't get it. Who else is in on this secret?"

"Enough to make it worthwhile to more than you. And if you consider sharing, you know the outcome."

Alice murmured something Hendra didn't hear as she left the room.

Hendra would make it up to her. She wasn't a flight risk; and no matter the veiled threats, Alice wouldn't tell anyone. She had kept a few secrets already; this would just be another. She knew the risks, and she knew the expectations of the wife of the Hendra. Alice might very well have expected to carry any children they were to have together.

Hendra needed a child of her own blood, and one she knew she could trust to take over the mantle of leadership. As much as she cared for the woman she had married, Alice wasn't the mother of a future leader. A future Hendra.

There was a single knock at the door before it opened and closed quickly. The man before her was tall and broad, his position evident in the way he moved. His face was well known in the building, yet he managed to walk around without being seen.

"Hendra," he said, standing to attention. Always a soldier. Even when doing his required duty by his leader. She nodded, and he bowed his head.

"Did you find her?"

He nodded once.

"Is it taken care of?"

He looked to the ground. She waited, although not as patiently as she would have liked to appear. But then, this man had seen far more of her and her weaknesses than anyone should. He was one of the very few she trusted not to share what he knew.

"What happened?"

"Sparrow."

"Haven't you sorted that problem yet?" she asked, not trying to hide her irritation.

He shook his head. "Too hard to pin down. But I saw one of them. I leaked his picture to the news and the enforcers on Urgway."

"The enforcers are looking for everyone. How do you propose to get her then?"

"She'll come looking for us. If she survived that bomb."

"And did she?"

"Last footage shows her leaping from a window. If she landed where we expected, we'd still be scraping her up."

"Not dead then. Why did it take so long to find her?"

"Changed her name, changed her world. I thought she might have lived with her war hero name for some time. Maybe I didn't know her."

"You should have done the right thing in the first place, Bear."

He flinched at the name.

"That was your call sign. The bear and the dragonfly. I'm surprised you managed to get anything achieved as Elite with those silly names."

"They weren't decided by us. They were given," he grumbled through gritted teeth.

She bowed her head to acknowledge what she already knew. "Your plan?"

"She'll come to Rennet, and we take care of her here. Maybe the Sparrow will take her out."

"Are you sure about them? You should have dealt with that properly."

"We left them with a reputation that should have ended more than their careers. They appear to hold a grudge."

"Against the Hendra?"

"We needed a scapegoat. They fit."

The Hendra leaned back against her desk and smiled. "You can deal with them, I assume."

He nodded and, as another knock sounded on the door, he bowed his head.

"Enter," she called, moving around to sit back behind her desk. When she looked up, the soldier was gone.

"Congratulations, Hendra," the chief scientist said, entering the room. He was tall and gangly, but brilliant.

"Thank you."

"I'm surprised you didn't have to use our services," he said with a grin.

"Who says I didn't?" Her tone was flat, and as the smile slipped from his pale face and his Adam's apple bobbed repeatedly, she saw that he understood the danger.

He stared for a moment. And then he nodded once.

"Not everything goes through you, Warren. And I thought you busy enough. Tell me how it goes?"

"They are mining far more than we realised. The quality is excellent, and it pools neatly in the mines. We're trying to contain it, but it takes some work to ensure stability. We can allow it to pool while we work on a solution, then bring it to the surface."

"It sits underground?"

He nodded.

"Is that safe?"

"Safer than trying to bring it up in containers. It doesn't like being contained."

"So I've heard."

"If we have too many more incidents like the one last month, it will come to the people's attention and questions will be asked. You were very clear in declaring the mining of rohen illegal, the risks and dangers to the people too great to outweigh the benefits of the metal itself. They tolerate the mines because of the money they bring to Urgway."

"Can you get it to do what you want?"

He nodded and then chewed on his lip.

"Warren, I don't have to tell you what we have risked here."

"I can," he said quickly.

She nodded once.

"What about this racer?" he asked.

"In hand." Hendra wondered why he would be asking.

"There's a rumour she's a hummer."

The Hendra stared at the man until he bowed his head and left the room. She looked back to the monitors above her desk and flicked through the various reports that had been coming in through the day. Not one of them mentioned that the woman might be a hummer.

The soldier reappeared behind the screens, his face serious. She wondered just how far he went when he hid in the shadows, and what he was privy to that she might not appreciate.

"Is she?" she asked.

He shook his head.

"You are confident in that response."

He bowed his head again, without saying a word, and strode out through the main door of the office. This time she knew he wouldn't be reappearing anytime soon. She looked back at the monitors on her desk and tried not to sigh. There was much she had to do before she could head home that evening. It was probably better to allow Alice to calm down first. She would make it up to her, but she hadn't been in the wrong, and if she had never told Alice the truth, she would never have known. It was better that she knew her place in the Complex.

"What exactly do you think you can do for her?" Reilly asked across the dusty table in the small drinking shack not too far from the mountains they'd hidden their ship in. They didn't really mix with the people here, except for some old friends they still met with when they could. Such as those hidden in the mountain. Old members of the Sparrow, those Reilly had risked by taking Isla with them when Gray had fallen out of the sky.

Gray shrugged. Isla didn't really need his help at all. If he hadn't gotten involved with the racing, she would probably be just as safe as before. He closed his eyes as he remembered her leaping from the building into the air over nothing. He had been trying to see inside, trying to get an idea of what she was doing, and he was thankful he had been there at that moment. If he hadn't, she wouldn't have survived.

"This is your obligation talking. Not that you think she needs looking after—we both know that girl can look after herself very well."

"Sure," Gray said. "Cut to ribbons and still walking."

Reilly looked at him seriously. "What did you see?"

"Too much," he murmured. "It makes sense now, why she ran. But not how she survived. I'm not sure she did. She sat so impassively during the hearing, taking in every word, every sound from that battlefield."

"You can't save her."

"I know that," Gray snapped. He wasn't sure why he was getting worked up, why it mattered what happened. But he had made a promise long ago to an old friend, one who needed to be sure she would be safe. He hadn't recognised her at first, as he didn't really pay much attention to the racers. He was too busy trying to work out what the connection to the races might be, what they were really up to. Then she had appeared in the pit with that old race helmet pushing down her hair, those bright red curls flying away from beneath it, catching the light just as they did in the image he had. He had known right then.

"She's going to go after whoever it is wants her dead." No matter how much distance she wanted to put between what she was now and what she had been. He knew it with everything he had.

"You would do the same."

"Perhaps." And they were, in a way. His name was also on that list, if only the name of the ship they had once belonged to. There was a mad series of knocks on the door, and Reilly climbed to his feet and opened it to a younger man. Gray had seen him around, but not for some time.

"You got to leave the planet," he panted.

Reilly simply raised his eyebrows.

"You've been rumbled," the boy said, glancing around behind him. "They got you up on the news."

"What?" Gray pulled the panel from his pocket and scanned the news sights. There he was, loud and clear, labelled as Sparrow. "Damn it," he grumbled.

"They gonna be looking for you everywhere."

He scrolled through the feed. Isla was still there, the same insane amount on her head. And although it didn't say dead or alive, anyone would know that was what that amount of money meant. Then there was Reilly, also labelled as Sparrow. But the amount was less. Someone knew who they had been, but Gray doubted they knew what they were doing now.

"Go home to your mother," Reilly mumbled, closing the door. "Where to now, then? They will be watching everything we do, every port. We need to get off planet, but where and how?"

Gray turned with a grin.

"I am not getting in that racer, or going anywhere with it."

"She might be our only hope."

"You have a hope, but it isn't related to keeping us alive."

Gray's cheeks betrayed him with a burn as the image of her naked, perfect other than the crisscross of scars, filled his mind. She was damaged both inside and out. "She is going to be headed for Rennet."

"We even think about Rennet, we are going to die."

"There might be another option."

"You would have to convince her of that. And I don't think you could convince that woman to do anything she doesn't want."

"No, but what might help us might help her."

Eight

Isla had her head under the front console, trying to familiarise herself with a ship she hadn't had any quality time with in far too long. Not that it needed maintenance. It was perfect, and she was soon lost to the wires and circuitry. Mac sat on the edge of the doorway, looking like he was keeping watch, but she knew he was watching her. Despite her wish that he didn't care, she understood his fear. They had found each other on this dusty planet by accident. They had worked well together so long ago, when she had been something else. She didn't want to lose him now. But given all that was happening, and that she wasn't quite sure who was behind it, he wasn't safe as long as she was around.

"Heads up," he whispered, and she put down the tool she had inserted into the underside of the panel.

"That is one amazing ship. We're looking for the owner," a familiar voice said. Isla tried not to groan.

"I don't think he's willing to sell," Mac said.

"He?" That was Reilly. The rifle was in reach, but Isla headed towards the door without it.

"We are a private yard," Mac said. She reached him just as he was lifting his bulk from the step. She put her hand on his shoulder. He looked up apologetically.

"How did you know?" she asked.

"Good guess," Reilly said.

"What do you want?"

"We have some heat."

"Don't we all?"

"We want to come with you," Gray said, stepping forward.

"To Rennet? You are wanted criminals. Do you want me to fly you into the middle of the Hendra headquarters?"

"Nearby would do," Gray said.

"This boy has a plan, and I don't think you'll like it," Mac said.

"I'm sure I won't. But I'll hear it." Mac grunted something under his breath. "It's ok," she said.

"Rennet is rainforest on one side of the planet."

"I was born on Rennet," she said.

He bowed his head. He knew. What else did he know about her?

"Who?" she asked, although she wasn't sure she wanted to know. "What do you think I can do for you?" she asked, redirecting the conversation and her own destructive thoughts.

"Just take us to Rennet and we can all learn what we need to do to make this end." Reilly shook his head. Either he didn't want to go, or he thought this was a bad idea.

"And how are we going to do that?" she asked, crossing her arms to shield herself somewhat from the grin he wore.

"Why would she go anywhere with you?" Mac asked, standing with a surprising speed that made Isla smile. "My girl owes you nothing. She puts herself in more danger going anywhere near Rennet."

Isla reached out again and rested her hand on his shoulder. "Both of you?" she asked.

"That's a fine ship, worth all the lamenting to get back to it," Reilly murmured, walking along the length of the ship. He reached out towards the hull, then pulled his fingers away from the dark metal as though he shouldn't touch it.

"She earned it," Mac grumbled. Isla sighed as she pushed past him and landed softly in the dust at his feet.

"A gift for duty served," Gray said, his face serious as she stared him down.

"She'll make any flight, but she's not designed for long haul or comfort."

"Just get us there and we'll keep an eye out for any danger to you," Reilly said.

Isla settled on the step Mac had stood up from. She looked at Gray, wondering if he was a man she could trust.

"Extra guns would be handy," Mac murmured.

"Thanks Mac, but I think I got it."

"I hope so, girl." Mac stepped away from the ship and disappeared across the yard.

"He doesn't seem to trust your judgement," Gray offered.

"He trusts. He just knows what lies ahead."

"Do you?"

She nodded once and stood up. "I got some work to do. Be ready at sundown."

This was probably a bad idea, she thought as she climbed back under the panel. But she was running out of options, and Gray knew it. She had nowhere to go, and no matter what she had done in her past or where she had been, someone wanted her dead. She needed to know who.

"What are you thinking?" Mac asked, his voice soft as he sat in the cockpit. She realised it had grown darker.

"That I'm not ready to die."

"And heading into the hornet's nest is going to ensure that doesn't happen?"

"Probably not," she said, looking out from beneath the panel as he sighed. "But I'm dead either way, and neither are the way I thought it would happen. I just need to find out why—who put a mark on my head. Get it removed and get back to my exciting life."

Mac chuckled, a warm and comforting sound.

"You could come with me," she suggested, even though she had told him he couldn't. She had wanted to keep someone safe and was both disappointed and relieved when he shook his head slowly. For a moment, it could have been like the old days, when she didn't know what she was headed into, but she knew who was with her, and that was enough.

"Do you think this boy will help?"

"I don't know," she said honestly. He was in this for his own reasons, only she wasn't quite sure what they were. And she was yet to find out who the mutual friend was that he mentioned so often.

Well, a couple of times. If she had any clue who, she might have a better idea as to where he fit in the picture.

"He might draw more fire. They've been trying to pin down Sparrow for some time."

She nodded slowly, refocusing on the work she was trying to do to the panel.

"What aren't you telling me?" Mac asked, his voice louder. Although she wouldn't look away from the panel, she knew he had leant forward.

"Nothing," she said, running her finger slowly along the wiring. The engines were cold, and yet she felt the hum of life beneath her fingers. She might not have had the chance to fly her ship often, but there was something familiar in it, something like an old friend. She knew she would have one on her side going into this, even if it was made of metal.

She secured the cover beneath the panel and climbed to her feet. "I just can't work out how Boss and the race fit into any of this."

"Any ideas on the bomb at the stables?"

She shook her head and tucked a loose curl behind her ear. "Change your mind."

He stood up then, wrapped his arms around her and pressed a soft kiss to the top of her head. The lotion had started working, and many of her cuts were already healed. "You know you are wanted throughout the Rohendra Complex."

She nodded against him, taking one last squeeze. The light was dimming outside. Isla didn't think the Sparrows, if that was what they were, had gone far with the amounts on their heads. But she wanted to go sooner rather than later, and they didn't have long before she would be flying off without them.

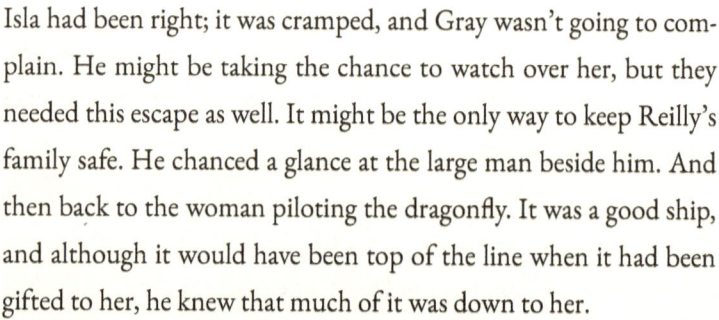

Isla had been right; it was cramped, and Gray wasn't going to complain. He might be taking the chance to watch over her, but they needed this escape as well. It might be the only way to keep Reilly's family safe. He chanced a glance at the large man beside him. And then back to the woman piloting the dragonfly. It was a good ship, and although it would have been top of the line when it had been gifted to her, he knew that much of it was down to her.

He also noted the Barilla not far from her reach. It had been unnerving when she had activated it. He knew too well that Elite weapons were imprinted to their owners and couldn't be used against them. But she appeared to have slept better with it in her hands than she had with only the duster after the last time he had saved her.

He wondered how they were going to leave the planet's surface without drawing more attention. It had been too long since he had been in space, and it had been far more heart wrenching than expected when they'd left the atmosphere. It had also been much faster than he remembered. He wasn't sure why, but he thought she might try and manoeuvre some different way. Yet when the roof opened, she went straight up from the mechanic's workshop. Straight into the air. No time for anyone to do anything other than hold their breath and hope they made it through.

"What did you think would happen?" she asked.

"Something."

"What kind of something are you hoping for?" Reilly murmured under his breath.

"I don't know," Gray said. "It seems too easy."

"Maybe I'm cashing you in," Isla said too chirpily from the pilot seat.

"Your head is worth far more than ours," Reilly said loudly.

"Which is why I'm flying. You might have flown me right into Hendra Central."

"We are just as wanted," Reilly said. "It would be condemning us all to death."

"I'm not ready to die just yet."

"You sure?" Gray asked, and she turned to glare at him before focusing on the panel before her. She waved a hand over the far end of the panel, then unbuckled and stood up.

"You've got some time before Rennet comes into view—start explaining why the Hendra wants you."

"We have a reputation," Reilly said, somewhat proudly.

"Do you?" Isla asked, crossing her arms. Gray noticed she didn't wince when she did so. "Why Rennet?"

"Hendra Central," Gray said. "You want to find out why they want you dead."

"And yet we can't land anywhere near the capital. We'll have to land in the forests on the other side of the planet. How is that going to help you?"

"You're right, it is a safer option. We can't just fly into the middle of it all and ask who wants us dead. The Elite will have us blown from the sky before we even think about our options."

"There are other ways."

Gray raised an eyebrow, but she said nothing further.

"We were enforcers," he said, and Reilly slammed a sharp elbow into his side. "Hey," he protested, "we owe her."

"We owe her?" Reilly asked. "Haven't we been the ones helping her?"

"Would you like to take it outside and debate who is helping who?" she asked, her arms still crossed.

Reilly shook his head. The expanse of space stretched out around them.

"We worked with the Elite."

"When?" Isla stepped closer.

"A couple years back, but we didn't like what they were doing. Or how they did it. And we, our ship, stood up to them. You can imagine how that went."

Isla nodded. "Why the sparrow?"

"It was our ship. A little like your dragonfly—only larger, held far more, travelled faster and further, and they used us to do their dirty work. When we stood up to them, they took us out. We made it home." He tilted his head towards Reilly. "But they never really let go. Not once we were seen with you."

"The others I saw you with?"

"Friends we collected along the way along with the remaining crew."

"You are planning a revolution," Isla said, her voice disbelieving.

"You have a problem with that?" Reilly snapped. "You've seen what they've done to the Complex. What the Hendra claims to do in the name of the people—but it only betters her and her kind. You were part of that."

Isla shook her head and headed back towards the pilot seat.

"You were. What do you think happened that day?" Reilly pushed. Before Gray could even shush him, the rifle hummed to life and she had it trained on them both.

"I know what happened." Her voice was soft, and yet there was both a sadness and a dark, dangerous soldier behind it. "I was there. I lived through every bloody moment. And then I relived it during the hearing."

Gray wanted to ask if she still saw it in her dreams, but he kept his mouth shut tight. This was a woman on the edge, and Reilly was poking her closer.

"We're not saying you are corrupt," Gray said, nudging Reilly again.

"Yes, you are," Isla said. "We were the Elite—we did all we could to protect this solar system, this way of life. And many died trying to do just that."

"You didn't," Reilly blurted.

"Someone is trying to make sure that's changed," Gray added quickly. "Why is that? What happened that day that a whole squad of Elite were overcome?"

She shook her head and headed back to the chair. She blew out a long, slow breath and buckled herself back in. It would be some time before they were close to Rennet. Gray wondered if they had hit a nerve. It was unheard of for the Elite to be defeated, at least by the general public, particularly to such an extent. As he watched the back of the woman's head, he wondered how much time she spent wondering the same thing.

The rest of the flight went in silence. They approached the planet from the far side, which, as he'd hoped, had far less security. Although, if he had been watching over the head of the Complex, he would have thought the whole planet would have better security. Either way, they landed in the middle of the forest, and Isla was out of her seat and into the forest surrounding the ship with barely a pause to ensure there was no one around.

Gray crept more cautiously from the craft. He couldn't see anything to indicate they had been seen landing, but there were also no animal sounds, and he was fairly certain they were being watched. "Stay with the Dragonfly," he instructed Reilly as he jumped down to follow Isla.

There was no response from Reilly, but Gray knew he would do as was needed.

Isla stood in the middle of a small clearing, flowers and creeping plants around her feet. Tall, broad trees loomed over her; long branches hung down around her. It was almost as though the planet had leaned in to see her. She stood with her eyes closed, taking deep breaths, and he was sure she smiled.

"Long time since you've been home then," he said. She nodded without moving, and he stepped forward.

"I don't trust you," she said without turning back to him. "Your ride is over. You can do as you please now."

"And you?"

"I have some things to do here first."

He opened his mouth to ask what as she pulled the outer layer of her clothing off, revealing a sand-coloured sleeveless top and exposing her scarred arm. He too had noticed the more comfortable temperature, but the air seemed damp, and he wasn't keen to get closer to the foliage than was necessary. Isla surprised him with a jump, and he watched as she pulled herself up into a tree.

"This is not a good idea," he called after her, then looked around to see who else might be watching.

"Lock the ship when you leave."

"What about the rifle?" He caught a glimpse of the bright silver amongst the leaves, and he bit his tongue. He was supposed to be helping her, not letting her loose in the forest to fend for herself.

He sighed and walked back to the ship.

"What is she doing?" Reilly asked, looking over the control panel. "She's made it so I can't start it."

"She asked us to lock up and leave."

"Where is she?"

"Climbing trees."

Reilly looked at Gray as though he had lost his mind. "You need her for whatever plan is forming in your mind," Reilly said, and Gray was almost disappointed that he wasn't as mysterious as he'd hoped. But his friend could read him no matter what he did; it had always been the case. And Gray was thankful every time he looked at him that he hadn't had to tell his wife he wasn't coming home. "So what do we do?" Reilly asked.

"We do what we came to do. Meet those we think can help and see what we can do to end Hendra."

Gray glanced back up into the trees. He had no idea how he could help anyone, let alone help her to do what she needed. He hoped, if she was from here, that she could find a way to discover what she needed without getting herself killed.

He was stupid to think her coming to Rennet would solve their problems. But he knew they would have scoured Urgway for her, turned the planet inside out. If he could find a way to work out what they were doing with the rohen, that would make a difference. For now, he had to focus on that.

Nine

The Hendra wanted to put her feet up, lie back and close her eyes, for no other reason than she felt ill. She hated feeling out of control, even of her own body. And the strange feeling had come on so quickly. When she had first learnt of the pregnancy, she had never felt stronger. The doctor had said he could give her something, but Alice talked of natural remedies, herbs and the like, and Hendra allowed her to dictate what she ate and drank.

She glared at the glass cup on the table, the green liquid filling it to the brim. Alice had said it was nicer hot, but it didn't matter what she did or how she took it—the liquid was bitter and only made her feel worse. Generally, she felt better than she had, or she might have thought that Alice was making a stand and ensuring she didn't deliver someone else's child. But she didn't really think Alice had it in her.

She pushed the cup further across the desk and tried to refocus on the monitors when Alice appeared in the doorway.

"Is it that time already?"

Alice shook her head, her eyes on the untouched drink. Hendra kept her eyes on the monitors.

"There is someone here to see you."

Hendra looked up then. She spent much of her time at a desk in her office or in their home, which was part of the buildings of Hendra Central. There were times she was off limits to everyone but family, unless it was dire, and she had left those instructions this evening.

She nodded once. Alice disappeared from the doorway, and the large soldier filled the space where she had been. Hendra sat her hand on the desk, and the monitors disappeared. "This had better be serious," she said.

"The dragonfly has been seen."

"Where you expected her to be?"

"She's on Rennet."

Hendra pushed herself up from the desk, fighting the wave of nausea and cursing her own weaknesses. "And her plan?" Her tone betrayed just what she needed it to, although this man was hardly intimidated, even by her. There had been a time she'd found that appealing; now she found it disappointing. It only took one not showing her the reverence she deserved before the whole solar system slipped into the same line.

He came forward and settled on the edge of the desk, leaning towards her. "I'm sure she will be predictable."

"I thought you knew what you were doing," she said, sitting back down. "I may need to have someone else look into this issue."

He smiled too comfortably. "I do know. And I know exactly where she will be."

A metal blade sat on the edge of the desk. It was an alloy. She would rather a pure metal, but it was too unstable. The knife had been a gift from a very talented scientist. Another she had briefly considered for the father of her child.

She laid her hand on the cool metal; it almost pulled the warmth from her skin. "Are you certain she isn't a hummer? Because if she is, there are those who might use her." She raised her eyes from the cool blade to his cool blue eyes.

He shook his head and rose from his reclined position to stand at ease before her, his hands behind his back. Although she couldn't see them, she could tell by the set of his shoulders that he was gripping them tight. If this girl was as suspected, he had not only missed it, but then allowed her to disappear into the solar system.

"You know where she might be, or where she is?"

"I will end this, Hendra."

"You had better, Colonel Calder, or I might need to revisit your worth in my Complex."

He turned without acknowledging her comment and left the room. She didn't look away from the door, knowing that Alice would have lingered. Particularly if she had taken the time to escort him to the office, but he might have gone to the residence first. It didn't matter. It was all business. That was what her life was, the business of the Rohendra Complex. Every meal, every party, every meeting was focused on that business. And everyone she met with was asking for something or trying to influence her in some way.

"Did I hear you say 'hummer'?" Alice asked.

She shook her head.

"Dinner is ready."

"I hope it is something tasty." She rose from the desk and kissed Alice's cheek as she met her in the doorway.

"It is healthy for the baby," Alice responded with a sweet smile.

"So, not tasty." Hendra allowed a little disappointment in her voice, but she smiled. Alice needed all the reassurance she could give.

"I hope so, but likely not. You'll be pleased to know I'm eating with you. I didn't think it would be fair if I ate slow-roasted Urgway buglets when you are eating plants."

"Now I want slow-roasted buglets."

Alice shook her head and pulled her into the lift to the dining room. The sooner this pregnancy was over, the better. All she had to do was produce a healthy child. Just one was all she needed to ensure her line. Alice could carry any further children, if they really needed them. If she could have bought a child, she would have, but there were expectations and laws to adhere to.

The meal was as tasteless as it appeared, and Alice smiled across the table as she chewed. Hendra stopped trying to look as though she might be enjoying it. It was as it was going to be.

"Why was that man here?" Alice asked before she pushed another mouthful of the sloppy green meal in.

"Sometimes it just can't wait."

"He makes me nervous," Alice admitted, looking down at her food.

"Colonel Calder?" Hendra reached for the large glass of water, longing for wine. "He is harmless enough—although not to our enemies, of course."

"You can't have any enemies left."

"I would like to think so, but unfortunately not everyone agrees. He fears that people will think I am compromised in my current position. An easy target."

Alice laughed, and Hendra looked at her seriously. "You would never be an easy target, even if you were on your deathbed. You would find a way to rally and overcome whatever evil is threatening you."

Hendra smiled. "True enough, dear."

"He thinks he is more important than he is."

"Does he?" Hendra wondered aloud, and she wondered silently if he had grander ideas now that he had managed to father her child. Although she hadn't told him, and he didn't appear interested in any way. They had done as they had needed, and when she'd shown no further interest, he had not raised it again. It wasn't like he was the only official she'd had her way with. There were others she was occasionally attracted to or wanted some power over—a way to test them. Only one of the few had needed to be dealt with, and the colonel had been happy enough to help. He hadn't been colonel then, but it had certainly helped him reach his goal.

"Are you going to tell me why he was here?"

Hendra looked up at Alice. "No," she said simply.

Alice opened her mouth and then closed it. She used to ask, when she wasn't included, what she thought she needed to know. But Hendra had only explained once that she didn't need to know anything, and if she did she would be told. Hendra looked after Alice, treated her as any good wife should be treated, and Alice supported the Hendra in everything. It wasn't for her to know the running of the Complex, and in many ways it would put her at risk if she knew more than she did. Not that Hendra would tell her so. They both had their place in the solar system, and Alice's task was being the wife. Hendra would allow her to feed her green muck and claim it was healthy. She would drink the green potions, and she would take the advice on caring for the growing child. But when it came down to it, Hendra was in control of the entire Complex, Alice included, and if Alice had to be reminded, then so be it.

"There was a minister at one of your parties…" Alice's voice died out as Hendra raised her eyes from the mess in her bowl, hoping now wasn't the time she would have to remind her wife of her place. "The colonel," Alice added weakly.

"What about him?"

"There's some question as to his training, and…"

Hendra didn't say a word. She didn't need to. Alice knew she had overstepped. She took another mouthful of the green slop from the bowl, and Hendra wondered if she truly thought it edible. Alice put her spoon down and waved the servant forward, her face paling as she did. Although they saw more than anyone would like, it seemed they were better trained than the wife.

"Bring the treat," Alice muttered, pushing her bowl away. The girl bowed her head, took the bowls and disappeared. Hendra put her spoon down. "I thought you could do with something a bit sweeter. You have been eating so well of late, and I knew you would miss what you usually have."

A bowl was placed before her, piled high with pure white ice cream.

Hendra blinked in surprise at Alice, who clearly wanted to smile but was swallowing down what could have been tears. She lifted the spoon and poked it carefully into the contents of the bowl, then lifted a taste to her lips. It was perfect. It was also extremely difficult to get. Milk was rare, and the fresh vanilla was even rarer.

"There are some pockets of the solar system that still hold secrets," Alice whispered.

"Thank you, my love," Hendra said, giving her a genuine smile and taking a bigger mouthful. It numbed her tongue. "You know secrets, Alice, far more than you should. I trust you to keep them, and that you won't listen to idle gossip."

Alice bowed her head, a smile on her lips again as she took a small taste of the ice cream herself. The servant stepped forward, but with a subtle shake of Alice's head she disappeared. Hendra wished she was sitting closer to her wife so she could have reached out and taken her hand. But Alice didn't need the reassurance, and Hendra didn't have the energy to provide it. As wife, it was for Alice to determine the evening meal, as long as it didn't clash with a meeting or function. She could have chosen for it to be served in the smaller room rather than the formal dining room. But then, traditions needed to be maintained—there was a new Hendra coming.

Ten

Isla woke to the sound of a big cat landing on the branch. The rifle hummed to life in her hands, but the shining eyes didn't shy away in the darkness beneath the branches. Isla stretched slowly. It had been too long since she'd slept in the trees, and it was the best sleep she'd had in a very long time. Despite the dark, she wasn't scared. The cat growled low and long, padding closer. Isla waited. When it reached her feet, it sniffed along her skin and then purred loudly.

Isla reached out and stroked between its ears. It was the best welcome home she could have asked for. It purred a little louder and almost pushed her from the tree as it rubbed against her. Then, almost standing on her, it rubbed a wet nose across her face.

"Alright," Isla said, "ease up." The cat rubbed her again, then jumped across to another branch and was lost in the dark. Isla had forgotten how secure she felt here, how the world was different from what she had woken up to amongst the bodies and hell in the dark that night. A night that had haunted her dreams since. Not this night. She breathed in the fresh air and sighed with the feeling that filled her being. It had been too long. She had hidden away on Urgway; maybe she should have hidden here. They would have found her—not that she knew who they were. But that didn't change the danger she was in.

She looked down at the forest floor and the fungi and other plants that glowed softy in the dark. She jumped down from the tree, landing lightly on her feet in the soft grass, and regretted wearing her boots. The dragonfly was dark. The others hadn't returned. She didn't know what they had planned, and she wasn't sure she wanted to. She had been so keen to learn who wanted her dead, but she felt so alive here it was hard to remember why she had stayed away.

"Rennet," she whispered as she knelt over a patch of iridescent red fungi. She held her hand out over it and they changed colour, becoming a pale green; she picked them quickly from the ground. She'd left her collecting bag in the ship, but she didn't think it would hurt to hold them for a little while. She saw another group the same and repeated her action. When she had her hands full of glowing pale green fungi, she headed back to the ship. She breathed across the panel, and it opened for her.

Something about being back on Rennet gave her a confidence she didn't think she had felt since that night. Since the day that photo had been taken. She dropped the fungi down and rested her hand on the floor beside it. A gentle click was followed by a panel opening. "Damn Gray," she muttered. He had her thinking about all sorts of things she didn't want to be thinking, and wondering about people long gone.

She pulled an old wooden bowl from the hidden space, scooped up the fungi and dropped it in. Then she pulled out a large pounding stick. Holding her hand over the bowl to keep the fungi light green, she pushed the rounded end gently into the soft flesh and it squelched quietly. She continued the motion for some time, allowing her mind to wander far away into a distant past and a fight they were confident was just the same as any other. And then there was nothing but blood. Despite the clarity of the nightmare, Isla struggled with the reality of that day. That they could be bested, that so many could be lost.

She shook her head slowly, refocusing on the contents of the bowl and allowing the hazy memories she had blanked out for so long to slip away. One of the counsellors at the time had suggested she would remember more if she didn't think about it, if she didn't try to think about it. But she had so desperately wanted to remember him, and others. And the harder she had tried to cling to them, the faster they had slipped away.

The fungi was now an opaque paste in the bowl. She rubbed a little between her fingers, feeling the slight tingle, and reached back into space beneath the floor for the bag that clinked with empty jars. Isla scooped the contents out of the bowl and sealed it tight inside one of the yellowed jars. It would last for years. She couldn't explain how—she'd tried, even tried to teach others—but there was something in the way she changed the plant and slowly worked it to a paste. An Elite medic years before had asked, but she couldn't tell him, and when he'd tried, he had nearly died from the fumes of what he had created.

She ran her fingers through her hair. She would need to do something with that too. But what she needed would be in another part of the forest, where there were more rocks than trees. She stood slowly and headed for the small bathroom, if it could be called that on the Dragonfly. She never thought she would need to travel so far, and yet here she was, a whole world away and home.

Would the Hendra be looking for her here? Would they think she travelled so far? Or even consider that she might want to return? As far as her history was concerned, what they might have on file, she was orphaned as a child. But it was more than that, something she couldn't explain except to someone who had grown in the same world, in the same way.

She was suddenly desperate to find those she had left behind. And she had left them behind so long ago. As ships had raced overhead, she had run away to find a different life, and it was only as she stowed the bag of jars away that she realised she'd never really let go of what she had learnt.

The sensor on the control panel pinged quietly. Isla cursed under her breath. She had become too complacent. In a single afternoon, she had slipped into ways she hadn't followed in years. Into a confidence she had thought long gone.

The sensor pinged again. Two. She slipped back into the cockpit, still dimly lit, and knew she couldn't be seen from the outside. Hoped. That was what the space-level tinting was supposed to do. But she'd peered into enough ships over the years to know that, with the right technology, anything was possible.

It wasn't the Sparrow enforcers returning, that was for sure; they wouldn't approach the ship in such a way. Isla growled under her breath and looked over her shoulder at the hidden panel in the floor, regretting not leaving some fungi as she had found it.

The Barilla hummed to life in her hands as she headed to the door. She placed a hand on the metal beside the door and took a deep breath as she readied the Barilla. With a nod, the door opened, and the man standing before her took a shot directly in the chest. It wasn't enough to kill, and from the sound alone she knew he was wearing armour strong enough to prevent most weapon blasts. She shut the door and raced back to the flight consol. She waved her hand over the controls, moved her fingers through the lights that danced before her and then squinted as the forest around her lit up like the middle of the day.

Another soldier stood at the front of the ship, shielding his face. Isla grumbled that they had found her so easily. She debated for a moment if she should take off and leave the others behind—not that she had promised them anything—or whether she should take these two out. Although she didn't know how many more were coming.

The man before her held up his hands and mouthed something. Isla moved her fingers through another part of the panel.

"I repeat," he said loudly, "we are to escort you, not harm you."

Isla looked around for the other man but couldn't see him. The one in front looked off to the side. Isla brought up the panel where a flashing red light showed the other soldier to be.

"Where?" she asked, her voice ricocheting of the trees.

"Central."

"No thanks."

He looked off to the side again. The movement was small, but she saw it. The inching towards the weapon on his belt. She turned the lights up, and his hand moved up to shield his face.

"Sargent Tarle, I don't think…"

"I think I do," she returned before he could finish the lie he was about to offer. "I'll come in when I'm ready."

"Will you?" he asked.

"Do you really want to try?"

He lowered his shoulders then, and the other man stepped forward. He was walking as though nothing had happened, as though he hadn't just been shot. She dimmed the lights. The man she had been talking to gave her a half-hearted salute, and they wandered into the darkness. She ran her fingers through the controls, watching the dots move further out from the ship. There didn't appear to be anyone around, but that didn't mean there weren't more just outside the perimeter of her sensors.

Other dots moved around her, but they were animals, marked differently. As she watched, more of them moved in closer to the ship. She left the lights on but dimmed them further. She didn't want any surprises, and they knew where she was.

Not that they had introduced themselves. But then, you wouldn't to someone you were about to kill. Isla sat back in the seat, closed her eyes and took a deep breath. At what point had she become the enemy of what she had belonged to? The ray of the Barilla bouncing from the armour replayed in her mind. It had pushed him back, but it wouldn't have penetrated his skin.

The searing pain of that night returned, the heat of energy cutting through her skin. It had seemed so unlikely, as though their armour hadn't even been Elite grade. And for the first time, Isla had the sick feeling that they had been sent out there to die. The armour they'd worn might not have been to grade, and they'd thought they were safer than they were. It had all been taken as part of the investigation. As part of finding out how a whole Elite group had been slain. The hearings suggested advanced weapons—something alien, at least to their solar system. Now Isla wondered if it was really that complicated. If not, that would indicate there'd been someone on the inside, someone who could have gotten at their equipment. Someone who had wanted them dead.

That raised far more questions than it answered.

⚬

Gray looked at the building before them and wondered if this was a good idea. Once they had met up with their contacts, gathering supplies, getting into the city wasn't hard, but getting into the building would be near impossible.

"Exactly what are we gaining from this?" Reilly asked. "Is it helping the cause? Is it helping us not get killed?"

"Depends on how well you avoid energy bolts or whatever tech they use to try and kill intruders."

"I hate you."

"Just as long as you watch my back."

The street around them was bright; the artificial light of the city almost kept it in perpetual daylight. For a moment, Gray longed for the dark, warm nights of Urgway that stretched out across the desert, where he could see the stars and distant suns and sometimes other planets in the solar system. The bright lights of the city took him back to when he'd been an enforcer and the world had appeared to be a very different place.

These people were not what they pretended to be. They weren't working for the good of the Complex as they claimed, and he didn't know how to fix it. He had an idea—to destroy them, to expose them—but he knew it couldn't be that easy. And his mind kept slipping back to a pretty redhead hiding in the trees. There was far more to her than he was getting at, but he still couldn't fathom why they wanted her dead.

"I feel uncomfortable," Reilly muttered.

"Stop pulling at it, you'll draw attention," Gray returned in a quiet tone. The enforcer uniforms they'd been gifted fit perfectly, although he hoped were current, as they updated too often—partly to ensure there were no counterfeit uniforms out there. They had been enforcers, so how hard could it be to pass as such now? Only looking at Reilly, you would never know it.

"We need more help," he muttered.

"We couldn't drag the team from Urgway into this," Gray returned. He wondered if Isla believed Hendra were behind so much of what was wrong with the solar system. He had tried to tell her, but she wasn't the sort to listen. At least she was safe out in the middle of the forest, unless some big cat tried to eat her, but she could probably defend herself better than he could in such a situation.

"Here," Reilly hissed, drawing his attention. Gray cursed himself for getting distracted. They walked around a corner just as two enforcers walked towards them, and he wondered why they weren't in a vehicle. One of them nodded as they kept going. Gray returned the nod, and they carried on without even glancing back. They cut around the building and then back towards the street.

"That seemed odd," Reilly muttered.

"As long as they don't think we are, that will help us."

The only person they could see inside the building was a security guard at the front counter. But he also might not be as he seemed. Any issue inside the building would be taken care of by soldiers on the premises; no one would call the enforcers. They might, but only if it was something huge. And then many more than two would turn up. Gray spotted someone moving through the lobby, and he dragged Reilly further along the street.

"They're headed for the main entrance." Reilly pulled his arm from Gray's hold and shook himself out. "We are not going to get past anyone to get into that building."

"No," Gray muttered, looking up as the building stretched away into the distance. But if the answers to what they were up to were anywhere, they would be inside Hendra Central.

Reilly nudged him. He brought his focus back to the lobby, where another man had entered the building. Gray stared at him. He had seen him before, he was sure. The man was dressed in casual clothing, not a uniform, and yet he wore it as though it were. The security guard saluted, and the man stepped up to talk to him. Then he indicated back outside the building, and Gray tugged Reilly towards the entrance so they could follow them.

The two men appeared to talk casually, but they couldn't get close enough to hear anything. They needed to look like they were on patrol, not following anyone who had been inside Hendra Central.

The street suddenly seemed very empty, despite the lighting, and Gray wondered again if this was a good idea. Something niggled at the back of his mind about the man before him. He knew there was more to this. More than just a catch up between friends or colleagues.

They turned into a small diner, and the young girl who greeted them seemed to know them, pointing them towards the back of the venue.

"You want to get inside," Reilly mumbled as they stopped.

Gray nodded. But they couldn't go in as they were. And he didn't want to risk being seen or identified by either of the men. If they were Elite, they would know Gray and Reilly, whether they had been around when the Sparrow went down or not. Their faces would be somewhere on a database. Although Gray hadn't noticed them flashing across any newsstands they had passed since arriving on Rennet. He pulled Reilly into an alleyway that offered a little more shelter from the lights.

"We'll wait," Gray muttered.

"Is this going to help us find what we want?"

"Maybe. That guy wasn't at the mine, but there is something about him."

"He was on the Sparrow."

Gray stood up straight, leaned back and took in Reilly. The man nodded once.

"He might not be in uniform, but I knew him too. I saw him." His jaw set, anger Gray had seen so many times before settled easily on his face. "I would never forget the way he moved, the lack of anything human inside him. If he is around, we need to be careful."

"Do you remember his name?"

"We'd be lucky if they told us anything that was real that day."

Gray nodded and looked back across the street. The two men left the diner. Gray wondered what could be so important they didn't sit down long enough to drink. A vehicle pulled up outside the building, the large man climbed inside, and it disappeared down the street before they even registered it was a military vehicle. The other man was gone. But they knew he hadn't gotten into the vehicle. Gray pulled Reilly further down the alley.

"Calder."

"What?"

"His name. Calder."

Eleven

Isla breathed in the scent of the forest and the cool morning air. There had been no sign of Gray and Reilly, and she wasn't sure if she should be looking for them or just grateful they hadn't dragged her into whatever they thought was going on—or whatever they were planning. It worried her that they might think they could use her for their cause, whether she agreed to being used or not.

The soldiers at the mine had been unexpected and, although Gray had helped her out, she wasn't sure she could trust him yet. He was convinced the Elite were rotten. But she had been one of them. She knew how they operated, and it was generally to order. There had been times since that bloody night when she'd wondered just who had sent them into that mess. Was it a case of not knowing what they were sending them into? Had their information been wrong, or had it been deliberate? She shook her head at the idea; it couldn't be true. But the hearing had not provided any reason as to how it had all gone so terribly wrong.

She looked up into the trees. She should let someone know she was back. But then, would that put them in danger? She looked back over the ship, took a deep breath and turned her back on it.

She wasn't far from the colony, and they most likely knew where she was. As she walked, she saw some small deer and large rodents. They looked in her direction, but didn't seem to worry about her. Then, out of the corner of her eye, she noticed the edge of a face peeking around the trees.

She walked on as though she hadn't seen it. The young were often sent out to scout or forage as a way to learn about the forest. She hoped they still knew who she was. And that she wasn't a threat to them. Another face appeared, and she stopped. They didn't usually send two. She wondered who else was hiding in the trees.

A whisper moved through the world around her, as though the trees themselves called to her and she was running, her feet light on the ground, her chest burning, the cries at the back of her mind growing louder and louder. Isla shimmed down into the ravine. Her body remembered the climb better than her mind did. She landed softly at the base of the rocky walls, her heart thumping in her ears, the forest screaming above her, to a sight she never thought she would find before her.

The buildings that had filled the small valley, tucked within the high, dark stone walls, were gone. They had either been pushed out onto the ground or burnt away. The empty shell of the ravine stretched out before her like a skeleton picked clean of the flesh that had once covered it and made it something softer, safe.

She heard the rocks move above her and stepped forward. One of the children from the forest dropped down beside her in much the same way.

"This is because of you." His voice was not accusing in any way, yet she felt the weight of what had been lost.

"When?"

"Days ago."

She turned and looked down at the boy, a child of no more than ten summers.

"Why?" she asked, her voice amplified by the empty stone. "Why didn't I come earlier?"

"It would have made no difference," another child said, stepping forward. She was older, yet not a child Isla knew. "It was long before you were coming."

At the far end of the valley, a large, raw mound stood screaming of the loss. Isla gulped down the threatening tears. It had been too long since she had cried. But it had been far too long since she had been home. Even after all that had happened, she hadn't returned home to heal. Hence the scars. Although she needed them. This was another she would wear.

"How many?" she murmured, as a hot tear surprised her by running down her cheek.

"Lost or survived?" an old voice croaked, and she turned to find an old man. He was nestled so deeply in the rock he was almost lost as he watched over the dead.

"Master," she whispered, bowing her head.

He waved the title away, but the soft smile she remembered was long gone. His hands were burnt, skin blackened, his leg at an unusual angle. How could it have come to this?

"Do you have a gifted one?" Isla asked, turning to the girl beside her, but the girl's eyes moved to the mound.

Isla looked around as the children started to move forward; there were only six of them. They ranged in age from the girl who might have been fifteen to a little one of five. She turned back to the mound, and her heart ached. So many lost. How big had the colony grown since she had left?

"Fetch the master's things," she snapped at the girl, looking around and then back to the top of the ravine, where she had watched the ships fly high above as a child. Did she have time?

"They are gone," the girl said, unmoving.

Isla growled something, and the child took a step back.

"You have seen my ship," Isla said. When the girl nodded, Isla stepped forward, took her face in her hands and breathed gently onto her face. "Go," she whispered. "Breathe onto the panel, find the floor that lifts—you'll know it." She tried to smile. "Bring the bag. All of it."

The girl nodded, indicated the boy follow and they were gone.

"That was a term you would never use," the old man croaked.

Isla turned and took him in. "I wasn't gifted, not like you wanted me to be," she replied. "And I learnt that any child here could have learnt as I did."

"Not all of them wanted to, and in the end, neither did you."

"Yet I used what I learnt from you nearly every day."

He laughed then, a hysterical cackle that echoed off the stone, and the children lifted their fingers to their lips as one. The motion broke her heart. If she had stayed, their future would have been something very different.

"This is not your fault," the master said, reaching for her. Isla reached her fingers back to his, desperate to hold him, desperate to believe him. But she knew the truth of it. Whoever it was that was so determined to kill her wanted to wipe any hint of her from the Complex.

Isla felt the movement of the approaching girl long before she saw her move down the stone from the forest above. She breathed out slowly. If it wasn't for the guilt of leaving in the first place, she would have returned here when she'd been injured.

She knelt down beside the man, held out her hand and took the bag from the air as the child dropped it. The bottles clinked together. "It is lucky for you that you taught me so well," she said, pulling out the new jar of white paste.

"When did you make that?" he asked, his eyes wide.

"Last night." She scooped out a thick handful of the gel and reached for his hand. He hesitated, which was something she had never seen in him before. "I made it correctly," she added.

"I don't doubt it," he said, yet the reluctance remained. "I'm not worthy," he murmured.

Isla looked up at the girl standing over her. "When did he last eat?"

"Not since…" She looked towards the mound.

"Make him some soup, something light and easy on his old gut." The girl nodded and disappeared, taking some of the other children with her. The boy waited with the smaller ones a short distance away.

"They need you," Isla said.

He shook his head.

"They are babies," she whispered. "The whole history will be lost if you allow yourself to be lost with the others."

The man looked over her shoulder at the little ones, then stretched out his hand with a sigh. He closed his eyes to the pain that was evident on his face as she tried as gently as she could to smooth the cream over his skin. It was absorbed quickly; his hands looked more red than black when she scooped more and motioned for the other hand.

"Who will teach them?" she asked as she rested the second hand in his lap and he laid his head back against the stone. The skin didn't look as tight, but it would take some time for his hands to be close to what they were. When he didn't answer, she asked, "What of the leg?"

He looked down at it. "It will take more than cream."

She nodded slowly. "Who were they?"

He looked up, a question creasing his brow.

"Those who did this." Her gaze rested on the mound.

"Soldiers, Elite."

"Elite? Are you sure?"

"I know what you were," he snapped.

"I didn't kill women and children," she retorted in the same tone, screwing the lid of the jar back on.

"Only men?"

"Soldiers, enemies of the Hendra."

He sighed and looked down. A lone tear ran down his face. "The forest will never forgive you."

"Maybe I don't deserve forgiveness." She stood up, then noticed the dried blood on the side of his head. She motioned the boy forward. "Water?" she asked softly. He nodded. She handed him a cloth from her bag, and he ran off. She looked back at the children sitting quietly in the dirt, watching her with wide eyes.

One small child stood and looked around at the others before walking forward. She stood close to Isla's legs as she looked over the old man.

"You could stay," she said.

"You won't be safe if I do," Isla returned. The little girl looked up at her with bright eyes, eyes that almost shone in the shadows of the crevice.

"You aren't like them," the little one said.

"I'm too much like them," Isla returned, squatting beside the child. "That is why they are after me."

"What do you know?" the child asked. She stepped into the space created by Isla's stance and put her arms around Isla's neck. Isla wrapped her arms around the child in return. She didn't understand the child's question. She was only little, after all; she might not realise what she was asking. "What did you see?" she continued.

Isla looked at her more closely, holding her out at arm's length. "What do you see?"

The child put her hands over her eyes. "Blood," she whispered. And as the boy returned with a wet cloth, she ran back to the other children.

Isla focused on the master for a time, wiping down his wound, applying more cream, and checking his body for further injuries and burns. She wasn't sure what she could do with the leg; the pain of trying to straighten it might kill him. She sat silently beside him until the eldest girl arrived with soup. Then she helped encourage him to sip it. As it grew dark, the children huddled together, and Isla remained sitting by her old teacher. He had been a father to her, although she was sure she had never lived up to what he had wanted her to be.

She heard the scared intake of breath as big cats wandered through the remains of the colony. She remembered playing with them as a child, much to the other children's horror. It was one of the reasons they thought she was gifted. But she knew the cats didn't come just to see her. They, like the forest, were connected to the people. A soft, long, warm body lay down beside her, and she ran her fingers through its hair. The children were too afraid of being discovered to light fires for warmth.

"The forest will provide," the master murmured, and the cat returned the sentiment with a soft growl.

"Watch him," she whispered, climbing to her feet, and walked back towards the children. Soft foliage glowed above them, a little growing in the wall of the ravine although much of it had been damaged with the fire that had destroyed the colony. It would return. She knew it would.

As she drew closer, a child squealed. Isla knelt beside her, pulling her into her arms, and then another was wrapped around her. A large cat purred and rubbed against her, and the children whimpered.

"They want to help protect you," Isla said, stretching out a hand to rub against the cat. "I haven't seen them this friendly for a while," she murmured, remembering the cat in the tree. A small boy reached out with her; the cat sniffed at his hand and then rubbed against it. He giggled nervously. And then it stretched forward and licked the face of the girl in Isla's arms.

"He is tasting you," the little boy whispered.

"He is saying hello," Isla corrected. The children settled amongst the cats, and Isla returned to the master's side.

"What did you see?" he asked, appearing to be asleep.

"When?"

"What do you know?"

"Master?"

"The child is right, there is more. There is a reason behind the carnage, the death on the field that day and here."

"You knew?"

"Of course. There are no secrets in the forest for those who know where to look."

Isla wiped at the tears as she leant gently on the old man's shoulder. "I don't know what I know," she whispered.

"Then go and find out. The forest will look after its own."

Isla sighed and rubbed at the furry head that nudged at her hand. She would, but not tonight.

Isla stood at the top of the ravine and looked down at the children moving through the valley space beneath. A cat sat beside her, looking over them as well. She reached out a hand and ran it through its fur, and it gave her a soft growl. She wasn't sure they could protect the children if more soldiers arrived. But they would do their best to help the forest people of Rennet survive.

She had left her supplies with the children, hoping she would be able to return to create more in time. As she turned and walked back to the ship, her hands ran over the bark of the trees and through the leaves of the plants that brushed against her. There was so much here that could help them—they just had to learn how to find it. She hoped the master would survive long enough that the way of the people wasn't lost with him.

The door to the ship stood open, and Isla cursed herself for not telling the child to lock up on her return. But as she drew closer, something moved in the darkness within. She had run off so quickly she had left the Barilla behind, but unless someone had her skill or was the original owner, they wouldn't be able to use it.

The cat appeared in the doorway, and she nodded slowly. They weren't just looking out for the children then. "You aren't coming with me," she said, running her hand across its head as she climbed aboard the ship. It pushed past her and out into the forest where it disappeared between the trees. She wondered what they could have done to protect them when the soldiers had come—surely the forest had given warning. But it was no use guessing at what might have been now.

Isla strapped herself into the cockpit, and the ship lifted into the air with a gentle hum. She wasn't sure what Gray and Reilly were up to, but she had to find her own answers. The Elite had to understand that a mistake had been made, that she wouldn't have created the havoc the race had become; and she had to believe there was someone at Hendra who would support her.

The distance between Hendra and the colony didn't seem that great as she travelled across the landscape. The city grew taller and bright before her, and much too quickly. It had expanded in the short time she had been away from the planet. She put the dragonfly down in a populated space, hoping no one recognised it, and was more thankful than she wanted to be that there was no one around to see her. Or at least not that she could see. The sun was only just starting to rise above the horizon, but the orange light was reflected off the shiny buildings. She missed the trees. There had been a time when she had missed this city, but it was fleeting.

She hid her ship where she knew it would be safe, and the owner of the garage would keep quiet if he recognised it amongst the ships in his yard. Then she headed back into the sparkling city and the long walk towards Hendra Central. Isla remembered the city being full of glass and metal, yet it looked different. Cleaner, perhaps. She wondered if that was due to her years in the deserts of Urgway.

Despite the early morning, there were people around closer to the centre of the city. Isla was sure she stood out somewhat in her dust-coloured clothing. Two enforcers walked towards her with purpose, and for a moment she thought they were Reilly and Gray, but as they drew closer and their weapons hummed to life, she knew they weren't. She glanced behind her and raised her arms into the air.

People around her murmured amongst themselves, and the enforcers stopped. She had left the Barilla on the ship. One of the enforcers motioned to the ground. Isla looked at it but shook her head.

"We know who you are," he said too loudly, seemingly just that little bit nervous of what she might do. His duster was aimed solidly at her chest.

"As does the rest of the Complex," she returned. "Take me in if you must, but I have a crime to report."

The other enforcer growled something and stepped in as though to force her to the ground.

"Someone slaughtered my family," she said, her clear voice echoing from the buildings in the now silent street.

"You are the murderer," the first enforcer said.

She tried not to sigh. "Even if I were, I have not been tried—and is the punishment the death of my whole family, and their family, and anyone living in the same village?"

A murmur went through the people around her. The enforcers looked nervously at each other.

"Does the crime of one mean a whole family pays?"

"That's not right," someone whispered not very quietly.

"She killed those racers," someone else said.

"But her family didn't."

"You don't have a family," the first enforcer snapped. "Orphan." The word spat with hate, as though it explained what she was.

"You are never an orphan in the forests of Rennet, although I am now," she said. They needed to believe they were all dead. All lost.

"Who?" someone in the crowd called out.

Isla turned to the people watching. "I don't know," she said. "Buildings burned to the ground, everyone slaughtered where they stood, including children. Babies."

Another murmur moved through the people.

"You could have done that yourself," the second enforcer said. "Once a killer, always a killer."

"I don't think the Elite like to be referred to in such a way," a deep voice said behind her, and a strange chill passed over her body. She turned slowly, but she didn't recognise the owner of the voice.

"Colonel," the enforcer stuttered. "She is a murderer on Urgway—there are warrants."

"For my family as well?" Isla asked.

"I think we can talk about this somewhere more private," the colonel said, holding his arm out to indicate the expansive building that was Hendra Central.

It had been some time since Isla had been inside the building, and suddenly it made her more nervous than the idea that the Elite were responsible for the colony.

"I thought the forest protected its own," the man said, a slight smirk at the corner of his mouth.

"Hard for a forest to stand against weapons of the Elite," she returned.

His face clouded, and something familiar tugged at her again. "Have we met?"

"Probably at some function or other," he said, looking ahead again. "How do you know it was Elite?"

"I was one, remember? I know the signs."

"The Elite leave no evidence, no sign that they were there."

She nodded. "Bandits or the like would have." She looked up at him and smiled. His face creased further. "Not quite as good as you think you are," she said. She wanted to smirk. She was clearly making the man uncomfortable, but she wasn't sure why. He, like everyone else, had to believe that everyone at the colony was dead.

"The Elite do not carry out such missions."

She shook her head slowly.

"Maybe your unit wasn't what you thought it was, if you participated in similar missions."

She glanced up at him then. They had done the dirty work of Hendra; the master had been right, and they had done things they shouldn't have. Things she wasn't proud of. But they had been the good guys, and she certainly hadn't slaughtered whole villages. The words of the child returned. What had she seen? What did she know?

"Tarle?"

She looked up at the man stopped by a door. "We carried out the good of the Rohendra Complex," she said. That was what she had learnt—that was who they had thought they were. "We are the law."

"Not any longer," the man said, his voice almost kind, as she entered the small room and sat at the table as indicated. So distracted by her thoughts, she hadn't even taken in the entrance and foyer of the building. The cold metal was smooth, fused to the floor, as was the stool. She had escorted enough people to rooms very much like this. Only she had never been able to ask the questions. She knew she wasn't going to be able to ask the questions this time either.

The door closed, and the colonel sat down opposite her. He was a large man and appeared even larger in the small room.

"Do you usually interrogate murderers, or are you here because you believe me about my family?"

"I believe something may have happened to them, but as the enforcer suggested, you may have done that yourself."

"Why?"

"That is something I would like to find out. Why did you come here?"

"Other than for my family? It seems someone is trying to kill me. It was suggested Hendra was that someone—and when they couldn't, they framed me instead. I'm here because I hope they are wrong and Hendra will help me clear my name and find who is behind this. That was my plan until I found my family."

"Orphan," the man said with little emotion.

"No one is an orphan in the forest," she repeated. "Even if you don't take into account my aunts, uncles, cousins, teachers."

"What did they teach you in the forest?" He leaned forward.

She had tried to share her connection with the forest once, with Bear. But he was too much a soldier, and he hadn't understood.

"How to live."

"You won't last the week if you don't help us."

"Help you?"

He nodded once and leaned back in the chair as she laid her hands flat on the table. She felt the metal breathe beneath her fingers. But before she could calm the growing uncertainty in her chest, the colonel reached across the narrow table and slapped her hard enough to knock her from the stool.

The door opened, and a young soldier appeared. "Report that we have captured Island Tarle, alias Isla Dee, and that she will be returned to Urgway to stand trial."

He bowed his head and disappeared. Isla rubbed at her jaw, her head spinning.

"What is really going to happen?" she asked.

"You will return to Urgway."

"Not to stand trial."

"How long have you had this *gift*?" He spat the word as though he meant plague.

"Gift?"

"Hummer," he breathed, but the word held more menace than his piercing blue eyes in that moment. For a heartbeat, Isla was sure he would kill her himself.

"Humming is a myth," she replied, staying on the floor as she massaged her jaw.

"We'll see." He lifted her to her feet by her arm, his grip tight, and she was marched out the door along the corridor into a lift. He waved his hand over the panel and they rose several floors, but there was no indication of what floor they were on. Maybe Gray was right and Hendra weren't keen to help—at least this man wasn't.

The doors opened onto a quiet floor. A large foyer stretched out before her, elaborately decorated with pressed metal walls depicting the landscape of each of the planets of the Complex. Two guards stood on either side of two large doors, the same shiny metal, only she couldn't quite make out the pattern. It seemed to come into sharp focus as narrow beams stretched out from a single point where the two doors came together.

Isla blinked with surprise. Was she actually standing where she thought she was? Not that she was quite standing; the colonel still held her too tight by the arm, lifted enough that she was on her toes. It kept her just off balance, and she knew it was deliberate. She might not have seen this man in the field, but he knew what he was doing.

"Colonel," one of the guards said as he saluted, but his gaze was locked on Isla. He made no move to open the door.

"She needs to see this."

"Is it your place...?"

The colonel stepped forward too fast, dragging her with him and growling as he did. The man moved out of the way as they pushed through the door.

"This had better be good," said a polite light voice, although there was just as much danger behind it as the colonel had shown earlier.

Isla gaped at the woman sitting behind an overly large desk. The flag of the Rohendra Complex was behind her, its inky black background and golden star the same shape as the etching on the door. The woman looked up slowly, her eyes narrowing.

The colonel pushed Isla forward, and she fell to her knees before the desk. She stayed on the floor, her head bent.

"You were right," he growled. Isla wanted to look up at the reception he would get, for no one would talk to the Hendra in such a way.

"Often," the Hendra said, her voice sweet again as she stood and walked around the desk. "And what am I right about?"

"She is a hummer."

"Really?" She sounded far too excited. She bent down over Isla, who remained unmoving. Just a sideways glance at the woman who ran the entire solar system might really get her killed.

"I'm not," Isla whispered. "I came to Hendra for help."

"Help?" the woman asked as though Isla had slapped her.

"My family..."

"Are not important. But you might be."

Isla looked up at the woman who ruled it all. But her angry glare was on the colonel.

"Why are you here?"

"I saw it," he said, still not using her title. Isla wondered what their relationship might be, and what they really wanted from her. "In the interrogation room, she was shifting the table."

An odd giggle escaped Isla before she could stop it. She wasn't quite sure what her gifts were, if that was what they were. Master had always been sure; she hadn't been. She had an affinity for metal the same way she did for the forest.

"I didn't believe you, but she is a hummer." He sounded desperate, surprised. Why would this man know anything about her?

"I will overlook that, now that you have her." The Hendra turned her attention back to Isla then and smiled sweetly. "Take her back to Urgway. Let's see just what she can do."

Without any further word or acknowledgement, he lifted Isla back to her feet and, still staring at the Hendra, she was dragged from the room.

"Colonel," the Hendra said as they reached the door. "Take some unknowns with you. I don't want the team in this. And then reassign them."

He nodded without turning back, and Isla was pushed into the lift. She watched the woman smile as the doors closed, and then they were travelling back down the building.

"She didn't look pregnant," Isla said causally. "Either it is still very early, or it is a lie. Just like everything else in the Rohendra Complex."

He growled something under his breath and knocked her hard into the wall. Isla slipped to the floor. When the doors of the lift opened, her blurry view was of what had once been her favourite place in the world.

Twelve

Reilly nudged Gray hard—too hard. He nearly yelped. It was enough to draw his attention from all the ships parked around the open space to the large man walking determinedly towards them, his face dark. Gray bit back any complaint he might have made. It had been a risk to get this far inside Hendra without being caught, and now they were done. But the soldier wasn't alone. He was forcibly directing a woman towards them. Isla.

She must have turned up here all on her own, believing Hendra would help and only getting herself into more trouble. And they were dressed as two enforcers wandering through Hendra Central, probably not very welcome either.

"Just what I need," the large man muttered, and Gray groaned inwardly. He knew this man. Calder, the man they had recognised the night before. He just hoped Calder didn't recognise them.

"How can we help you, sir?" Gray replied curtly.

"Take this woman onto a transport. The entire Rohendra Complex is after her, and I want her returned to Urgway to stand trial before the city decides to take her for themselves."

Isla didn't even look up. She hung from his large hand and then slumped forward as he dropped her into their waiting arms.

"Which ship?" Reilly asked, glancing around at the oddly abandoned space. "You got a pilot ready to go?"

"I will pilot," Calder growled. "This way." He pushed past them, striding ahead.

Reilly had taken Isla's arm, but he was barely holding her up.

"You aren't helping yourself," Reilly mumbled.

Calder stopped and turned back. "She talks too much. Had to shut her up."

Gray noticed the growing bruise on her face, and her fat lip. She must have taken some heavy knocks.

"Get her on that one." Calder pointed across the hangar at a very bright ship on the far side. "Strap in and prepare to go."

"Should we tell the captain we've been reassigned?" Reilly asked loudly. Isla groaned as she leaned into him.

"I'll sort out the captain," Calder said, striding away, and Gray wondered if he was collecting anyone else to come with them.

"Run," Isla whispered.

"He'll hunt us down."

"He will kill you when we reach Urgway." She looked up then, the spark lost in her eyes. "Go home," she whispered to Reilly. "Don't let them take your family."

Gray had stopped just before the ship Calder had suggested. He wondered at the man's rank that he could do as he pleased, but then he had always done that. Whatever he had been or was now, he was someone they didn't want to be close to.

"What propaganda is she spouting?" Calder snapped, appearing silently in the tight space of the ship. He pushed Gray out of the way and roughly strapped her into a narrow seat. "Never thought you would be labelled an enemy of the Complex." He sounded excited by the idea.

"Wasn't she a war hero?" Reilly asked.

"Not anymore. Maybe she was behind the attack on her unit; maybe there were mistakes made."

"Maybe I should have been killed with them," she whispered.

"Traitor," Calder growled, leaving them standing in the small space of the aircraft while he moved through to the cockpit. They threw themselves into seats on either side of Isla as the engines roared to life. Reilly was still buckling up when the ship lifted from the ground and headed out of the building over the waking city below. It was lost quickly from view as they headed out of the atmosphere long before they should have.

"This is a nice vessel," Gray said. "Maybe we should have signed up for Hendra rather than the enforcers."

Calder glanced over his shoulder. "You might be Hendra material, after all. I've been asked to reassign my help on this mission."

"My wife would be so proud." Reilly beamed as Isla whimpered something.

"If she gives you any trouble, just knock her out. Probably best she isn't shouting slogans when we land."

"Sir," Reilly replied.

"Where are we going to land?" Gray asked. "Once people know we are there, it will be hard to contain. Do you want me to call ahead for more enforcers?"

"No need," Calder said.

Gray wanted to ask more, but the man wasn't going to give him anything. At this stage, they would all be lucky to get out of this alive.

The impact of what they had fallen into hit Gray when they landed and the door slid open. There were no crowds, and there were no soldiers. They were at the mine. The only ones around were miners and a couple in worn suits who appeared to be tired office workers.

As he unbuckled her belts, Gray whispered, "Where is the dragonfly?"

"What did you say?" Calder was far too close behind him. Gray stepped back and allowed him to pull Isla from the seat by the front of her clothes. She appeared to have given up, which surprised him. She had faced hard enough times before; she might have run away, but she hadn't given up.

"The dragonfly. Wasn't she gifted some amazing ship?"

Calder glanced at the woman in his hands and then back to him. "You want it?"

"Really?" Gray asked, trying to sound like Reilly, but sure he only sounded disbelieving.

There was something in the grin Calder returned that made Gray even more certain they were not going to survive this. Someone cleared their throat, and Calder indicated they climb down. The scrawny man in a worn mining suit nodded once and disappeared.

Reilly stepped out into the heat and, Gray realised, shade. Gray followed, wondering who had known they were coming. A long protective cover had been placed from the ship out to the opening of the mine. It was held up with thin poles, and it moved a little too much in the hot breeze that carried dust across the open space.

Calder nearly nudged him out into the sun as he pushed past, Isla slung over his shoulder. He stalked directly towards the mine, and Gray struggled to work out just what they wanted from her—or was this the way she was going to disappear?

"I am not going down there," Gray said quickly.

"You don't have to." Calder snapped his fingers, and the man who had met them reappeared. Gray pulled his weapon as the miner's duster hummed loudly to life.

"But I could if you insist," Gray said.

Calder shrugged, as though it didn't matter to him either way, and Gray followed him into the dark. A pale yellow light flared to life as Calder stepped into a metal cage, and it moved unevenly as the man stared at him. Reilly stepped in after him without hesitation. Gray was sure his nerves were showing as he followed. The gate swung closed with a squeal and an echoing clang. Before Gray had a chance to work out how they would tell the cage where they were going, it dropped away beneath his feet and they were plummeting down.

The metal they mined was so unstable that if this madman didn't kill them, they would likely die anyway. If they survived the lift ride.

The lift stopped with a jolt. The large man shifted Isla on his shoulder and pushed open the gate. A string of poorly illuminating lights reached into the darkness beyond. Gray worried more than he had before about this woman. A woman he had promised to look out for and had left to wander into Hendra Central on her own, and who was now to be left in a rohen mine along with him and Reilly.

Although why here, he couldn't understand. Did they not want her surfacing? There was something she knew that someone else did not want her sharing. But Gray wasn't even sure Isla knew what that was.

The lights led to a low-ceilinged chamber with two large open vats of liquid metal set into the rough floor. Gray stopped as the colonel continued forward. This stuff was unstable at the best of times, let alone so much of it swirling around in one place. There was a bitter metallic smell to the air, and he felt the temperature shift. It was cool, but it wasn't.

The colonel walked directly to the closest vat and dropped Isla onto the floor before it. She groaned and put a hand to her head. "Here we are, hummer. Show me what you got."

She squinted up at him, then looked over the vat. Gray put his hand across his mouth and nose, trying to block some of the metallic taste as he wondered if this was what would kill him.

Calder grabbed Isla's arm and lifted her to her feet, and Gray was sure she would drop back to the floor if he hadn't maintained his tight grip on her arm. "Go on," Calder growled. "Hum." His voice was a little muffled. Gray noticed the well-fitted skin-toned mask he wore. He wondered if it would be enough to stop the fumes. Regardless, it only reinforced the idea that he wouldn't be taking any of them out of the mine with him.

"I'm not what you think," she whispered.

"Hummer?" Reilly asked, looking warily at Gray. It wasn't the first time he had heard her called that.

"They are a myth," she said. Her voice lacked any of the strength she had exhibited earlier, and Gray again wondered what they had done to make her give up.

"What can she do?" Gray asked, stepping forward, trying to put himself between her and the vat without getting close to the odd metal. He glanced over his shoulder, the taste permeating every sense. The metal pool shimmered as a ripple moved across the surface. "Did you do that?" he asked, looking back at Isla.

"Move," Calder grumbled, pushing Gray to the side. He lost his footing and nearly fell into the second vat. Thankfully, Reilly was close enough and grabbed him, pulling him to safety. "Do something!" Calder screamed at Isla, taking her by the shoulders and shaking her.

She shook her head, and he swung her around to face the vat. His knuckles were white where he gripped her arms. Gray wondered if she could do anything in such a state, even if she wanted to.

"Hum!" Calder demanded.

The ripple that had crossed the vat disappeared. The temperature fluctuated again, and then there was an odd calm in the chamber.

"Even if I could, which I can't," she wheezed, Gray wondering if the fumes of the metal were getting to her, "I wouldn't do anything for you." She swung her leg back, but he was too quick for her. He spun her around again to face him.

Calder grinned too broadly as he gave her a shove backward. As Gray reached forward, she tumbled back and into the vat.

"What the hell?" Reilly growled.

In the same instant, Gray shouted, "No."

"She had better be right," Calder said. "Or I win either way, Dragonfly."

"I thought she was going to trial," Reilly murmured.

Gray had taken a step forward, disbelieving of what had just happened and that he'd had no chance to stop it. No moment of warning of just what this man was capable of.

"I'll be upstairs. Let me know if anything happens."

"If anything happens?" Gray asked. "She's dead."

"Maybe. Probably." Calder disappeared into the dark corridor that led from the chamber.

The temperature in the room slowly fell. Gray studied the still vat of metal.

"Did he call her *Dragonfly*?" Reilly asked.

Gray stared at him for a moment, trying to take in where they were, what was happening. "Dragonfly?"

"He called her *Dragonfly*," Reilly articulated slowly, as though he were a child. "He knows her. He knew her."

"The entire Complex knows her. She is the only one to survive that carnage. She's a hero."

"She's gone," Reilly said quietly, looking at the metal. "Maybe we were right—they were trying to kill her. But why?"

Gray shook his head, looking back at the too-still metal pond. Hadn't it rippled when they'd arrived?

"We are going to die down here too," Reilly murmured, coughing and pulling a face at the bitter taste in the air. "He might have needed some help, but he isn't coming back. Reassigned. My arse."

Gray would have laughed if it weren't so frighteningly true. No one knew who they were, where they were, or could raise the alarm that they were missing. Calder had wanted some fall guys, and he'd managed to find those he had failed to kill the first time around, although Gray was certain he hadn't recognised them. He wouldn't have expected them to be walking through Hendra, and he wouldn't have taken any risks dragging them along here. If he had recognised them, their cold dead bodies would be lying on the hangar floor back at Hendra Central.

The metal moved, the smallest ripple crossing the surface. Gray stepped forward. Another followed. He had no idea just how unstable this stuff was or how it worked, but the third ripple identified for him what was wrong—it moved from side to side in the vat, not in a ring pattern as he would expect of water. But then, this didn't move like water; this was very different.

Before he could grasp exactly what was happening, the rohen began to rise. He moved back against the wall, tugging at Reilly's sleeve as he had been rooted to the spot.

"What the hell?"

All Gray could do was stare as the metal not only rose up above the edge of the vat, but into the air. Once it left the confines of the vat, it spread out like small droplets. Gray looked around in wonder, sure his jaw dropped open at the sight of Isla standing in the middle of the vat. He stepped forward and looked down. It was deeper than he had imagined. He wondered how they moved the metal, or whether they siphoned small amounts out at a time.

The small metal spheres moved around the space as Isla stood with her hands in the air, her eyes closed. She looked calm, lost to whatever she was doing.

"Hummer," Reilly whispered, and her eyes shot open.

Reilly stepped back as Gray stepped forward. A strange noise emanated from the metal moving just above his head. As he looked up, she closed her eyes again, and the balls moved closer to the earthen walls of the chamber. And then, in a heartbeat, they were gone. Gray blinked, unsure of what he had seen, then looked back at Isla on her knees in the bottom of the empty vat.

He leapt over the side and knelt beside her. As she slumped into him, he closed his arms around her.

"Where did it go?" Reilly asked, leaning over the edge.

"Home," she whispered.

"Come on," Gray said, lifting her from the floor into his arms. Reilly leant over the side and took her from him. As Gray climbed out, he looked to the other vat. The rohen bubbled and churned as the temperature in the room rose and fell, the air thick with fumes. He was starting to feel lightheaded.

He waved Reilly forward, directing him towards the dimly lit corridor and hoping they could find a way out. As Reilly's hold on Isla tightened and his face paled, Gray turned slowly back to the vat.

The metal had lifted out like a giant silver wave, reaching for them. Reilly turned, but Gray grabbed him, wondering if it wanted her. Isla had been under or within the metal for some time and didn't appear to have been damaged by it, aside from the semiconscious state she had seemed to maintain since Calder had dragged her across the hangar. Except when she had been standing in the vat. She reached out a hand, and the metal met her fingers.

"Go home," she whispered.

It pulled back, then reached out and touched the earthen floor. It seemed to spill out from the vat across the floor, surrounding them but never touching them, and then it too was gone.

"Where?" he murmured.

"Back to where it belongs," she whispered, her eyes closed and her head resting against Reilly's shoulder.

Gray stared at her, wondering just who this woman was and what she could do. Then back to the empty vats. They would never get out of here, and it would be worse if Calder thought they had stolen the metal.

"Your call sign was Dragonfly," Gray said, trying to work out what they could do.

"A lifetime ago," she whispered.

"Calder called you Dragonfly."

She shook her head once. "The colonel? It was my call sign on mission. It was only used on mission."

"Only on mission?" Gray asked. She lifted her eyes towards him as something else passed across her face he couldn't quite read.

"There was someone who used it all the time." She closed her eyes again and leaned into Reilly.

"Who?" Gray demanded as Reilly shook his head.

"It doesn't matter. Do you have a way to get us out, or are we going to die here?"

"You are actually quite hard to kill, so I think our chances are good." Gray's anger at the situation was evident in his voice.

"You've surprised me by surviving this long; maybe you are right. Put me down," she added as the lift at the far end of the tunnel made a squealing noise to indicate it was moving.

"What do you think you can do?" he asked as she sank to her knees on the ground, pushed her fingers into the dirt and closed her eyes.

"You have a better chance without me," she said. A sad smile lit up her face as the molten metal filled the ground beneath her, and then she was gone.

"Who is this woman?" Reilly asked.

"More than I imagined," Gray said, trying to hide the smile that seemed determined to stay on his lips. "But we need to find a way out."

"Out? Did she go out? Do we need to find her?"

"I have a feeling she will find us. But right now, we need to get out before the colonel decides we can be more help—or worse, that he no longer needs our help. We've just witnessed something else he'll need to remove us to cover up."

Reilly jogged behind him towards the lift shaft. If they called it back, the colonel would know they were trying something. He prized the metal door open, scowling at the noise that filled the corridor, and then looked into the shaft.

"Down?" Reilly asked.

"Where is your trust?" Gray joked.

"Gone with the rohen. If they find us here with the metal gone, we are dead whether he misses the girl or not."

"There is a connection," Gray said.

"Really?" Reilly crossed his arms. "I might have said the same. The man who tried to kill us is now trying to kill her. And it appears he has risen to the giddy rank of Colonel."

"What if he already tried?"

Reilly paced back and forth across the space. "She got away."

"I mean before, when the whole unit was killed. What if he was behind it?"

"He wasn't around then, not in this part of the solar system. He was off building his own unit, one we ended up with. One that tried to kill us."

"Are we sure?"

"Not of a single bloody thing. I just watched liquid metal pull a woman into the earth."

"She spoke to it as though it was alive," Gray muttered, looking back into the shaft and then up. He could see a distant glow of dim light against the side of the shaft. "There—maybe if we could reach that tunnel, we could find another way out."

"There is only one way in and out of a mine."

"Nothing is as it seems here. I'm willing to bet there is another way out."

"Why do I think you are betting with my life?"

Gray didn't say anything further as he reached into the shaft and climbed onto the narrow ladder that ran the length of the lift system. As he headed up, Reilly sighed loudly and then climbed up behind him. He was dying to say something else, Gray could tell by the heavy silence, but their voices would travel in the shaft so it was best to keep quiet. And they needed to move fast, because they had no idea how long it would take until the lift was moving again.

"What do you mean *gone*?" The Hendra stood behind her desk, trying not to look as pissed off as she felt.

"This was your idea," he said, that defiant grin on his face. She wanted to slap it away, but as he was only present via video com, she would have to wait. At some point she had found that grin intriguing, enticing. Now she found it annoying. He held up his hands, but the look didn't change. "She is a hummer," he conceded.

"And she stole the rohen?"

He shook his head and then nodded.

"Where is my metal, Colonel?"

"I don't know," he said. She glared, but it made no impact. He looked down rather than directly at her, clearly trying to work out what had happened. She could almost see the cogs turning.

"You haven't seen this skill in her before?"

He shook his head again.

"Colonel, you are on thin ice here."

He looked up and nodded slowly, his features more serious. "At Hendra, she showed some skill with metal and machines, not enough to convince me it was anything other than skill. She has a way..."

"Are you still attached to this girl?" Hendra interrupted, disappointed that his voice indicated there was more to his feelings than he had admitted.

"I was never attached," he said, but the look in his eyes said something different. "She had a way with animals and plants. She grew up in the forest, and it was a skill her people had. There is no metal out there. Not on Rennet. There was no sign of a connection when she was Elite."

"Is there something of these forest people we can use?"

"They are gone."

"Where?"

He raised a defiant face towards her, and she sat down with a sigh.

"Tell me again what happened in the mine."

His focus moved back to the floor at his feet. "I threw her in the metal. It was still and silent, the enforcers watching over her..."

"And..." she prompted.

"I knew them," he muttered.

"You have taken out others you have known."

He lifted his eyes to her again. "These are people I *have* already taken out."

"That is what you said about Island Tarle."

She could see him reaching for the com controls. "Colonel, I'm not finished. Where is my rohen?"

"I don't know," he grunted, and the screen flicked off.

She leaned back in the chair, tapping her nail on the lacquered armrest and staring at the blank monitor.

"He is not respectful enough," a soft voice whispered from the side doorway. Despite her best efforts, the Hendra jumped.

"Alice, you can't scare me like that."

"Nothing scares you." Alice stepped out carrying a cup of steaming green liquid, and Hendra's stomach knotted at the idea of it.

"He thinks he is more important than he is," she muttered, reaching for the cup, which Alice held too tightly in her hand. She looked towards the door and then back to Hendra. "What is it, my love?" Hendra asked softly as she stood, the cup still too tight in Alice's hands. She worried if she tried to pry it free, it would burn them both.

"How do you know that man?"

"Like every other man or woman who walks through that door—they are members of my realm."

Alice looked at her for the first time.

"He does as he is told. He works to protect the Complex."

"And is he doing that?"

"Not very well today. Perhaps he was more damaged than I thought."

"When?"

She looked at Alice then, smiling sweetly as she sat the cup down on the desk, her earlier concerns gone. "You have met him before."

"And he was too casual then. Where is the respect? Where is the reverence you are owed?"

"If only it were that easy, Alice." Hendra leaned forward and kissed her cheek, and Alice raised a hand to Hendra's abdomen.

"It won't be easy for the baby either, will it?"

Hendra shook her head. "But he will be all the stronger for it."

"He?" Alice asked, clearly surprised. "Do you know the gender?"

"Just a feeling."

"Will you be disappointed with a daughter?"

"Never. How could you ask that?"

Alice shook her head, gave her another small smile and, with one last look towards the double doors that led from the office, she turned and disappeared back through the other entrance.

Hendra looked at the green cup and shivered, then followed Alice through the doorway only to find there was no sign of her. She stood in the private lounge off the office looking around at the warm, comfortable, empty space and wondered where her wife would have gone so quickly.

Thirteen

Isla sat in the middle of the small cavern and shivered. The temperature was cool, and she could feel metal on the other side of the stone and dirt. It was as though it was breathing, which scared her far more than anything she had faced before. And she had faced far worse during the training they'd said she would never complete; in some difficult situations, she'd thought she would never survive in the Elite.

She had a way with machines, with ships. Her own dragonfly seemed to bend to her will. But she wasn't a hummer. It wasn't a thing. And yet, the foggy memory of the metal flowing around her reminded her so much of the foliage and forest she had grown amongst.

"Master," she whispered, "is that what you meant by gifted?"

There was no answer from the dark world around her, but she felt the metal come closer, and small fungi growing along the base of the cavern started to glow a pale blue. "Don't you start," she told it, and it faded to nothing.

She wanted the release of tears, but there was nothing there. Isla had no understanding of what she was or how to find it. She was far from home, a home she should never have left. She lay back down on the floor, pulling her arms around herself and holding tight, but the shivering continued.

Amidst all that had happened, she had seen Gray and Reilly dressed as enforcers. They had been enforcers, hadn't they? The colonel had been what scared her more than any of the strange things that followed.

He knew her, but she didn't know where from. They hadn't worked together. She would have remembered. He was built like Kalli, but the similarity stopped there.

At the thought of him, she sobbed. Kalli had been everything. Her whole life, right up until that moment when the world around her disintegrated and went dark. She dug her hand into the cold dirt beneath her, desperate for something to protect herself from the dark, a weapon of some kind. That was another skill she had, another force she didn't understand. But she had never questioned it. Never shared it with anyone. Gray had noticed. Gray had noticed a lot of things, and he was always so close. She remembered the warmth of his body as she leaned into it. The strength behind it. Where were they now?

Her breath caught in her throat as the dark closed around her, and then a soft blue light filled the space. Although she didn't want to admit it might be for her, she sniffed back the tears and ran the back of her hand over her nose. She shivered again and curled up tighter. The ground around her warmed, and she snuggled into the earth, reminded of the forest and the warm nights. She closed her eyes.

Soft voices filled her mind as she dreamt of the forest, but they were not voices she knew. Not the voices that had filled her childhood. With a gasp, she opened her eyes to two silhouettes in the pale blue light. She wondered if the warm cat curled at her side would attack, and then her fingers moved in the thick liquid surrounding her.

The world glowed a brighter blue as the startled faces of the miners turned and ran from the cavern. The metal around her became solid, lifting her from the ground and pointing her in the opposite direction.

There was nowhere she could go, but it pushed her on. She staggered into the dark as more voices echoed off the stone. There was only solid wall ahead of her. She moved along the stone, her hands held out and her eyes closed to the darkness. The voices grew louder, but she wasn't sure if they came closer or echoed.

A cool breeze crossed her skin, and she squeezed her body between the rocks. The shivering started again as the air grew colder around her, although she continued to work her way through the small crevice. Catching her skin on the rough rocks, she held in her grunts and cries of pain at the deep scratches. Then the world was slipping away again as she slid down a gravel incline. The noise echoed too loudly around her, but there was nothing she could do to prevent it or her downward fall.

The voices behind her were long gone. She stumbled across a hard floor and fell to her knees, sure her clothes were in tatters, her skin grazed. She'd dealt with worse, only now she seemed to be deeper in the mine. The temperature was warmer, and the air carried the metallic scent of the rohen the world seemed so desperate to have. Behind the smell of metal, she could just pick up the scent of foliage. She stepped forward, the ground hard beneath her feet—and then it was soft, as though she had walked onto grass. She squatted and felt the soft, cool narrow blades beneath her fingers. She wasn't sure if it was a moss or grass. Nothing could live down here in the dark.

"How?" she breathed, squinting into the soft glow of light surrounding her.

Different fungi made the world around them glow in various colours. She looked up at what could have been tall trees. So similar to her childhood home, she wasn't sure what to make of it. Perhaps she was still dreaming. Perhaps she was lost somewhere in the ground, unconscious and dreaming of a world that did not exist. She could hear a breeze move through the leaves, the rustle comforting and yet unsettling at the same time.

There was no one here. She moved forward into the warm environment. The shivering had stopped, but her skin stung. The world around her looked surreal, in yellows and blues and greens. Then a red glow drew her eye. She moved slowly through the leaves hanging down from the trees, pushing her way through, feeling the familiarity of them as they brushed over her skin. She stopped. There, in the base of a tree, grew a fungus she knew. It glowed a brighter red.

Her relief at seeing it was almost overwhelming. She looked around for a rock or something that had been hollowed out, finding one that looked as though water had run through it. But despite the foliage, there didn't appear to be any water down here. Isla ran her tongue over her dry, cracked lips at the thought of it.

She picked the fungi, not waiting for it to change, yet it changed colour in her hand as she plucked it from the ground and dropped it into the rock. She found a small branch not far away, as though it had been left for her. Breathing out slowly, she tried to calm her nerves and bring herself out of whatever dream she had fallen into. She slowly worked the fungus into a paste, holding her hand over it, trusting in the odd light of the cavern that it was turning white.

She hoped in that moment that the master had been able to use the ointment she had left him with and that it was helping him in some way that would help the people. She sucked in a sob, thinking of the loss and the death and how it had been her fault. Because she had survived, they'd had to die.

Her skin burned from the gravel rash. She rubbed a small amount of the ointment between her fingers, then pulled at the remains of her clothes and smeared it liberally over her damaged skin. The relief was instant.

Standing in the middle of the forest, covered in ointment and wearing very little in the way of clothing, Isla worked her way back into the trees. The little cavern was larger than she had first thought, and higher. She pulled herself up into the branches and moved through the trees, working her way higher and higher.

How had no one discovered this place? Maybe someone had and they were watching her. Not that it mattered if they were—she felt safe and comfortable in the treetops. The world glowed gently above her, and she reached out to touch the soft mosses that grew over the hard stone. It didn't appear to be disturbed down here, yet she sensed something else, something from within the stone on the other side. She wondered if that was the rohen. It was strange how it had pooled around her, but she had an odd memory of it hovering in the air above her. She wasn't sure if that had really happened.

"Dragonfly," she whispered. Her voice carried around the cavern. Why had Gray asked about her call sign? It had once been secret, or at least just used within the Elite. And then only when they were on a mission. Kalli had called her Dragonfly all the time. And although she'd been tempted, she'd only referred to him as Bear when she'd needed to. When they'd made her retell that day and explain what they were hearing on the recordings. She'd called them by call sign then, every one of them. So as to distance herself from the people—the friends—she had lost.

And then she had become lost herself. Only someone had found her. And not to shake her hand, as too many had wanted to do in the beginning, but to kill her. Gray was so sure it was the Elite, yet they were her family. She gulped down the rising bile as she thought of the forest people again. Her actual family were gone, and the Elite had done that. Despite her wanting to believe something very different.

"Why?" she whispered on the breeze. Why would they do such a thing? What did she know that they wanted her silenced, despite her not knowing at all? Isla had no idea how long she had been beneath the ground. The colonel had taken her down. She rubbed at her sore jaw, yet the ointment had gone some way to relieve the pain of that too. And then she had disappeared from there, but again she didn't know how. She had slept fitfully for some time. It might have been that Gray and Reilly had hidden her and would return.

Although they wouldn't find her now. And somewhere in the back of her mind, she wasn't confident that was what had happened.

Isla must have drifted in the tree, for she woke to the sound of voices. She lay as still as she could, listening to the trees. The breeze had stopped, and she knew any movement would give her away. Although, that might not be the only thing.

"These look like her clothes," a deep voice said, gentle, concerned. She squinted down through the branches to the two shadows on the floor of the cavern beneath her, longing for more light. The fungi along the cavern floor seemed to glow a bit brighter, as did the moss above her.

"What is this?" a second voice asked, and she knew they had dipped their fingers in the ointment.

"That is hers too."

"Gray," the second voice chastised. "I hardly think you know her well enough to know that this pile of cloth is her clothing and that goo is her making."

At the sound of his name, Isla moved quickly through the branches and dropped down in the clearing before them. Gray smiled, his relief evident, and Reilly looked away.

"Isla," Gray said, stepping forward and closing his arms around her. Although it was comforting, it was strange at the same time. "We were so worried."

"You are naked," Reilly muttered.

Isla pulled the material from Gray's hand and wrapped what remained of the sand-coloured cloth around her. "Sorry," she murmured.

"Are you alright?" Gray asked, his hands too quickly finding her shoulders. She pulled away from him.

"I'm not quite sure how I got here."

"What is this?" Reilly asked, still not looking at her even though she had covered up. She was sure more of her body was exposed than he was used to, and more of her scars than he was aware she carried.

"An ointment. I grazed my skin falling down through the rocks."

He looked at her then, stepping up, and before she could step out of his reach, he ran a rough hand over her arm. "You seem ok."

"It is good ointment. What have you done to your face?" she asked Reilly, stepping closer, the dark line evident in the blue light of the cavern.

He shook his head. She squatted down, scooped out some of the remaining ointment and then wiped it quickly over his cheek. He cried out and stepped back, reaching for his face.

"Don't touch it yet," she said. "Give it a chance to work."

"A chance?" Reilly squealed.

"Are you alright?" Gray asked, but she wasn't sure who he was asking.

"It feels better already. What are you?"

Isla shook her head as Gray removed his jacket. Although it was dusty and part of the arm was torn, he placed it around her shoulders.

"It isn't cold," she said.

Gray shrugged and turned his attention to Reilly.

"I'm not a hummer."

Reilly opened and then closed his mouth.

"My teacher called me gifted as a child. I didn't like the term; I didn't like what it meant my life would be. I shouldn't have left," she whispered.

"You did something with the metal," Reilly said, but she shook her head as he spoke.

"I don't remember."

"What do you remember?" Gray asked kindly. Too kindly. She wasn't sure how to deal with his friendship in that moment, if that was what it was. He had given too much for her already.

"I told you to run," she said. "You don't listen, do you?"

"We couldn't leave you. How do you know him? How does he know you?" Gray asked quickly.

"Who?" she asked, but she had an idea of who he was talking about. She shook her head and held up a hand. "What do you want to do?"

"If you're asking whether we want to camp here forever or try to find a way out, I think I know what I would prefer," Reilly said.

"Does he think we are dead, or are they looking?" Gray asked.

"I saw some miners in the tunnels," Isla said, but she wasn't sure where that was, nor if they were still looking or thought she might have died somewhere in the dark. She shivered involuntarily and pulled the coat around her closer, thankful in a way that he had provided it. It hadn't been so long ago that she couldn't stop shaking.

"What do you think I am?" she asked, focusing on Gray only to realise he was staring at her. She looked down for a moment to see that she was covered. Not that it mattered—he'd seen her before, and she didn't care what he thought, did she?

He shook his head once, and Reilly mouthed *hummer*. She wanted to roll her eyes at the idea, but a part of her thought they might actually be right.

"I don't know what that means," she said.

"Yes, you do," Gray whispered. Although she knew he wanted to step in close to her again, he stayed where he was.

"I think we should find a way out of here," Reilly said, looking back towards the way she thought they had entered.

She shook her head. She wasn't sure why, but this was the most at peace she had felt for a long time, like she had in the forest. She wanted to stay.

"We can't stay," Gray said, and Isla looked down at the soft grass and her marked bare legs. "Did you have boots?"

She looked around and nodded, finding them where she had removed the damaged clothing. Which was doing very little to cover her. She slipped her arms inside the enforcer jacket and sat on the soft grass, taking a moment to run her fingers through the cool blades before putting her boots back on. Gray unnerved her more than she wanted to admit; he watched too closely.

He nodded once and held out a hand to help her back to her feet once she was laced in, and then they were moving across the cavern in a silent line.

"What if the mine is working against us?" Reilly asked up ahead. They had been walking for longer than she'd expected and still hadn't found the cavern wall, nor a possible exit. His voice didn't echo as much as she would have expected from the walls around them, but the gentle blue light of the fungi had gone out. "I'm sure it isn't," he muttered as the smallest glow lit the ground at his feet. "I don't like this."

"Just walk," Gray suggested, but again his eyes had found her in the dim light as the wall ahead opened into a rough tunnel.

Perhaps he didn't trust her. But then, she wasn't sure she trusted herself in that moment. She had no real idea of what she was, what she was capable of, or what those who had already tried to kill her might do.

"They want you alive, I think," Gray whispered, too close again.

"You don't know that."

"He didn't bring you all this way to kill you. It was something to do with the metal. A test of some kind."

"If you use that word again..." she threatened, but the usual strength behind her words was gone. Gray held his hands up in a defensive motion, the smallest smile lifting the corner of his mouth. Isla looked away and back towards Reilly disappearing ahead of them.

Whatever gift she may or may not have, the foliage of the mine was showing her a way out. Or at least she thought it was. The whole time they walked, she could sense the metal behind or within the stone she passed. At times she put her hand to the wall and felt it flow closer. She hadn't seen it again, and she wasn't convinced she had seen it in the first place.

"They think I can draw it out," she whispered. "They think I can help them."

"Now they do, maybe." Reilly stopped ahead of her and turned back. He looked nervous. What would he do to her if he felt threatened? Her hand still rested on the rock, and she could feel the metal pull at her.

"Do you think they could find the cavern?"

"Not if the cavern didn't want to be found." Gray's hand rested lightly on her shoulder. As soon as she looked up, he removed it. "They haven't found it yet, and they have been digging and drilling in this place for a long time."

"They might pull it apart even more now that the metal reserves are gone."

Gray nodded solemnly. There was peace within the rock. She took a deep breath and moved her hand, then stepped up to walk beside him as they continued down the tunnel.

"I still can't believe I saw you do what you did," Reilly murmured.

Isla didn't fully believe that she had anything to do with the freeing of the metal.

"What are we going to do if we manage to get out of here?" Reilly asked when she didn't speak.

"We'll need to find a way off planet, find my dragonfly," she replied.

"And then what?" Gray asked. "Do we take on the Hendra?"

"Why did you step in?" she asked, stopping again and making Reilly sigh with frustration. "What did you hope to gain by following me here?"

"That wasn't our intention when we entered Hendra Central. In fact, finding you was something of a surprise. Maybe we should have just left you to the colonel to..."

"You aren't even sure what he wanted me for. You're right, he didn't drag me here to kill me—they wanted something else, wanted to learn something. What did he say after he dropped me in the vat?"

"You say that so calmly," Reilly muttered.

"I don't really remember it. And not that he called me dragonfly—you mentioned that several times already."

"He said, 'She had better be right.'"

"Who is the 'she'?" Isla asked.

"The Hendra?" Reilly suggested.

Did the head of the whole solar system really think she was some threat, or that she could be used in some way to help them? The Hendra knew the dangers of the rohen; she had outlawed it herself. And yet her own Elite had been sent after Isla and killed her family. "Why?" she murmured. "What do I know?"

"That seems an odd question," Reilly said, looking more at Gray than at Isla. "Why wouldn't you know what you know?"

Gray raised his eyebrows.

"Everyone keeps asking the same questions, and I still don't know the answers. More than my body was damaged that day. Even listening to all those hours of recordings..."

"You don't have to do this," Gray said, stepping closer.

Isla nodded slowly, but she needed to talk this through. Despite all the talking she'd done at the time, she'd never really told anyone what was going on inside of her. "It never felt right."

"Talking?" Reilly asked.

"What happened that day. It was just not right. I spent some time recovering after the attack while they stitched me back together, tried to put things where they used to be." Her hand moved over her heart, and she was reminded of the thick material beneath her fingers. "Why do you insist on helping me?" she asked, looking at Gray. But as he opened his mouth, she shook her head. "I remember something different. Something I can't quite grasp. Something that scares me in the dark," she whispered, looking down.

"What?" Reilly prompted after too long, but she could only shake her head again. She didn't know, couldn't quite put her finger on it.

"Do you think someone told you what happened, altered your memory of that day?" Gray's voice was firm, no longer coaxing. She looked up at him, his face intense in the dim light. "Do you?"

"Ease off," Reilly said, putting his hand on Gray's arm. "We know full well just what the Elite and Hendra are capable of in the name of the Complex. And what they will do to cover that up."

"The Sparrow," she said. "My unit," she added slowly.

"Don't force it," Reilly said, pushing Gray, who still stood rigid before her, and taking her arm. "Let's focus on getting out. Then we can uncover what they are, and what they are trying to do."

"Or have already done," Isla murmured. She allowed him to take her arm, and then she heard voices. The three of them stopped dead as the lights of the fungi went out.

Isla closed her eyes to the dark. Her hand longed for a weapon as she thought about the odd feeling she got at night, the fear that set into her bones. A counsellor had claimed it was the trauma of the day. She might have even given the symptoms a name, yet Isla had always known it was something else. Not just surviving the blood and horror of the attack. Something had been in the dark. Something far scarier than anything else she had ever faced.

A hand closed around hers and tugged her along the narrow cutaway through the earth. She searched the dark around them, putting her hand to the wall. They weren't in the mine. They weren't in a section created by man, and if the cavern had gone unfound for so long then perhaps this path had as well.

A light formed ahead of them. Round and bright, not natural. Then the world went dark again as a sheet of metal flowed from the rock above. A cry of help went up from the other end of the rough path, and Gray squeezed her hand tighter.

The metal filled the space, and then they watched as it turned to stone. Cutting off their exit and protecting them from whatever was on the other side. Maybe it wasn't the Elite that wanted her here. The rock to the side of her disappeared where her hand rested against the rough surface, replaced with the same liquid metal. Her hand moved through it.

"We can't move through that," Gray whispered.

As she opened her mouth to say she couldn't either, it disappeared, pulled back into the rocks. A new path opened up before them, lit by softly glowing fungi.

"Did you do that?" Reilly asked.

"No," she said. "I didn't."

"Could there be another?"

"Another what?" she asked.

"Hummer," Reilly whispered, and Isla tried to ignore the strange feeling in her chest as she followed the new path.

The light shone brighter, and she raised her arm over her eyes. Many loud voices filled the tunnel, yet she wasn't sure what they were saying. She heard Reilly grunt, or was it Gray? Then rough hands closed around her arms, and she was dragged into a brighter light.

"How the hell did you find your way out here?" a stern voice asked. It had a strong Urgway accent, reminding Isla of the lessons she had taken and the time she had practiced to sound more rounded, more like the Elite. They weren't to sound like any one region, any one planet, for they represented them all.

"How did ya get in there?"

"Shaft," Gray grunted, and Isla realised then that he was doubled over on the ground. She tried to reach him, but she couldn't get out of the hold around her arms. She wondered at what point she had lost the strength that had earned her the place she'd held in the unit.

It all kept coming back to the Elite.

"What are you men doing..." a more rounded voice asked. Isla peered at the silhouette in the tunnel entrance that looked so different from the ones surrounding her. He was short, thin and dressed very differently. "How the hell?" he asked.

"You seen her boss?"

"With the colonel..." he stammered. "What are you doing down here? This isn't connected to the mine."

"Then why are there miners in it?" Isla asked, trying to sound tougher than she felt in that moment.

She thought Gray made a noise, something like a laugh.

"Get her out of here."

"What about these guys?"

"We're just three friends hanging out in a cave," Reilly murmured, just dodging the punch one of the miners swung at him and moving into the oncoming fist of another. "Do we look suspect?"

The man stepped into the light of the miner's helmet and looked at them, then back to the men who had knocked them to the floor. "Enforcers?"

"Exactly," Gray murmured from the floor. "Wait until our captain hears about this—and not to mention the colonel. We were with him earlier."

"I saw him come out alone," the thin man stammered.

"You sure?" Gray said, climbing slowly to his feet. "How did we get from the mine to here then?"

The thin man looked past them into the cavern, his face screwed in concentration. Then he took the helmet of the nearest man and pushed past them all into the cavern. Isla had to strain against the hold the men had on her to see what he was doing. But what had been an opening behind them was sealed shut. She wondered if the rohen had something to do with that. But she might never know. Perhaps she had been in this cave the entire time and had dreamt the whole thing.

But as she looked at Reilly, the growing bruise on his jaw and the healing wound on his cheek told her that she was mistaken.

Fourteen

G ray watched the woman sitting in the corner. Her brow creased as she thought over something, and he wasn't sure what that might be. Who she was, perhaps? Or what she could do? He had never in his life seen anything like what he had just seen. He had heard stories of hummers all his life. Those with an affinity for metal or machines. And he had been sure she was one the moment he'd seen her with the ship. The response of the Barilla to her touch had confirmed it. The weapon knew what she wanted, even though they all knew it had been imprinted to someone else.

Isla had denied the humming. She admitted a skill with animals and plants, which she had proven when she'd healed Reilly's face and likely her skin. She raised her green eyes towards him, and he held them for only a moment before he looked away. This wasn't the strong woman he had met in the desert, the one who had blown up a building and jumped into nothing. Something the colonel had done or said had broken her, long before he'd dropped her in the metal.

Or had it? She had survived that day, that terrible attack, and then relived it over and over—and that hadn't managed to break her.

She was stronger than that. Stronger than he would have been, and stronger than she herself realised.

"What are you doing?" he asked.

She glared at him. He smiled, seeing a little of the woman he had met before return. "Thinking," she said.

"About what?" Reilly asked before Gray could.

"How to get out of this?" Gray prompted, not wanting to be left out, as he glanced at the grubby miner standing against the wall. The man looked like he wanted to be in the room less than they did.

"How we got into it," she whispered, looking towards the doorway as the thin man entered.

"The colonel is returning. He said you were doing some groundwork for him. Although what that could be without my knowledge, I have no idea." He was clearly annoyed, and Gray wondered just how much power this little man had.

"So, you could release the cuffs then," he suggested.

"Not likely."

"Working for the colonel," Isla said, holding out her hands, "means working for Hendra. *The* Hendra."

The little man seemed to think about it for too long, rubbing his fingers together. All the while, Isla sat still with her hands outstretched.

He nodded once, and the miner stepped forward and undid them. Isla nodded to the others, and when the man didn't move, she coughed politely. The miner stared at the little man first. "Working for the Hendra," she repeated.

He scuttled into action and unbuckled their cuffs, taking them away. When Reilly rubbed at his jaw, Isla reached for it and then pulled her hands back. Her face was hard to read, and Gray realised he might have been mistaken about her state of mind.

"How long have you worked for Hendra?" she asked the man.

"Hendra? We are mining rohen. We don't work for Hendra."

"And yet you do the bidding of her lapdog."

He pulled himself taller, but it did little to make him look any more in control. "If you don't want to be shut down, you do as the colonel asks. No matter what business you are in."

"He'll be pleased to know that."

"He already does. It is why we allow them entry, and to take what they want."

"You don't mine all this for Hendra?"

"Who are you? Because there is no way you are working with the colonel if you ask so many questions. Anyone who knows anything of the colonel knows you don't ask questions. People who do..." He leaned forward, almost into Isla's face. "Don't live very long."

"So that is your reason."

He scoffed and turned towards the window. In the distance, Gray was sure he could hear a ship coming. He looked to Isla to alert her, but she seemed to have already noticed, for she wiggled a little closer to the edge of her seat. Gray was reminded of how little she wore.

"Should we ask him? You and me, when he arrives?"

"Are you dim?"

"I could be," she said, shimmying forward a little more, and what was left of her clothes exposed quite a lot of her slender, muscular leg. When Reilly coughed, Gray realised he was staring as much as the man she was trying to distract. She hadn't seemed that concerned when he'd seen her naked, but she clearly knew how to use it when she had to.

"What do you want?" he asked, exasperated, his eyes never leaving her legs.

"Let us meet the colonel on our own terms."

"What does that mean?" the man almost whined. She stood up and glanced ever so briefly towards the door, and if Gray hadn't been watching her, he would have missed it. With a clean swing and a charming smile, she knocked him out cold.

"Wow," Reilly breathed.

"Come on," Gray said, following her to the door and into the corridor. The sound of the ship landing in the middle of the site echoed from the mine tower and vibrated through the building.

"Now what?" Gray asked, grabbing her arm as she made for the door. She turned her glare on him. "Are you going to knock out the colonel?"

"No. I'm going to steal his ship."

"She's mad," Reilly whispered. "I love it."

Gray wasn't sure if he should try to stop her or try to keep up. As men rushed towards the ship, they slipped out of the building and out of sight of the landing site. The engine silenced. Isla waited perfectly still, her body pressed into the hot wall of the building.

"He's alone," she whispered as the crunch of the colonel's boots echoed just as loudly as his ship had done. The door banged shut to the office building. In the same instant, Isla broke into a run, and it was all Gray could do to keep up.

The door of the ship still open, she leapt aboard without hesitation. As he followed, Gray wondered if there was a chance someone else might be aboard. But the ship was empty. Gray wondered what this colonel did that he travelled alone so often—and just who he did report to if he was working on his own.

In that moment, when he knew they had been betrayed on the Sparrow, he'd thought the man had gone rogue. He soon realised that he was working for the bigger picture, and the Sparrow no longer fit in it.

The door slid shut behind Reilly, and the ship lifted quickly into the air.

"Maybe I should fly?" Reilly suggested. Isla nodded but didn't leave the controls. They sat down, strapping themselves in hastily to the same hard seats they had occupied not so long ago, and yet it seemed like days. Gray licked his lips for the first time, realising just how dry and cracked they were. In no time at all, he felt the gravity fall away; they went from pushed hard into the seats to held only in place by the wide belts. Beyond Isla at the controls, only darkness stretched out before them.

He nestled back into the seat as Isla activated the onboard gravity, which was quite weak compared to larger vessels. She left the controls. Gray was tempted to release his safety belt as she opened a narrow locker on the opposite side of the ship between similarly hard seats.

"They'll be looking for us now," Gray said.

"They can't track this. That is part of the reason he prefers it. Hendra might know where he was headed, but not exactly." She handed him a narrow canteen, which he sniffed at before he drank.

He nodded thanks and passed it back, but she shook her head. He handed it to Reilly. "Can any ship be truly untraceable?"

She smiled then and removed the jacket he had lent her. She reached up on her toes, more than her long legs exposed beneath the ruin of her clothing, and a panel he hadn't noticed near the roof line slid open. Isla pulled out a uniform, held it out at arm's length, crinkled her nose and then threw it at Gray.

"I can't dress as Elite."

"You can't stay as you are. Ship or not, the colonel will have a way to let them know we are coming."

"Coming?" Reilly asked. "We are heading back to Rennet?"

"What would you rather do?" she asked, holding out a black suit. There were no markings to indicate it was Elite, yet Gray recognised it for what it was. Before Reilly had the chance to answer, Isla allowed what was left of her clothes to fall to the floor and stepped into the suit. Although her body was still marked by the heavy scarring of her surviving that day, she was beautiful.

"Why didn't you use your cream to heal those?" Reilly asked as she zipped up the suit.

"Some things can't be healed," she murmured, then reached back into the locker and pulled out another suit like the one she wore. She threw it at him.

"Can you fly?" she asked Gray.

"You've seen it," he said, standing and finding himself closer to her in the small space than he expected.

"I've seen you crash. That might work too."

"I am not crashing this ship."

She shrugged and pointed towards the controls. "Let's find my dragonfly and a way to the Hendra."

"*The* Hendra?" Reilly asked. "I'm happy to start what we thought we were starting. It is time for a change—but you can't walk into the middle of Hendra Central and accuse the head of the galaxy of I'm not sure what."

"We need to know why she wants me dead, or at least what she thinks I can do with her metal."

"I'm not sure she wants you dead," Gray said, trying to focus on the controls. "Not now."

"But what does she want?"

"Her metal back, would be my guess," Reilly said. "What did you do?"

"I'm not sure," Isla admitted, sitting down beside Reilly and strapping herself into what had been Gray's seat. Gray wished Reilly was at the controls. "I can't remember what happened. I could feel it though, even in the cavern amongst the trees—the metal was there within the walls."

"It was the strangest thing I had ever seen," Reilly murmured.

"Any chance there is a weapon or three on this vessel?" Gray asked.

When there was no response, he turned around to find Isla sitting with her eyes closed. Then she was out of the seat, opening the door of another hidden locker at the back of the small ship. Barilla rifles,

Stardusters and other, larger weapons he couldn't name were held in place. She gave him a smile as she indicated the locker.

"That might see us through," he murmured, turning back towards the controls. "Maybe."

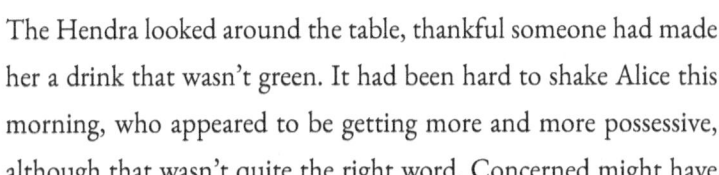

The Hendra looked around the table, thankful someone had made her a drink that wasn't green. It had been hard to shake Alice this morning, who appeared to be getting more and more possessive, although that wasn't quite the right word. Concerned might have fit better, but she knew that Hendra wasn't a woman to be fussed over; rather than endear her, it was wearing Hendra out. And she had far more important things to be worried about.

"Are you sure on your intelligence?" Chief Victor Sem of Rennet asked. She raised her eyebrows in response. He coughed politely but didn't look away.

"Yes," she enunciated slowly. "I am."

"The rohen is too unstable to do anything with," Chief Sem continued. "How do they think they could move it, if they could truly extract it? I've heard rohen has a mind of its own."

"Rohen is a metal, a very dangerous metal, and that is why I stepped in to regulate the industry as I did. It can't think for itself."

"Regulate?" a voice at the far end of the table queried—possibly louder than intended, for every other member at the table turned that way. "You outlawed it," Chief Dekka Brown of Draroh muttered, then pushed himself up from the table. His old frame was stronger than it appeared. "You drove it underground so you could have more power over the market and fewer eyes watching you."

"Really, Chief Brown, that is a serious accusation."

"Your father would be ashamed." His voice was low and even, but it cut her deeply.

She sighed and made no response. She wouldn't give him the satisfaction. Her father had put the idea in her head as a child. The number of times he'd talked about having control of the rohen market, how that would strengthen their hold over the Complex... He just hadn't thought of a way to do it. She had. And then she had learned something unexpected about the metal, something that had reinforced she was doing the right thing.

"You are very quiet on this matter, brother." She looked to her left, to the tall man who said very little and seemed far more than the ten years younger than her he was. He wasn't a man; he looked like a boy skiving off school.

"Would you heed me if I offered comment?" Solon didn't look up from the monitor before him. She waited, but he didn't raise his eyes, and Brown coughed again at the other end of the table. She wasn't sure if it was his age, some dreaded, lurking illness, or if he was trying to be polite, but she found her hand moved to her belly all the same. The brother she rarely saw smirked. "Be careful, sister. They may realise you are human after all."

He pushed his chair back, the legs scraping across the hardwood floor. She relished the wood, the rarity of it, as it was no longer harvested. Brown winced at the noise, as did someone else, and Hendra wondered again why she needed to explain herself to these people.

It was her solar system, after all, to do with as she saw fit. Only they insisted she include them in major decisions. *Damn history and the rules of governance.*

The problem tonight, she thought as she refused to watch her brother leave the room, was that the news was out about an illegal mine and enforcers needing to be called. She had not sent them anywhere near the mine where she had sent the hummer—but however it had happened, the news was out. And Calder, for all he was worth, had gotten himself trapped on Urgway.

"Is it true she is a hummer?" asked Chief Ebberah Slar of Oric, the only other woman in the room, not that it mattered that she was a woman. The only important factor was that she was weak in Hendra's eyes.

"Do they exist?" Chief Sem asked.

"Hmm," Brown offered, and Hendra looked up towards the end of the table.

"No," she said. "They are myth."

"Much of what we didn't understand was thought to be myth, and now that we understand it..." Sem trailed off.

"Is there evidence of hummers outside of the stories we heard as children?"

"I'm surprised your father told you stories," Brown offered. Hendra glared again at his grey hair, wrinkled skin and dull eyes. "I would have thought he told you only what you really needed to run this solar system."

"That includes the beliefs of the people. However mistaken or limited they are."

Brown cleared his throat again. "Can Calder shed any light on this?"

She shook her head and sat back in the soft chair.

"Chief X'ang, you too are very quiet."

"I, like your brother, feel that I have nothing I can bring to this conversation that you would listen to. I'm sure if Calder had made it back from whatever mine you tested this hummer in, he would have said everything you needed said."

Hendra stood slowly from the chair. Her hands gripped the arm-rest longer than needed. She leant forward over the table and eyed Chief Bind X'ang of Urgway, but he didn't give her the reaction she wanted. Their fear was evaporating. Her brother was right—they were starting to see her as human, rather than the formidable power she was. She would have to rectify that. Even if she had to use these people to make the point.

"What makes you think I placed her in a mine?" she asked, looking around the table again. Who did these people think they were to question her? And how had her plans, or any hint of them, escaped into the atmosphere of Urgway or beyond?

"It is what I would have done," X'ang said, pushing his chair back with more control. As he stood and bowed his head to her, she wondered just who was telling who what.

"The mines are illegal."

"The need for rohen hasn't changed. You claimed the reason you changed the law was from a concern for safety. But we all know it was for the control of the rohen. I think you might find that rohen is much harder to control than you expect. Even with a hummer."

"As Chief of Urgway, I suppose you think you know best," Hendra said.

"I've seen it. I've worked with it long before I moved to such a position, despite what my father had hoped for me. And..." He leaned forward. "It wasn't on Urgway." He grinned too easily as he left the room. She turned her attentions back to the remaining three at the table.

"He's right, Hendra—no matter how much control you think you have, it isn't the same in reality. The metal is considered unstable for a reason." Victor looked towards the door but didn't move. As Chief of Rennet, he lived not far from the building they met in, and she didn't think he held quite the same power as the other leaders as she too resided on planet.

"It is a resource," Ebberah said. "One the Complex needs, although how it differs from the other metals we use for ships and the like, I couldn't begin to understand."

Hendra was tempted to say something about just how little of anything Ebberah seemed to understand. But it was Brown who put his hand on Ebberah's and gave her a soft, friendly smile.

"The liquid is"—he looked to Hendra—"*was* essential to our interplanetary transports, and the metal moves in such a way as to be able to create the smallest of wiring and conduct, so much more than other metals. It was used in control panels and communications."

Ebberah nodded slowly, seeming to take in every word, but Hendra doubted the woman truly understood. "I tested that once," she said, leaning towards Brown as though it were a secret.

And that seems to give credence to my edict that it is not safe, Hendra thought. It would explain why Ebberah was so vague, and yet she managed to run a whole planet. At least her officials kept the planet running, the smallest in the Complex; it was one Hendra rarely visited, not worthy of her time. But if the metal had made it there to be used for various items, it would be interesting to find out just what they did with it.

The conversation wasn't going as she wished, and Hendra wasn't going to argue any further with them. She bowed her head, and they returned the motion before climbing to their feet as she waved them from the room.

When she entered the sitting room off her office, she was surprised to find her brother and not Alice.

"You are yet to congratulate me," she said, sitting opposite him in the deep chair.

"I remember sitting in here as a child, waiting for Father to finish some meeting or other and spend some time with me—but I can barely remember him."

"You were young when he died," she said, and he raised serious eyes to hers. "What do you want?"

"Why should I want for anything?" He lifted his long legs off the table that separated them and leaned forward to support himself with his elbows on his knees. "I have what I need."

"A small planet of your own," she murmured.

"A family, and none of the pressures of the Complex resting on my shoulders."

"I appreciate the position I'm in." She looked at him staring at her across the room. "Family?"

"I hope you pay your wife more attention than you do your brother."

"I thought she would be waiting," Hendra said, looking around. "Do you have a wife?"

He nodded slowly. "And three children."

"Three?" She was openly surprised. "Why did I not know this?"

"I am sure there is very little you don't know. But then, did you need to know? Does it affect your ability to rule? You have your heir." He lowered his eyes to her midsection. "However you managed that."

"Do you really think we were both born naturally to Mother?" She scoffed.

"It was never a secret," he said, standing, and she realised just how tall he was. Was it possible he had grown? "The only law that matters in the Complex is that the Hendra must be mother or father for the offspring to stand in line." He stepped close and looked down over her. "Until this child is born, I am still next in line, sister. And at your age, it is a precarious thing."

She stood quickly. "Alice is ensuring we are safe."

Solon smiled, a smile she couldn't read, and he left through the private exit. She wasn't old—not in terms of a leader, not in terms of a mother. It was not a concern her doctors had raised at any stage. And he was so young, too young to be married with three children. She would need to look into that. Perhaps he had married an older woman with children already. But those children would still inherit his place, perhaps. He had taken over from an old chief who had outlived a single son. Lines could change; rulers could be unexpected. Except the Hendra. That was always a certainty.

Once she had Calder back on planet, she would send him off to find out just what her brother was up to.

Fifteen

Isla ran her hand over the ship and sighed. It felt as though she had been away forever. Whatever the time away had been, it was down to her. She had stupidly walked right into the middle of Hendra Central expecting them to be understanding, believing, on her side.

"Who are you?" Gray asked. He had watched her even more closely since finding her in the mine. Annoyingly so, and annoyingly close.

She rested her head against the cool metal and breathed in the scent of it. She wasn't anyone of any consequence, yet so much had happened.

"Island?" a soft voice called behind her. She turned to find the old mechanic she had learnt so much from when she had first joined the Elite, or at least Hendra, between the long hours of training.

"Sam," she whispered, feeling better for seeing him, yet it took her back to a world she'd thought she had left far behind. She reached out her hand, which he looked at for too long before pulling her into an awkward embrace.

"I thought you had gone off somewhere to die," he whispered, his voice catching in his throat. "And yet you managed to hold on to your retirement gift."

"Luck," she returned, breathing in the comfortable and familiar scent of the workshop on his clothes. "Thanks for watching her."

"One look and I knew it was yours. You have that special touch."

"I learnt from the best," she said, leaning back and taking in his sad face. "Sam?"

"It isn't safe," he said, his hands too tight around her arms. He glanced past her to the men standing by the dragonfly.

"They are friends," she reassured him. "Also, on the wrong side of the Elite."

"How did it come to this, Island?"

She shook her head. There was something that would answer everyone's questions, especially her own, yet she couldn't find the information.

"What has happened to you?"

"Too much," she murmured. "If only I could remember it all," she added under her breath.

"I thought you would want to forget." Sam walked around her, running his hand over the metal of the dragonfly in same way she had. "You could always ask the memory collectors."

She stared at him as he turned slowly, opened and closed his mouth, and then grinned at her. "I was joking," he said, glancing at the others. "If you believe in stories like that, you might as well believe in hummers."

Gray looked Sam up and down, then turned with raised eyebrows. "How many grease monkeys do you know, exactly?"

"All of them," Isla said with a smile, but Reilly was not looking happy at all. Standing back, he was looking quite edgy. "What is it?" she asked.

"We don't have time for this. They know where we were headed; they are going to find that Elite ship..." He waved vaguely back towards the door of the workshop. "And then they are going to quickly work out where you are."

Isla looked back to Sam. Maybe Reilly was right. Maybe the memory collectors were myth, but then maybe they weren't. Isla had seen some strange things in the last little while. She doubted she was a hummer, but she had a strong sense of the rohen. Even now, standing in the middle of the yard, she could feel it around her—in the ground beneath her feet, in the ship so familiar to her. The more she thought about it and searched it out, the closer it came and the more distinct the feeling became.

"Memory collectors," she said.

"Escaping the Elite," Reilly said.

"Maybe we could do both." Gray suggested. "Where would we find a memory collector?"

"I was making a joke," Sam reiterated slowly, as though Gray were dim. "They are a story from the old times. These boys aren't very bright, Island. Ditch them as soon as you can, or they'll have you chasing hummers."

"You so sure they don't exist?" she asked.

Sam rolled his eyes. "There are some gifted with a feel for machines; you are certainly one of them. But if you could talk to metal... it isn't like it could talk back."

Isla looked down at the ground beneath her feet and wondered just what the rohen was trying to do. Was it trying to keep itself safe? If it could, perhaps it wouldn't have been mined in the first place. Unless it wanted to be. She shook her head and stepped forward to take Sam by the shoulders, then kissed his cheek.

"You are not what you were," he murmured, "and yet just the same."

"Reilly is right. They will come looking, and we can't be here when they come."

"You were them not so long ago."

"And now they want me, *us*, dead. Calder—do you know him?"

Sam shook his head.

"You know everyone," Isla said, reminded of the time they'd spent talking about the Elite and soldiers while she'd learned to repair and build ships.

"Something odd with that one," he muttered.

"Like he keeps trying to kill us," Reilly said behind her, and she smiled.

"Something else," Sam said, stepping out of her reach. "Go, as far away from him as you can." He ran a hand through her hair, capturing a curl and tucking it behind her ear, where it sprang straight back out. "You were never to blame for that day. You are the hero they say you are."

She shook her head. He nodded slowly, his hand squeezing hers tighter.

"You were always the hero. You were the best of them all." He walked quickly across the yard, his head down as though he didn't want to say goodbye. She wondered what he knew of Calder and why she hadn't heard of him before. If he was Elite, they must have crossed paths.

Isla climbed aboard the ship and settled into the pilot's seat. Sam was right; they had to get as far away from Calder as they could. But she had no idea where that was, or where she might find the memory collectors if they did exist.

The others followed, Reilly muttering as he buckled himself into his seat. "Bloody hummer. Now we're looking for mythical men."

Isla put her hands to the controls, and the engines roared to life. She lifted her hands slowly, the ship lifting from the yard without hesitation. She didn't look for Sam. He would be tucked away somewhere, hopefully pretending they had never been there. With her back to Gray, he couldn't see her close her eyes, yet she felt his gaze on her. She tried not to shiver. He was helping, maybe. And he seemed to have worked out a few things about her she didn't even know herself.

Isla focused on the rohen, searching for it within the ship. It flowed through the metal walls around her, beneath her feet, within the chair and most importantly, around her fingers.

She took a deep breath, feeling the pull of the metal, then thought of the memory collectors—the name, the stories—not that she had any idea of what they really were. The ship shifted beneath her; the flight path came into focus and then was gone.

"Do you know where we are going?" Reilly asked.

She shook her head, but the ship seemed to have some idea. She rested her hands against the control panel while her dragonfly, or the rohen within it, decided where they were going.

"Isla?" Gray asked after a while, and Isla opened her eyes to the dark world around them.

"Are you going to tell me the reason you are here?" she asked, getting in before he could ask whatever it was he wanted.

"I made a promise," he murmured. She turned and looked at them.

"Just tell her," Reilly groaned.

"Kalli," he said reluctantly.

Isla felt the air leave her body. Before she could find the words, it was as though the rohen called to her from the ship and soothed her in a way. She knew he had lived a life before she knew him, before he had joined the Elite. And he had been there some years before she had joined. Before she'd learnt what it was to be Elite. "Why would he ask that of you?" She was surprised at how level and together she sounded.

"He didn't," Gray said, looking at Reilly as though he could explain. "He..." He shook his head.

Isla tried to be patient, tried to look as though she was giving him the time he needed to find the words to explain this to her in a way that made sense. Because it didn't. Kalli knew she could look after herself. And although there had been something very special between them, it had only been over the last year that they had worked together.

"When?" she asked, finding it harder to keep her voice level. She used to do this every day—she used to be able to portray herself as strong and independent and unflappable and now, with one name, she had come undone.

"We were children together, school friends."

"What did you promise him?" she asked, unbuckling and stepping forward, aware that what Gray thought he was doing was not something Kalli would have asked of him.

"When he joined up, when he left…" he stammered, his eyes not resting on her.

"Gray!" she snapped, and he finally looked at her.

"He asked me to watch over his life. Although we'd be far away from each other, I promised."

"You failed there," she muttered.

"You're not dead yet," he returned, his gaze studying the black nothing beyond the ship through the narrow forward window.

"Gray," she said evenly, "this doesn't make sense."

"He made me promise. We were only boys, yet I had to keep what I could of it. He was scared, and the training was intense. The calls grew further apart and then stopped. When he died… when the news came of his death, I felt like I had failed him. And then there was something on those recordings that day…"

"What recordings?" she asked slowly, but she knew what he was going to say.

"Of the day he died."

She took a step back and he looked at her again, something lost and sad in his bright blue eyes.

"There was something odd, something that wasn't him in the way he spoke."

"He wasn't a boy anymore."

"You were all I had left," Gray continued quickly. "All I had of a promise I couldn't keep. I thought if I could keep you alive, keep you safe..."

"I don't need you to keep me safe." An odd feeling grew in her chest, that he would care so much. But he wasn't worried for her; he was trying to keep a promise he'd made to a boy too many years before that he wasn't capable of keeping. "Soldiers put themselves in a position of risk. It is what we do, risk ourselves to ensure everyone else is safe. You can't stop that. I couldn't stop that. I couldn't stop what happened that day, and it wasn't just Kalli we lost. It was everyone."

Gray nodded once.

"To keep this promise, you followed me?"

"Actually, I lost you after the hearings, and then we were working on what had happened to the Sparrow, what the Elite were up to. When their focus moved to a racing crew on Urgway, I followed and found you."

"You have no obligations to me. I have probably saved you once or twice. Call it even."

"This isn't finished."

"I need to find the memory collectors," Isla said, and he gave her the same exasperated look. "Something changed—something happened for that unit to be slaughtered. I know what it is, only I don't. Somewhere deep in here"—she tapped her temple—"is the answer, and I need it. I need to know what happened to him."

Gray nodded. "Let me help. Let me find out with you. He wasn't the boy I knew in the end."

"The things we see in the Elite can change you."

"It was something else, something I can't put my finger on. He joined Hendra to help people, but I don't think that was what he was doing when he went into the Elite."

"The man I knew wanted to help the entire Complex." Isla smiled for the first time at the memory of the large man directing them into a mission. His blue eyes locked on hers, willing her to stay safe. Although he had wanted that for all of them.

"Let's hope your memories remain the same," Gray murmured, looking away again.

Isla felt more uncertain than before as to what had happened that day as Kalli smiled at her from her memories. It wasn't a friendly smile but was like something Colonel Calder would wear. She shivered.

"If you lost contact, how did you get that image?"

He put his hand to his chest as though feeling for the pad in his pocket. "It was made public record after that day."

Isla hadn't heard that. She had moved through that time in a fog, but now it was time to go back and learn what had happened, do what she could to right the wrong of so many deaths.

She strapped herself back into the pilot's seat and ran her hands over the controls as the whole dragonfly hummed around her. It somehow felt different and yet just the same. She tried to concentrate on what she needed, but that was made difficult by the whispering men strapped into the space behind her. She should have left them behind, ensured they returned safely to their families, or at least Reilly.

She turned around. Gray lifted his eyes to hers, and the conversation stopped.

"What are memory collectors going to do for you?" Reilly asked. "If they even exist. And how do they get at the memories? Crack your head open and look?"

She laughed at the idea.

"What will happen when you remember?" Gray asked, his voice serious.

Isla stared back out at the nothingness. Despite the clarity of what she had relived that day, it seemed oddly foggy. As though there was as much in her memories as out before her in the emptiness of space. A distant planet came into view. Oric. She doubted that the memory collectors were there if they did exist, and yet that was where they were headed to. Maybe her memories were just as this planet, perfectly formed but just out of view.

"Maybe that depends on what I remember," Isla returned, conscious of the fact that it had been some time since he had asked the question. There was a relief at the idea that she would discover what she seemed to have lost that day, and a nervousness as well. Maybe Gray had a better idea than she did of what she might remember or what might have really happened.

"Could it be as easy as someone hid them?" she wondered aloud. "You said something was odd. It hasn't felt right. I remember it; I can still visualise everything that happened on that recording as though I'm reliving that same day over and over again. Although detailed, the recording doesn't answer any questions. Why we were there, where the attack came from or who was responsible." She took a deep breath, suddenly transported back there, her hand itching for a Barilla as the darkness closed in around her. "The look on all their faces despite the dark, the flashes of weapon fire, the limited light—I saw them all go down. I saw them fight for their last breaths." She was talking faster, the words running over each other. Then Gray was standing beside her, his hand on her shoulder.

"You have interesting scarring for energy flares. What did they use?" Reilly asked.

She looked around at Reilly, and Gray growled something too low to hear.

"It's true," he said, holding his hands up.

Isla could taste blood on her lips, not only her own but the spray of others', and something else. Maybe the master was right all along and she was gifted. "Metal," she breathed.

"Metal?"

"There was metal. They used metal."

"Rohen?" Gray asked.

She shook her head. She wasn't sure how she knew, but she did. And she wondered why the idea had never come to her before. She had thought the wounds were so deep they had to put her back together, but it was something else that had felt wrong. Her fingers ran over the dip in her collarbone. The bone was perfectly healed despite the raised skin, but she remembered a dip, a chip in that bone when she had awoken after the surgery. When she had cried out and they had put her back to sleep to allow the healing to occur in a safe, dark place.

"Isla?"

She refocused on the men before her. Reilly looked as though he wanted to ask something, and Gray was focused on her fingers working over her skin. She turned back for the controls, placed her hands over the display and closed her eyes. She had to remember.

The ship turned a few degrees to the left and then accelerated towards a destination only her dragonfly seemed to understand.

Despite her best efforts, Isla couldn't keep her eyes open. The ship was steering itself, and all she was focused on was that they were getting closer to Oric. Reilly wanted to relieve her in the pilot seat, probably just to feel as though he was in control of something.

She gave up the seat without a fight and headed into the narrow bathroom that ran down one side of the dragonfly. The hot shower failed to clear the fog that had settled over her, and she changed into a suit too similar to what she had taken from Calder's ship. She fell into the narrow bunk longing for the Barilla or the old duster, but she had managed to sleep over the past few days without either of them. Even though that had been a very different form of sleep.

As she closed her eyes, she felt cocooned in the soft hold of the rohen. The warm liquid enveloped her without suffocating her, giving her the same feeling of safety she'd had in the mine. The security that nothing could reach her helped her relax into sleep. She had once felt that same security in a distant hospital bed as people had stood her around whispering, wondering if she would survive. No one from the colony had come; they hadn't been sought. She wondered then if they really thought she would survive. And why they had tried so hard to keep her alive. If the Elite and Hendra were behind the recent attacks, why had they gone to such lengths to save her six years ago?

A flash of metal caught the light. The vest that should have protected her from the most determined enemy fell away as though it were made of linen. Isla sucked in a breath as she searched the darkness, her hand to her chest, the pain intense. Loud screams filled the world around her, and she couldn't find Kalli.

She sat up, her hand rubbing over the skin at her collarbone, and sighed. That was new. She hadn't had that dream before, but maybe she was searching for something. Maybe she was so fixated on trying to remember what had happened that day that she was making things up.

The ship lurched sideways, and she was nearly thrown out of the bunk. "What are you doing to my dragonfly?" she asked as the door opened and she scrambled out into the cockpit.

"Someone is trying to stop us reaching wherever it is we're going!" Reilly growled, his hands working through the control panel. "She only really likes you," he muttered.

Isla was beside him in a heartbeat. She moved her hand over the side of the panel to reveal the image of ships surrounding them. "Where did they come from?"

"Not around here," he said. "I can't shake them." The ship lurched again to the side as a volley of fire ricocheted off the hull.

"She's tough," Isla said, patting the panel beside her as she looked up at Gray. He was still watching her too closely, and she was not certain it was for the right reasons. Nothing was as it should be or as she'd thought it was. She longed for the simple desert and the races. Although those had never quite been what she had hoped they would be. "Move over." She nudged Reilly out of the pilot's seat.

"I can fly her," he grumbled as he gave up the seat. Isla belted herself in securely, trying not to wince as the belt cut into her shoulder and wondering just what her memories could do to her if she managed to remember the truth of the day. That was, if they could get out of this and find the memory collectors.

An alarm sounded through the cabin. "Sit," she said as she waved her hand over the control panel. Another ping echoed through the ship. "Yes?"

"Island Tarle. You are wanted in connection to an illegal mine on Urgway. Please halt your travel and hand yourself in."

"Do I know that voice?" Reilly murmured as he strapped in.

"Calder," Gray said as Isla thought it.

"You are responsible for the illegal mine," she said. "I'm not handing myself over to you to be killed or used for whatever you think you can do with the rohen."

Silence followed. Another hit shuddered through the dragonfly, but it wasn't aimed at destroying them, just slowing them down.

"He's not going to stop," Gray whispered.

"I will find you," the cruel voice whispered over the comms as Isla closed her eyes and wished them far away. The ship stopped dead in space.

"What the hell?" Reilly breathed. Then they were thrown back against their seats as the ship sped through the stars, travelling far faster than the small vessel should have been able to. Isla watched the control panel, where there was no longer any indication of other ships.

"Did we sustain any damage?" Reilly asked once he got his breath back.

"No," she said, pushing her hands through the controls. At least not enough to slow them down. But she could feel the metal moving around them, covering what might have exposed them to the vacuum of space. There was rohen in the ship. Isla wondered then if it was in every ship. Had something of the metal made it beyond the ban, or had it been there already? *What does Hendra want with it?*

A large moon came into focus as they moved into its orbit. Isla focused on the planet beyond it, far too close. "Is that natural?"

"Oric's moon is famous," Reilly said, moving around behind her and looking over her shoulder. "So low that the stories talk of being able to touch it from the mountaintops. Have you never been here before?"

She shook her head. The smallest planet in the Complex, Oric was of little political importance, although Isla thought Kalli had visited on missions long before she had joined the Elite. As with all previous missions, the reason was not talked of, if he even knew it. They had done as they were told and more often than not, they didn't even know the reasons behind it.

"Are the memory collectors on Oric?" Gray asked.

"I don't know."

The ship pulled up suddenly. The two men were thrown back as it circled around the small moon, and then they were landing on the far side.

"And yet here we are," Gray murmured, wincing as he stood from the floor.

"I'm not in control of this," Isla said, looking out onto the dark surface. "Is there anything here?"

A faint glow shone in the distance, and Isla was reminded of the fungi in the forest and the caves. It shone brighter for a moment before going out.

"I don't like this," Reilly murmured.

"If they are able to help, it won't matter."

"How can you be sure what they will do, or what they want?" Gray asked, his hand too tight around her wrist. "You have no idea what you are doing."

"I need to know," she said, pulling from his hand and reviewing the console before going to the door.

"Is there even an atmosphere?" Reilly asked as she put her hand on the panel beside the door.

Isla stopped. She was too keen to find out what was there. She reached for the cape, but wasn't here, lost somewhere in a forgotten racer. She took a deep breath and pulled the narrow mask from its place against the wall. She pressed it to her face, turning to see Gray nod his approval. She had always found the mask constricting, too close to the skin, and although it might have helped her to breathe, the proximity seemed to make it harder.

"Have you got enough of those for us?" Gray asked.

She ignored him, opened the door and was hit by a cold, dry wind. Her eyes watered from the constant blowing, and she wondered if she would find goggles like she'd had in the Elite. She had used them far more than she'd expected then, and she was missing more and more of her equipment.

It was as though allowing herself to think about that time again was bringing more than she'd thought she remembered to the fore. And then a dark shape loomed before her. As she reached for the duster at her hip, something hard smacked into the back of her head.

Sixteen

Gray watched the closed door after Isla had walked out into the dark. He stepped forward to place his hand on the panel.

"I think we should wait," Reilly said. "She knows what she is risking."

"Does she?" Gray asked, turning on him. "She doesn't even believe Hendra are really trying to use her or kill her."

"I'm not sure they know what they want with her. They didn't know what she was," he insisted. "She's a hummer. She led us here, found her way here with only a thought."

Gray looked back at the panels. There was more to her relationship with the ship than he'd thought. Did they know what they had given her, or had she changed it enough to create what she needed? She had worked on it well enough when they were in the yard. She had spent a lot of her life with mechanics, it seemed, both in the Elite and beyond.

"But we don't know what they will do if she manages to find these people. What if they are not what she thinks?" The door opened. Gray sighed with relief, then stepped back as a tall, dark, hooded figure stepped into the cabin. The wind blew around them, and

Gray wondered what was next as he stared at the figure, whose face was hidden beneath the hood of the black cloak.

"Come," the figure said with a deep, rumbling voice that seemed to vibrate through Gray in much the same way as the ship had during flight. He held out a hand that was still lost within the sleeve, but two masks were extended beyond the rough black cloth. He remained unmoving as Gray and Reilly looked at each other. Then, with a noise of annoyance, Reilly reached out and took them, handing one to Gray.

The hooded figure turned slowly, his face still covered, and stepped out into the darkness beyond the ship. Gray took a deep breath, affixed the mask and followed. He wondered just what Isla had dragged them into as the wind cut across his exposed skin and pushed against him. Even though he was still dressed in the Elite uniform, it was cold, as though the cold of the wind pushed through the thick material and wrapped around his skin.

He reached out towards Reilly, but something hard pushed into his back, and he brought his hands back into this chest. He tried to turn, but the same hard item kept him moving forward. With the howling of the wind around them, he couldn't hear any sound to indicate if it was a weapon. And then he thought he couldn't see the man before him any longer. His feet slowed as he feared he was lost or they were being led far away. Then he was shoved from behind, causing him to stumble.

"Where is Isla?" he called into the wind, but his voice was pulled away before it could reach anyone. He stumbled again as his foot hit something, and then he was climbing steps, the world around them still dark. He raised a hand to shield his eyes as a wide door opened and flooded the landing with a soft yellow light. He turned, unable to see the face of the man behind him hidden in the shadows of his hood. The light stopped there. Not illuminating the steps or where they had come from.

The hooded figure ahead of him coughed politely, and Gray followed him through the door after glancing back at Reilly, who raised his eyebrows. They walked a few paces inside, and then Gray stopped. The enormous open space was filled with light and nothing else. It was hard to determine what the smooth white walls were even made of.

"Isla?"

Another shove from behind.

"We only want to help her."

The man they were following stopped and turned slowly, looked down over him as though taking his measure, then turned back and started walking again.

"Are you memory collectors?" Gray asked.

"We do not like that term," a voice whispered behind him. "It is not what we are."

"Then what are you?" Gray asked. But he was met with silence. They followed the figure in the hope that he was leading them towards Isla and that she was alright. "Why are we here?" Gray asked.

The figure continued in silence, and Gray started to think this was a very bad idea. Before he knew it, they were back in the dark. He followed close behind, wanting to hold onto his cloak like a child might so that he wouldn't get lost, but the further they travelled the more he began to wonder if they were men. Maybe they were another race altogether. There were other races in the galaxy, some very like him, others very different. He considered the squat frangar who looked after the paddock for the racers. The creature before him stopped and turned slowly.

"You are clear," he whispered, the sound echoing around the empty space surrounding them—or at least Gray had thought it empty, for they had walked and walked through the darkness and come close to nothing. But he didn't understand what the words meant. Was he cleared to find Isla, or clear of some other test? A soft chuckle filled the world around him, moving across his skin like the wind, pushing into his unsteady thoughts.

"Come," he whispered, and a door opened at the far end of the room. It seemed as though they had walked so far already. He wondered if this was a temple or series of tunnels beneath the surface of the small moon, for someone would have seen them otherwise and the memory collectors wouldn't be the myth that they were.

Again, the light shone from within the doorway but didn't shed any light beyond it.

"Reader," the creature whispered.

"Excuse me?"

"We are Readers."

"Have you been reading us?" Gray looked around; Reilly had disappeared. Panic set in.

"You are safe." The quiet voice was still undecipherable. He couldn't determine quite who it belonged to. "It does not matter."

"I suppose it doesn't, as long as Isla is safe."

The hooded figure bowed, and Gray stepped forward to a narrow bed, stretched out beneath a window. There was no one else in the room. He looked beyond the space to find that there was dim lighting on the other side of the window. Isla was lying on the narrow bed under a window in an identical room. He looked up at the reflection of his own worried face and the hooded figure behind him.

"What are you doing?"

"Reading," he whispered.

Gray sighed. He wasn't going to get anything like this, and the idea occurred that maybe this was an opportunity for him to help.

"You share memories."

Gray turned and took in the figure. "Share?"

The figure bowed his head.

"We only met recently."

"But you have shared much since you have met. You can help her."

"How? It was hard enough knowing that she had to relive that day over and over. If it isn't what really happened, and she has to relive a different day... it hurts just to think about it."

"Do not try, just be."

"Isla has been trying."

"We have prevented that."

Gray wasn't sure he wanted to know how they had prevented such a thing, but Isla was where she had wanted to be. "Can you find her memories?"

"They were not lost," he said, turning and leaving the room. The door slid shut, and the light dimmed to a similar fashion of the neighbouring room. Isla lay too still on the bed. But whether someone was watching from the other side, Gray couldn't guess.

He wasn't sure what he was supposed to be doing. He stood for a time and watched her. She didn't appear to be distressed, yet there were times he wasn't even sure she was breathing. She lay so still. He wondered at the scars on her body, the deep lines that crossed over each other as though she had been stitched back together badly.

He sat on the edge of the cot, allowing the idea of her naked body to fill his mind. She didn't think she was worth looking at, he realised sadly. For such a beautiful woman, it was a shame. He shook his head, trying to dispel the image. That wasn't why he had followed her. He'd just needed to know she was safe. She might have dragged them here, but he wasn't convinced these people, or creatures, could do as she thought they could.

What might the truth of that day do to her? Someone had hidden it for a reason; what that might be, he couldn't even begin to understand. It wasn't hard to believe the Hendra could be involved in destroying so many lives—lives that worked to do her bidding, her work in the Complex.

Calder came to mind, the horror of what he had done and then pinned on the Sparrow more recently. Was there a connection? Was there something more that linked him to Island Tarle, the strangely confident woman? No matter what she had been through, she was still strong, sassy, and determined to jump in where she was likely to get shot at.

Why did he think he could save her? She was right; she had saved him more often than he had managed to help her. On Rennet, he had left her in the forest to further his own interests, find out what he could on the Elite, prove they were not what they were thought to be. Find something to pull the people of the Complex together for a different future.

Gray hadn't learnt how she had ended up with Calder. He hadn't asked the important questions. He wondered what they were doing. What were they really trying to find?

He closed his eyes, remembering her disappearing into the foliage in the forest, and breathed out slowly. He had walked away from her. His view shifted, and it was as though he was in the tree watching himself and Reilly walk away. A moment of fear washed over him, as though he didn't want to be left alone, but the tree was comforting. The smells and sounds of the forest soon blocked any uncertainty.

The next moments were unclear. Flashes of images were accompanied by overwhelming feelings, and he couldn't quite see what was going on. Large cats, soft yet scary, children in a cutting in the rock, an old man, loss. Overwhelming loss and guilt.

He sat up, sucking in a deep breath. Just what had pushed her out of the forest? Why had she walked straight into Calder? Or had he found her?

There was far more to Calder. He remembered the man's confidence when he had first come aboard the Sparrow. He remembered the excitement of the opportunity, the way the Elite looked down at him as though he wasn't worthy of their attention, that they weren't really working together and he was disappointed. Not that he wasn't good enough, but they were so full of themselves. Isla never gave that impression. Gray wondered if she would have been different, had she been among the group that had worked with them at that time.

He didn't think she would have supported what they'd done to the Sparrow, or would she not have been given the choice? She might have thought it was for the greater good of the Complex. That was what they did, wasn't it? Worked—or at least did the dirty jobs that were needed and no one else wanted—for the protection and development of the Complex.

She had run away. When he'd found her, quite by accident, in that pit, with her long red hair poking out from beneath the old helmet, he had been so relieved he had wanted to hug her. But she wasn't the sort to get close to anyone. All those years and she had chosen to be alone. He had dragged her into their cause under the pretext of helping her. Although in a way, it was true. He had saved her. After all this time, someone wanted her dead, although he couldn't understand why—particularly when she still remembered nothing, how had she become a threat?

Or had they wanted to draw her out? Attacking her made her a threat, and they could eliminate a criminal more easily than a hero. The race footage had been doctored. He had stepped in because he had wanted to help her. If he was honest, it wasn't Kalli driving his need to do something—it was Isla. She was more than he'd ever expected and, despite her best efforts, she wasn't as tough as she appeared.

Something banged on the window between the rooms. He turned, blinking into the dim light, wondering where his mind had wandered to, and looked up at Isla's face pressed against the glass.

He was on his feet, his hand pressed where her breath was fogging the glass. She closed her eyes. When she opened them, she nodded once. With a serious face, she turned away.

"Do you remember?" he called, but she couldn't hear him. Instead of walking towards the narrow bed, she opened a door, and he looked around the room and did the same. He found her just inside the doorway. She rubbed at the back of her head. "Isla?"

"I'm not keen on the dark," she admitted, and he looked along the dark corridor that stretched into the distance.

"Did you remember?"

"No." She sounded distant. The light in the hallway grew a little, until it was as dim as the rooms they had left. "How do we get out? How did I get in?"

"I don't know. You were already here when I arrived."

She nodded once, as though knowing what he meant.

"I dreamt of the forest," he stammered. She gave him an almost panicked look, and he bit his lip.

A hooded figure stood at the end of the corridor. They headed towards it together. "Did they not want to help you, or could they not help you?" Gray asked.

Isla moved slowly but steadily towards the figure at the far end of the hall. When he opened his mouth to ask the question again, she held up a hand. She had heard him; she wasn't ready to answer. The figure bowed a head, and she did the same.

"It is as it should be," he whispered. Isla sighed before he turned, and they followed him further along a dark corridor. Before Gray realised it, they were in the brightly lit room he had entered, and

Reilly was sitting against the wall. He scrambled to his feet when he saw them. Without even acknowledging him, the figure continued towards the door.

When it creaked open, a grey light covered the world. Although Gray was sure he should be able to see Oric, he could only see black sky. Distant stars twinkled, and he stopped on the step, staring up at them.

The door banged closed behind them as Isla skipped down the steps and into the sandy world before them. In the distance, Gray could just make out the dragonfly sitting blacker against the grey surface. The cold wind that had battered them the previous night was gone, but the temperature was still very low.

Isla rushed ahead, walking faster than he would have expected after her slow movement inside the temple or building they had left. Gray turned and looked back, only to find nothing there but sand. Isla moved quickly towards the dragonfly, and Reilly pulled at him to hurry up.

But as they reached the dragonfly, more shadows appeared from around the back of the ship, and he knew these were not the hooded figures he had seen but something else. He hoped with everything he had that they weren't Elite.

Seventeen

"I made sure you were given every opportunity, Colonel, and yet you still manage to disappoint." Hendra leaned back in her chair and waited while he stared her down from the other side of her desk. Nothing was going to plan. And with word of her use of the girl out in the world, she wanted an easy fix. If anyone should be able to do that, it would be Calder.

"She had help."

"The two men you put her with. Elite? Enforcers? You didn't seem sure last time we spoke."

"Enforcers. The Sparrow."

"You are making a mess of things," she chided. His frown deepened. For a moment, if she had been anyone else, she might have been scared. But he was the one who needed to be afraid. "I'm tired of repeating myself with this matter. Either get her working on our side or remove her from the picture and find another who can do as I need."

"Hummers are hard to find."

"Or is it just hard for *you*? How long exactly did you spend with this girl? Years, wasn't it?"

"Two," he said with a nod. "There was no indication. And there is no hint as to where they have gone."

"She'll resurface soon enough; she doesn't seem to be able to remain hidden. Put your feelers out and when you get an idea, you can go to work. In the meantime, I have another task for you."

"I am not some pet," he snapped.

"You are what I deem you to be, or you'll go back to the heap I found you on."

He ground his teeth, and she clenched her fist.

"My brother," she said.

"Ineffectual little..."

"Careful, Calder; he is still my brother."

He nodded curtly.

"I want to know more about him. It appears he has been keeping things from me—a wife, children. I want all the details and what other secrets he may have."

Calder turned without another word and disappeared from the office. Hendra tapped her fingers on the desk. Nothing was as she needed it to be. Calder was meant to be hers to do as she directed, and he had started to think for himself. When he had called in help, it had been from those he should have disposed of years ago. Maybe her judgement was off; perhaps he wasn't as reliable as she'd thought. Although he had managed to do just what she needed him to previously. And she had rewarded him very generously. Extremely generously. She would need to ensure he wasn't going rogue, or she would have to end the relationship. Her next in line wasn't quite ready to take over yet. It was never too early to prepare for the worst.

Alone in her office, the monitors blinking around her, she put an indulgent hand to her belly. The doctors had told her she would not have her own, that Alice was her only hope at parenthood and an heir, and yet it had been surprisingly easy to fall pregnant.

Alice would have to provide some support to be of use, to help her raise the child while she continued to do as necessary for her Complex. Her own mother came to mind, what little she could remember of her. The sacrifices, the abuse.

Hendra had married Alice because she cared, a rare show of feelings, and she knew that no one was as loyal to her as Alice. She glanced at the doorway then, half expecting her wife to be standing there to comment on Calder's lack of manners, lack of respect, or query why she kept the man around at all.

But there was no sign of her or the hideous green drinks she required Hendra to force down. Not that they seemed to make her feel any better; she still felt unsettled, and her brother's words, and his threats, came to mind.

She ran her hand over her belly again. She didn't appear to be growing in any way, but it was still early. There was time, and her doctor was not concerned. Not in any way at all.

Hendra longed for Alice in that moment, to wrap her arms around her and reassure her that everything was well. That the world was as it should be, despite all the work she had to do to make it so.

Waving her hand over a panel, Hendra shut down the monitors and stood slowly from the desk, then headed into the neighbouring sitting room. All she could think of as she passed through the room was her brother's long body and longer legs stretched across the space. He wanted it, despite what he had said. He wanted her place in the solar system. But she wouldn't let that happen.

The whole building was quiet and, for a moment, she wondered if something had happened. There was no sign of the usual guards, or of Alice, anywhere. Hendra checked the old timepiece she wore from her belt. It was late. It was always late when she left, but she needed the darkness to bring those she didn't want others seeing.

Although it appeared that the council had heard of her plans and that she had used Calder. He was head of her Elite, after all. It was only standard that she should meet with him. But not so late or so often, and he didn't have a set meeting like the other heads of services did.

The Elite were outside of that, outside of the usual. Everyone in the Complex knew it.

"Hello?" she called. As her voice echoed from the stone walls, she headed back to her office to find Alice waiting for her. "I couldn't find you," she said, unsure now why it had mattered so much.

"I've been here," Alice said, pointing out into the main office beyond the door.

Hendra looked about for the green juice, but there was nothing.

"Are you hungry?" Alice asked.

Hendra nodded, wondering what hideous health option Alice had prepared.

"Lovely, we can head home if you are ready. I have a quiet supper waiting."

Hendra allowed Alice to lead her through the outer offices and the lift that would take her the short distance home. Despite the cool evening, Alice couldn't seem to stop smiling.

Eighteen

Isla felt foggy, as though she couldn't quite remember where she was or what she had been doing. She had slept, she remembered that much, but she didn't think she had dreamt. Gray was there, telling her of the forest, and she wondered what the hooded figures had done. Readers. She wasn't sure why the word was so clear in her mind when nothing else was. What had they read?

The ground raced up to meet her as Gray tumbled forward, pinning her to the ground. The unnatural noise around came into focus. The wind had died, but the sound of whooshing overhead was odd. All she could see were legs. She heaved at Gray, but he didn't move, and then the sound suddenly made sense. As an energy bolt skimmed off the dragonfly, the fog filling her head lifted.

A soft breath against her neck told her Gray was still alive, but she had no idea for how long. On her stomach in the dirt, she couldn't get a good position to determine who these people were or what they wanted. The grey light filtered across the sandy, rocky ground, some of which was pushing into her under the weight of the man atop her. Something warm and wet was soaking through her suit. She looked back in the direction they had come, but there was nothing there.

In a heartbeat, the weight lifted and he was gone. She missed it instantly. Then she was hoisted so quickly to her feet that her head spun. She still had no idea who these people were. They wore black, blending into the dark sky behind them, no marks to indicate who they might belong to, but they were not Elite. That much she was sure of. They all wore tinted visors that hid their faces. She looked again towards where they had come from, and there was no indication a building had even existed. Perhaps it had all been some strange dream on the dragonfly.

She wanted to lift her hand to her head, but they wouldn't let her. Her arm was starting to hurt. They were holding it so tight. She couldn't see Reilly or Gray amongst the bodies crowding around her. Then the engines hummed to life, and the bodies surrounding her thinned as they raced forward. The dragonfly lifted into the air. Reilly, it had to be. She only hoped he came back for them, and that he didn't damage her ship in the meantime.

It was then she saw Gray, slumped over someone's shoulder. The shielded faces turned back to her as though she might be able to answer the question of where her dragonfly was headed. But she could only shrug her shoulders, although that was extremely difficult with the tight hold they had on her.

And then, as her feet left the ground and she was sure the circulation was being cut off from her hands, she saw another ship. A darkness against the sky. She lost sight of Gray again as the bright light of the ship's interior made her squint. There was nothing to indicate who these people were or what they wanted. She was carried through a small cargo hold, along a narrow corridor, and into a small cabin with a bunk and a desk.

As she was released, she turned, expecting the door to slide shut behind her but finding one of the figures between her and it. The visor withdrew, and she sat slowly on the bunk. He was an older man, with neat greying hair and weather-worn skin.

"What are you doing on Oric's moon?"

"Memory collectors," she said simply.

The man squinted as though trying to read the truth.

"Readers," she tried again.

"Don't exist," he said, looking at her as though she had lost her mind. And she might have.

"What do you want?" she asked.

"I am asking the questions. And I asked you what you were doing here. Are you looking for a place to hide? We don't want the enforcers or Elite turning our planet over trying to find you."

"Why?" she asked.

He opened his mouth and then closed it, his face growing hard. Isla cleared her throat. People had tried to intimidate her before, and it hadn't worked. She had been too well trained. And even though she might not have used those skills recently, they never went away.

"You know who I am," she said.

He nodded once.

"I haven't done what they claim. They want to use me."

"That is what Hendra and the Complex do. They take what they want to make them stronger, no matter what it does to the rest of the solar system."

"Then why bring me here?" she asked again.

"Maybe I want to use you for myself. A bargaining chip, or a sacrifice."

Isla kept her breathing steady.

"I haven't decided yet," he continued, trying to sound casual. Isla was certain he was following someone else's instructions and none of this was his decision to make.

"The man who was with me, he isn't a part of this."

"The Sparrow. Of course, he is. And someone else the Elite would give anything for."

"Is he ok?" Isla asked. She didn't want to care, but the man kept throwing himself in after her, no matter what she wanted or who he might have known.

The soldier's hard face gave nothing away. He let out a frustrated sigh, turned and left, and Isla caught the profile of another man waiting outside the door as it closed. She counted slowly to one hundred, stood, crept towards the door and placed her hand over the lock. A loud beep sounded, and someone coughed politely on the other side. She sat back on the bed. There was nothing in the room, no drawers in the simple desk. The chair, when she gave it a gentle tug, was built in; she couldn't move it. Likely welded to the floor. Although it didn't look like a cell, that was exactly what she was in.

There wasn't even a porthole, only a strip of light that ran across the ceiling. No light switch. As she lay down across the bed, she wondered if they might turn the lights off. She wasn't ready for the dark, although she had managed to survive it without a duster recently. At some point soon, she would learn who these men were connected with. She sighed, frustrated that she hadn't been paying enough attention. She had come all this way to find answers and had found nothing but more confusion—and might just have gotten her only friend killed.

It was a long time before Isla felt the hum of the engines and the movement of the ship. She had been away from the world a long time, and things changed—people changed, power changed. The Elite might not be what they had been before. They might not be spread through the solar system anymore. Maybe Colonel Calder was all they had left.

After the horror of what had happened to her unit, Isla thought the number of applicants for the Elite would diminish, but they had surged, at least initially. Waiting for the hearings one day, she had watched a whole group of new recruits jogging from the building, far more of them than her intake. It had scared her, firstly, that so many would be prepared to sign up for what they had to know was so dangerous. She hadn't fully comprehended that when she had joined; she'd just wanted to fly. And that there were so many more out there, trained to the level she had been... the danger they could be to others.

She'd had that thought so many times, that it could have been her unit on the other side of the bloodshed. They had been before, if not to that extent. They had eliminated threats, a lot of threats, and her unit had become one of those threats to someone. Maybe she had survived to remind others to toe the line. Although she still had no idea why they would be a threat, what they had learned or known that had meant they needed to die.

She closed her eyes and tried to remember the hooded figure in the darkness. She knew immediately that he was the reason she had come, the reason the ship had determined where she needed to be, but he wouldn't speak. She remembered nothing until Gray had been there, standing in the unnatural light, directing her out. What had happened? What had they done? She didn't know anything more. In some ways, she thought she knew less. Did they work to help someone remember what was lost, or did they take it for themselves?

The term memory collector suddenly seemed to mean something very different. Gray. What if they gave her memories to Gray? She closed her eyes and imagined the forest she had grown in. She knew every tree; she could smell the leaves, the damp ground after rain, the feel of an animal's fur, the large cats, the small deer.

They hadn't taken those—they just had not returned what she had lost of the Elite, and of that day, and perhaps the lead up to it. She had been so focused on that day, on the memories that she did have, the whole thing recorded, step by bloody step. But she couldn't remember the lead up to it either. The conversations, the travel, where they might have been. None of it.

The engines stopped, and the humming she could feel through every fibre of her being ceased, although something lingered, as though she knew it was there. What had that metal done to her? She stood then, placing her hand against the wall. She took a deep breath, closed her eyes and almost saw the flow of metal beneath the surface, but she was sure she imagined it. The door opened. She opened her eyes to the surprised face of the guard on the other side.

"You are to stay inside," he said, looking along the hallway and then at her. She nodded, and the door closed again.

She hadn't even put her hand near the mechanism that opened the door. It was on the smooth, cool metal wall. She looked over her hand, trying to determine what she was although she had no idea. She put her head to the cool surface as she longed for a shower, and another door slid open to her left.

Inside was a small bathroom that had been sealed over and lost in the wall. As she stood in the doorway, the other door opened again and the older man sighed.

"I want her cuffed. She could be capable of anything."

"And I might not need my hands to do it," she muttered.

He ignored her. She held her hands out to allow the young soldier to cuff her, and then she was directed out into the hallway. Narrow as it was, it was filled with more soldiers. They might not have been Elite, but she knew them for what they were. In a way, she was curious as to what they wanted, what they thought she would give them. She would follow until she found Gray and knew that he was alive.

Exiting the ship was a surprise, for they were right in the middle of a city. She glanced around, trying to work out exactly where they were. The low moon in the sky above indicated they were on Oric. People moved around them as they crossed from the landing pad to the building they were attached to. It was a crowded city, filled with tall, bright buildings, but she had to admit it was pretty, and in some way it reminded her of the forest.

The people they passed didn't even look at them. The older man ahead of her, so far the only one to talk to her, nodded as two stopped before him. They raced off towards the ship, and she tried to glance over her shoulder to see where they might be running and if it involved Gray. Urgency meant he was still alive, at least.

They entered the building. Several similarly dressed men standing by the door saluted, and they continued into a cramped lift. The doors closed quickly. It shot upwards at a pace that made Isla stumble, although the bodies tightly packed around her prevented her from going anywhere.

Many of them were a good head taller than her. She wasn't one of the taller ones, something someone had said would do her no favours in her early days of training, and yet she was faster than all of them. That had served her better than height would have.

The lift opened to a small lobby and large, ornate dark grey doors. There was something familiar in them, and yet she couldn't place it. As she stepped forward, the doors swung open. She half expected to see the Hendra sitting behind the desk, but instead it was an older woman she couldn't quite place. Like the doors, it felt as though she should know this woman, and yet she didn't.

"Isla," the woman said sweetly, standing up and coming around the desk. She was tall, slender and elegant, dressed in long flowing skirts overlayed with a long top, all in white. Her hair was dark and tipped with silver threads, highlighted by her clothing, yet she didn't appear old. Her skin was flawless.

Isla only stepped forward when she was nudged firmly from behind.

"I understood you preferred Isla. Would you rather I call you Island?"

"Isla is fine."

"Your Grace," someone muttered behind her.

"Excuse me?" Isla turned to see who had spoken.

"Some prefer to have their title used, or at least the honorifics. I'm not so fussed about such things."

"I'm sorry," Isla said, taking another step forward in the hope she was outside the reach of the poker standing behind her. "Who are you?"

The woman laughed, a soft, friendly sound although it made Isla edgy. She was not what she pretended to be. "I am Chief of Oric, the leader of this planet and counsel woman of the Rohendra Complex."

Isla bowed her head.

"You can call me Ebberah, my dear, for I think we will be firm friends."

Isla waited. With a subtle nod, the men that had shown her into the room disappeared—all but the older one, who remained by the door. So these were her men, her force. Likely more trustworthy than an Elite force who would report to the Hendra. Isla held out her hands.

Ebberah seemed to take a minute longer before nodding, and the soldier stepped forward and removed the cuffs. Isla rubbed at her wrists. The cuffs hadn't cut into her, but she needed to make a show of her own.

"My friend?" she asked, looking around the large room as though Gray might be standing back in a corner. But there was no sign of him or where he might be.

"He is being cared for," Ebberah said, looking at the man rather than at Isla. "An unfortunate event, don't you think, Hari?"

The man cleared his throat.

"What do you want?" Isla asked.

"Have a seat," Ebberah said, indicating a long table at the side of the room. There were two places set at the end of the table, cloche-covered trays sitting just beyond each. Isla sat down where she was directed, and Ebberah sat beside her as the soldier stepped forward and lifted the covers. The smell of fresh eggs and meat made Isla's mouth water before she could control it. "I didn't think you would have had the chance to eat well in the last few days. Please, help yourself."

Isla surprised herself by reaching for the serving spoon and heaping eggs onto her plate, then the tongs and meat. She wasn't quite sure what kind of meat it was, but it was dark, and she had killed and prepared enough of her own meat in the forest to believe it was safe. As she did this, the soldier poured what appeared to be tea into the chief's cup and then hers. Ebberah didn't seem to have any issues serving her own food.

"I believe a good breakfast is the key to a productive day," she said, but she didn't touch anything on the plate, sipping from the tea instead. "Please, eat."

Isla pushed mouthful after mouthful in, the tender meat melting in her mouth and the eggs light as air. She hadn't eaten like this since her days at the academy.

"What do you think I can do to help you?" Isla asked between mouthfuls.

"Maybe I am to help you."

Isla laughed. Picking up the cup, she leant back from the table. "No one wants to help me. I appear to be very wanted for various reasons, none of which seem to make much sense. I'm an old soldier and of no real use."

Isla sipped from the cup as she watched the chief scoop up a small spoonful of eggs from the plate before her. She savoured it and took another, not acknowledging Isla, and then she set her utensils down and waved a hand over the plate.

The room suddenly swam in staff in starched white uniforms as the table was cleared, and if Isla hadn't maintained her hold on the cup, it would also have been taken. The look on the chief's face when she turned back to Isla reminded her of the soldier who could look both friendly and harsh. These people might seem like they were easy, but they were far from it.

"You are a hummer," Ebberah said, her voice flat. "There are many in the Complex that would use you."

"Hummers are a myth," Isla said.

Ebberah turned to the soldier who had returned to the door, and he stepped forward.

"She opened the door to the room, despite the locks, and opened a hidden internal door."

Isla laughed. "I opened doors and you think I'm a hummer. Surely others can open doors."

The scowl deepened on the chief's brow, and Isla sipped at her tea.

"There is something about you. I know what Hendra wants," Ebberah said, leaning forward, her face too close to Isla's.

"I don't think the Hendra even knows what she wants, other than power. Or what her people are doing for her. I think she surrounds herself with people she can use and appears to give them power, but they are doing what they like."

Ebberah waited.

"Calder," Isla said, taking another sip of her tea.

Ebberah stood, pushing the chair back and looking towards the soldier. "He is her puppet."

"He might have his own agenda. What does he get by doing her dirty work?"

"Whatever he wants, I should imagine," Ebberah muttered.

"And what does a soldier want?" Isla asked, looking to the man by the door. He sighed, looked to Ebberah and then left the room.

"She isn't working for the good of the Complex," Ebberah said, appearing more restrained and composed than she had moments ago. "She isn't what she should be. Not that any Hendra has been."

"What of the brother, then? Would he be better? Or the child, when old enough to rule?"

Ebberah moved back to her desk and sat down, running her hand over the surface. A screen shone to life. "The brother is inconsequential. He doesn't appear to want the power."

"But you do," Isla said. The screen disappeared and the scowl returned. "You want to be Hendra."

"I want a different way," she said. "I don't think it should be only one in charge, working for their own power."

"What do you think she wants with the rohen mines?"

"You believe she is involved?" Ebberah asked, her voice soft again, as though she didn't know where the question had come from.

Isla leant across the desk, her hands sensing the metal within. She briefly wondered what might happen if she called to it, if she could call to it. "You are not helping yourself," she said honestly. "You run a whole planet—maybe not the solar system, but a planet—and its moon is enough that others might want to take it from you. It might be that if this little Hendra heir has siblings, they might one day rule in your place."

Ebberah sat back and nodded slowly. "That may very well be how the Hendra's brother got a planet of his own. We don't know what he does there, or what he might do to help his sister."

"Does he help her or himself?"

"We may never know," Ebberah said.

Isla stood at the window and looked out over the city that sprawled around her. The view was amazing. The lights were dazzling even in the daytime, great billboards showing a variety of advertising and news flashes. Even from this distance, she could see them clearly. She had the fleeting thought that if she had chosen something very different, she might have lived a life in a city like this. But with all the movement and bustle, bright lights and pretty buildings, it wasn't anywhere she would have been happy.

Not that she was really happy living the life she had been up until recently. She wasn't sure what the last few days had really meant for her, but it was purpose. Far more purpose than she'd had for some time. It reminded her of her time in the Elite, which seemed so long ago, as though it was stories from another person's life.

"Reilly?" Gray moaned behind her, and she turned from the view to find him trying to sit up in the narrow bed in the centre of the room. People moved around him, nurses or doctors, she didn't know. They were all dressed the same. None of them had spoken to her, but they had allowed her to stay.

"He's gone," she said, and he focused his far too blue eyes on her. Her relief that he was ok was surprisingly overwhelming. She didn't need this with people—she didn't need to get attached to anyone. She had survived the last six years without doing so. There had been some exceptions, some mechanics, but nothing like she feared she might care for this man.

She wanted to turn back to the view, but instead she stepped forward. Despite the movement around them, she sat on the edge of the bed. He clutched at her, more desperately than she imagined he might.

"Not dead," she said, and she could see the instant relief on his features as he lay back. "He took the ship and left us."

"He might have thought us already dead."

"You, certainly. I thought it myself." She wanted to reach out and take his hand, but she didn't. His bare chest was covered with monitoring patches. She looked at one of the people dressed in white, and they looked at someone else.

"He'll survive," the second one said before disappearing.

"I didn't know you could afford such care," he said, looking around the sparse but clearly expensive room.

"I can't." Isla stood up, walking back to the window.

"You going to tell me?"

"The Chief of Oric, Ebberah."

"First-name basis?" he asked casually. "Do you remember?"

She shook her head.

"Ok, fill me in."

"I'm not sure I can." She turned from the view as he grunted while he worked his way back into a sitting position. "It was the chief's personal forces that collected us on the moon, or the like. They thought we were spying or hiding, and she wasn't sure if we were working for Calder or the Hendra."

"The Hendra? She shouldn't suspect her of wrongdoing, should she?"

"Where did they shoot you?"

He ran a hand over his chest. She wanted to look away, but she maintained eye contact.

"Did the Readers help you at all?" he asked, something of concern in his voice.

"Readers?" she asked, trying to read his face. "Where do you know that word from?"

"They told me." He took a breath and then swung his legs around from beneath the sheet. "They were doing something to you, or letting you remember. I don't know."

"You mentioned the forest," she said, stepping closer as he stood staggering from the bed. She put her hands out to hold him up, and he rested heavily on her shoulders.

"It was fragmented," he muttered as he sat back on the edge of the bed. He sighed, and she was thankful he was not naked. "I couldn't understand what I saw, but it was as though I saw what you did."

She stepped back from him.

"The forest, only in the forest—and children in rocks?"

Isla nodded. Why did she think he was going to be able to remember for her, or help her? Again, she was saving his life, and yet he was in danger because of her.

"Ebberah wants me to pretend to help the Hendra, to learn what they are doing."

"She wants to overthrow the Hendra?" he asked, his voice rising.

Isla put her finger to her lips. "This is her domain, but you don't know who might be listening."

"I don't think anywhere is outside the Hendra's reach."

"Exactly, so let's just keep our thoughts to ourselves."

"What of my thoughts as to why the chief has kept us alive, and that you are still looking like an Elite soldier?"

"She gave me a dress, but I don't know."

"A dress?" He smirked. "Do you know how they work?"

Isla walked back towards the door. "Any chance Reilly might return my ship?"

"We can't exactly walk free on this planet or any other," Gray reminded her, standing again, but she didn't move to help him and he was steadier on his feet. "You want to help her?"

"I don't know what I want," she said, heading out through the door and nodding to the guard who stood there. Another appeared further along the hallway; Isla walked towards her and then followed her back to the room she had been given.

It was large, much larger than anything she had lived in. The main living area contained a small kitchenette, a dining space that could have seated eight quite comfortably, and a sitting area that rivalled the chief's office. The bedroom was off the main area and almost as large; Isla shuddered to think how many could fit in the oversized bed. The bathroom was bigger than the dragonfly with a walk-in shower she could have slept in, a long bench with two basins, and a toilet tucked discretely behind a tinted screen.

Isla had been air drying for as long as she could remember, but there were soft, large and very white towels hanging from various bars around the room. Although she hadn't used them yet, she liked to run her fingers through the delicate material. She could quickly go soft living like this.

The dress hung on a hook by the shower. There were others in a small walk-in space off the bedroom, along with pants and shirts, and Isla wondered who had been moved out for her to move in. Or had she been placed here for a reason? She was about to touch her hand to the wall when the main door opened. She headed out into the living space to find the soldier who had dragged her here, Hari, and Gray.

"You are to dress for dinner. Her Grace likes finesse. You have been provided with the appropriate attire."

Isla opened her mouth and closed it as he bowed his head to her and then turned to leave the room, Gray a step behind.

He stopped and held up a hand.

"Where do I go?" Gray asked.

"You stay here," he said as though Gray were a child. "You may appear as guests, but you are still to be watched, and it is easier to watch over you together."

Isla groaned. Gray looked around the space as though he were lost.

"Dinner," the soldier said again and was gone.

Isla watched Gray for a moment as he scanned the room, looking past her into the bedroom and then raising his eyebrows when he saw the bed. He opened the cupboard, and she understood the clothes. Then he disappeared into the bathroom. When he whistled, she followed him in.

"This is big enough that we could shower together."

"Not going to happen," she muttered.

"Nice dress," he said, heading back out into the living area. "You start, I'll follow."

Isla washed as quickly as she could, regretting the loss of her lotions again when she tried to tame her hair. The soft, creamy material was not what she would have worn, but it covered her arms and her scars, and it fell to the floor. It was comfortable and didn't look too odd once she was standing before the mirror. She slid open a drawer to find it filled with bottles and jars and a toothbrush.

Finding something that might have been similar to her own hair product, she ran her fingers through her damp hair. It was still a mass of red curls, but it wasn't as frizzy as usual and she was enjoying wearing it out for the moment.

When she emerged into the main living space, Gray was lying back across the seating, his head back, his eyes closed. She put a hand to his shoulder and he jumped.

"Your turn," she said.

"I expected you to take longer. Don't women take longer?"

She glared at him. Without really looking at her, he rose slowly from the seat and disappeared into the bedroom. Isla sat on the edge of the seat, unsure what she should do with herself. She hadn't really thought of herself as a woman; she was still just a soldier deep down, and as a child she had been gifted, never expected to do anything but follow in the master's footsteps. She thought she had been making choices all those years ago, but she hadn't. *You can't change who you are.*

Isla stood slowly, smoothed over her dress and stepped back to the wall she had been inspecting when Gray had arrived. Taking a deep breath, she pressed her palm against it, closed her eyes and slowed her breathing. She might not believe she was a hummer, but there was something she had, some gift the master had seen. She could feel the rohen in the world around her, flowing along narrow channels behind the panel. She longed to feel its warm embrace as it flowed towards her. But when it shifted course, she wanted to follow it instead. Patterns became clear. Although she didn't understand them, she sensed something within the rohen's flow. Listening, watching. The whole building was the same. It was not only alive but watching everything she did. She stepped back from the wall and looked around. Everywhere, every room of this apartment, every space within the building.

She didn't know who or why, but it made her nervous, very nervous. They might be testing her. She was a prisoner here, not some guest, and she was starting to forget that already. The Hendra could very well be behind all this.

"Stop," she whispered.

"What?" Gray asked, too close behind her. But she focused on the wall, feeling a shift in the pattern.

"Stop," she repeated and breathed out slowly as her knees buckled. Gray had her in his arms, sitting on the floor.

"What are you trying to do?" he whispered, still too close. She felt off, woozy, tired.

"They are listening and watching."

Gray looked around the room, his arms remaining around her.

"Let me go," she said more firmly, and he looked at her as though just realising he had hold of her. He cleared his throat. She climbed to her feet, allowing him to hold out a hand to steady her. They couldn't even look after themselves at the moment—how were they going to face whatever might be planned for them here?

"What did you do?" he asked, standing over her. He smelt different, as though he had been in the forest. She looked up as he blushed and stepped back. "You don't like it. They had a spray, and it has been so long since I got the chance to dress up."

Isla laughed. The relief that he was human, a real person, when she was sure she was surrounded by so much that wasn't as it seemed.

She nodded slowly. "It is nice," she admitted, and he coloured further.

The door opened, the soldier looking about before his gaze locked on them standing by the wall. He stepped back, and they moved in the same motion towards the door.

Nineteen

G ray was sure he had never felt more out of his depth as he
followed along the hallway behind the stern soldier and Isla,
who looked amazing in the light-coloured flowing dress. She was
covered, he noted, although the dress fitted snugly against her body
and left little to the imagination. Although it covered her skin, he
could just make out the raised crisscross of her scars. Despite the
scarring, he thought exposing her arms and neck might have been
more appealing.

He wondered if she had selected the dress, or if it was something
that whoever was behind all this had chosen. He had found it hard
to believe they were staying in the care of the chief of Oric, or that
she might be capable of acting against the Hendra. The woman had
a reputation of being ineffectual. It was rumoured that her council
ran the planet, and that she had very little input.

As they entered the large, white room, he stopped, wondering just
what he had walked into. A long table ran the length of the room.
The walls were blank and the table simple, as were the chairs. Even
the floor was the same colour and, he wondered if it was for effect or
some greater reason. Surrounding the table, on the white chairs in

the very white space, was a group of people he had never expected to stand before.

The head of the table was an elegant woman in white who stood as they entered—the chief. Gray stopped and bowed his head.

"Your Grace," he said.

"We don't worry about that here," she said, indicating a chair in the middle of the table on her right. Isla was already moving to the one opposite. She didn't appear to be as fazed by their company as he was, but he did note that they were dressed similarly to those around the table.

"I won't introduce you to everyone," the chief said as she sat back down. "They are my advisors and counsel, and I have told them everything."

"A risk," Isla said. A murmur went around the table.

"I see that you have worked out our security system," the chief said, her eyes on Isla and her tone no longer as friendly.

"I only asked for it to stop," Isla said, looking over the plate before her. Gray wondered what she had done. He wanted to ask if it involved rohen, but he wouldn't say that aloud here.

"How can a hummer do such things?" asked a man several down from Gray.

"If we find one, we can ask," Isla returned.

There was a small amount of food on the plate before him, and no one was eating yet. Isla looked disinterested in not only the food, but the company.

"How do you feel?" the chief asked Gray directly.

"Much better, thank you," he said with a bow of his head.

"Well, it was my man, or one of them..." The chief looked around the room, and Gray noted the soldiers positioned by the door and at the far end behind the chief. "Who shot you."

"Quite accidently," the soldier by the door added.

Gray tried to smile and looked back to his plate.

"As we are all here," a rotund woman several seats down from Isla commented, "perhaps we could start."

The chief waved her hand over the table, and the group began to mutter amongst themselves as they played with the small amount of food on their plates. Gray looked up to see Isla looking at hers as though she wasn't quite sure. The man next to her leant in and whispered something in her ear. She nodded once and tasted a small amount of the food. When she raised her eyes to Gray, he smiled, and she pointed with her fork to his plate.

"Is it good?" he asked her. The table dropped to silence.

"It is the table of the chief," said someone a few seats down. "It is all perfect."

"It may not be as you are used to," the chief said. "You may meet more familiar dishes as the night carries on."

Gray bowed his head to her again, then swallowed what was on his plate in two bites. He wondered how much would be on the next plate and when it would arrive. He felt as though he hadn't eaten in days.

"Send for the next and leave us," the chief said. The soldier at the far end of the room opened the door, and a line of people dressed in white moved through the room. They cleared the table and placed another dish before him, this one larger, and as they disappeared from the room, so did the soldiers.

"Wine?" the woman next to Gray asked, holding a narrow decanter over a tall glass before him. He shook his head, and she poured more into her own.

"Tell us the plan, Ebberah, now that you have found a hummer. Or was it that you stole the Hendra's hummer?"

Several people looked to the chief at the end of the table; most looked to Isla, who appeared more interested in the plate before her.

"I am still to determine what the Hendra was trying to do, what she wants to do, and what controlling the rohen means."

"Control of the world," Isla said. "All of them."

"There isn't that much rohen out there," someone scoffed.

"It is everywhere," Isla said.

"You can sense it?" Gray bit his lip, but it was too late—the question was out there. Isla raised her eyes to his but said nothing.

"What can you tell us?" the chief asked.

"I don't understand it," Isla said. "I don't know whether I am a hummer or something else. I just know the rohen is there."

"Where?" someone asked.

"Everywhere," she said seriously, turning to him.

"What can we do?" a younger woman asked the chief. Before she could answer, Gray had opened his mouth and then closed it. He was an observer here, not a participant.

"He has heard the stories," said the woman beside him with the wine, laughing, "and believed them."

"I don't..." Gray started.

"As long as Hendra believes." The chief stood slowly from the table and walked to Isla. "Show me." She held out a hand, which Isla ignored as she pushed the chair back from the table.

She moved over to the wall and closed her eyes, pressing her hand to it. She seemed so calm, but Gray worried what might happen. Would the rohen steal her away again? He stood also. But before he could move around the table, the chief gave him a look that would make even the Hendra wither as she held up her hand.

In the silence of the room, Isla's slow breath echoed from the walls. The wall beneath her hand shifted, a strange pattern covering it in the bright silver reflective metal he had seen in the mines. He sat back down. It pushed out from the wall, wrapping around her fingers, trying to pull her away from the room, or at least that was how it appeared. Then it was gone, the wall white and perfect. As the chief wrapped her arms around Isla, pulling her to her chest and whispering something in her ear, everyone else at the table was on their feet, running their hands over the walls and speaking loudly.

By the time they made it back to the room, very little had been accomplished. A lot had been said. The ideas of those at the table had all differed in what they thought should be done next. The chief had listened, mostly watching Isla, who had sat silently in her chair and moved the food around her plate. There was far more going on inside her head than she was sharing, and Gray wanted to share her load, if only to take that look from her face.

He wondered if Reilly had any idea where they were, or if he was coming back. As they entered their allocated apartment, Isla surprised him by grabbing at his arm. Her legs went, and he put an arm around her, pulling her close and then directing her to the seated area. He still couldn't quite grasp where they were or what was expected of them, but he doubted Isla had any better idea.

She nodded slowly, and he moved to the small kitchenette for water.

"I don't think you ate enough," he said, holding out the glass. He waited for the standard snappy response, but she just stared at the floor. He held the glass out for a moment, then sat beside her and pressed it into her hand. He wasn't sure, but he thought there was a slight tremor there. He waited. This woman didn't like to be pressed, and it had clearly taken a lot for her to draw the rohen from the wall.

"How did you know it was there?" he asked as she lifted the glass to her lips. When she didn't speak, he prompted, "The rohen."

"It's everywhere."

"Everywhere?"

She nodded slowly. He looked around the room. No wonder... If she was surrounded by the stuff, what was it doing to her?

"In the walls, in the ships, in the food," she whispered. "Everywhere."

He reached for her, but she moved away. "I'm ok."

"You don't look it."

"You were the one who was shot," she said, looking at him. "How do you feel?"

"Like I wasn't shot," he said.

Isla sat the glass down on the table and looked around the space. "You take the bed."

"It is big enough..." She glared at him, and he raised a hand. "I won't turn it down."

"Do you think she is just testing us for Hendra?" Isla asked. "I wish I could turn it off."

"It is possible, but I don't know." He didn't know how to help her.

She lay down along the length of the sitting area, pulling a cushion beneath her head and rolling to face the wall. He glanced around for a blanket, but the space was warm. After too long watching her, he reluctantly turned away.

Twenty

"I am tired of these same excuses," Hendra said, standing by the window and looking out at the dirty city beneath her. At least she thought it was dirty... All those people, if only they would do as she directed, it would be much easier, much cleaner.

"I have tried," Calder growled. "She must have friends. She must have allies protecting her."

"Raise the reward on her head. Repeat the news loops. I thought the ship had been found."

"The dragonfly." Something in his voice made her turn from the window and take in the big man. "It was found, but it only had one man aboard."

"And?" she prompted.

"We will break him."

She turned back to the view. "Why do I need to tell you how to do your job? You have worked for me long enough, been granted many advantages for that work." She turned back to him. "I saved you."

Calder's jaw was locked—she could see the muscles tight beneath the skin—but he bowed his head once.

"You knew what it would mean, what would have to happen, and yet you regret it."

"Never, Great One."

"It wasn't a question. And you only use that term when you want something."

There was too long a pause, and she stepped forward. He looked at her as though trying to judge whether he could tell her what was on his mind. She might not use it as he planned, but that wasn't why he was to share all information he came across.

"How do you feel?" he asked.

The question made her step back, and it took all her effort not to put her hand to her belly. "Fine," she muttered.

He looked her over as though not believing her.

"I am with child," she said. "There is bound to be some sickness in the beginning."

"Hmm."

She was struggling to read him, and it frustrated her. "Tell me," she demanded.

"I have heard some whispers from your household."

"You have crossed a line, Colonel."

"It is my job to keep you and your universe safe."

"Solar system," she corrected. He had a flare for the dramatic that she had only recently noticed. "My household is Alice's domain, and she is quite capable of ensuring the staff do exactly as she says."

"That is not the problem," he said quickly.

"You would dare to accuse Alice?"

He bowed his head.

"Of what?"

"It isn't clear, but I fear for your child."

Hendra clenched her teeth. She very nearly questioned if he feared for *his* child. But she had not confirmed for him that it was his, nor anyone else's. Alice was aware that the child had not been conceived as it should have been, but Henra wouldn't tell her who had been involved.

"She may be trying to replace it with another, one of her own."

"She is my wife," Hendra insisted. "She is the mother of this child. This, as any more children we have, is her child."

Calder raised an eyebrow, but she ignored it. He might be well aware that she hadn't done things as she should, that the child—whether his or not—had been conceived in the old-fashioned way. Perhaps she should have married a man as her father had wanted, but then it would have been for alliance and power, just as any match would have been with him involved. Alice was different. Alice was outside of that world.

There was a knock at the door. Before she could answer it, Calder had turned and opened the door himself. A servant entered, bowing his head to the colonel as he pushed a tray.

"As you ordered, sir."

"On the table," he directed. Hendra raised her eyebrow at the presumption, but she was curious to see what the man was up to. He was surprising her in ways she didn't want to be surprised of late. There was a connection to the hummer, no matter what he claimed. She could see it, she could feel it, and it was preventing him from doing the job he should be doing.

The servant laid out placemats, utensils, and glasses. A pitcher of clear water was placed in the centre of the table, and Hendra realised just how thirsty she was. When Calder indicated the table, she sat down. He poured water while the servant placed the covered dish before her. She could smell the meat, even through the cover, and then he lifted it with a flourish. A pink chunk of meat, the juices pooling beneath it, sat in the middle of a large plate.

"Orician buffalo," the servant said, "with slow-roasted vegetables, all hand selected by the colonel."

Hendra gave Calder a quizzical look. "You are buttering me up for something." There was a second plate on the tray, but the servant waited. "Join me," she said. The man placed it on the table and left.

"I thought you could use the red meat." He settling into the seat down the table a little, as she was at the head, and sprinkled salt from a dish across the meat.

She nodded and cut into it, watching the red juices flow across the plate. She pushed too large a piece into her mouth, but she had never tasted anything so wonderful. It was tender, and tasty, and it felt like her body came alive. "Alice won't like this," she mumbled through the next mouthful, then cut into an oily roasted root vegetable she couldn't identify and didn't care to. Her world was filled with flavours she had been estranged from since the moment Alice had discovered her news about the baby—which was when it had been publicly announced.

Hendra lowered the fork to the plate and wiped the back of her hand across her chin. Calder laughed at the motion, but he was right, and she really did not want to admit that. As much as Alice loved her and was willing to sacrifice for the position she was in, she was not happy about the child, not initially, and that may have been Hendra's fault. But then, Alice couldn't be privy to all news before it was announced, including the announcement of their child.

"What would you do about Alice?" she asked as she moved the food around the plate. Calder's smile slipped as he watched her plate rather than her.

"Not what you would want me to," he said, and she understood his honesty.

"Then we wait, but you may watch. Put a man in or the like," she added with a wave of her hand.

Calder nodded once and tapped her plate with the edge of his knife. "Eat the meat," he coaxed. Although the earlier joy had gone, Hendra cut into the thick slab and pushed the meat into her mouth. It didn't quite taste as she had hoped it would, and yet it was far more enjoyable than the green teas and juices Alice had been feeding her.

At the end of the meal, as she gulped down another glass of water, she felt calmer and less nauseated than she had in what felt like forever.

"Better?" he asked, and she remembered him in the room.

She nodded and pushed up from the table. "Enough for today. You have things to be getting on with. You aren't growing soft, are you, Calder?" He stood from the table and dropped the napkin that had been across his lap beside the plate.

"I don't do soft. I do practical."

She nodded and watched him disappear from the office before she returned to her desk and the reports requiring her attention.

The door clicked open without a knock, and the servant returned to collect the plates. They knew when she had someone with her; there was someone outside the office at all times, whether she was there or not. Otherwise, half the solar system would be barging into her office with various demands.

Calder hadn't mentioned her brother. She flicked the monitor off. She had asked for him to find the hummer and find out about her brother, and he had returned with some rubbish about Alice. Was he deflecting again? There was something with the dragonfly girl. The war hero. Calder had promised it was only to be able to do the task he'd needed to do that he had used her and the unit. Yet he continued to exhibit a hesitation when it came to the hummer. Although he had thought he'd killed her at the mine. Twice now, he had killed her and she had survived. Hendra was starting to wonder if the girl was even human in the first place.

———◆○◆———

Isla struggled to fall asleep on the padded seating. It wasn't that it was uncomfortable; she was starting to think it might be because it was too comfortable. Whatever the issue, her mind wouldn't allow her to slip into sleep. She had left the light on. Gray was already snoring in the neighbouring room, not that she thought he would comment on whether she needed the light or not. She felt somewhat lost, and it had been some time since she had truly felt that way.

Even when she had found the colony gone, the whole village lost but for one old man and a handful of children, she'd had purpose—it had given her purpose. But she still didn't know who she really was or what she could do. What would she want to do with such gifts? And if she'd had them all her life, why was it only now she could sense the rohen? It was more than sensing; it was almost as though it called to her, wanted her to find it.

Everywhere. She had tried to impress that upon the crowd she had been paraded before this evening, but they hadn't quite gotten the sense of it. It was everywhere, in everything, on every surface, everywhere she went, in everything she touched.

She sat up and ran her fingers through her hair, catching them on a snag. She didn't think she could find what she needed on Oric to make her hair treatment. The creams in the drawer had gone some way, but it wasn't the same. Maybe she needed a weapon. Not any weapon in particular, just something that could hum her to sleep and protect her in the dark.

Her fingers traced the scars that covered her skin, despite the fact that they were beneath the material. She knew exactly where every one of them was. She could almost taste the metal and the blood. She squeezed her eyes closed, and it was as though something sharp sliced through her skin. Metal cutting deeper and deeper. Her breath caught, and she struggled for breath. Rohen.

Her fingers stilled over the raised skin. The doctors hadn't pulled her back together—or maybe they had, but the damage hadn't been caused by any battlefield weapon.

She shuddered, remembering the first cut, the ease with which it had passed through her clothing, her armour, her flesh. It burned. There was no way she could have defended herself against it. In the dark, surrounded by the smell of death and blood, Isla couldn't make out what was attacking her. Another sharp burning blade cut deep into her back, and she cried out. Hot and sharp across her arm—she dropped her Barilla, unable to hold anything. She could hear the screams around her, unable to determine which were theirs and which were hers.

In a flood that lasted only seconds, the entire attack replayed through her mind. A pale blue light reflected on metal in the dark. Her whole body filled with burning, searing pain.

She sucked in a breath and opened her eyes to Gray's worried face, his hands hovering as though wanting to hold her. But he hesitated. No. It wasn't worry—it was fear. Her whole body shook. She felt the pain of the blades as though they had only just sliced into her, and she looked down at the odd crisscross pattern of red stripes across her pale dress.

"Shower," he said. "I'll find help."

"No." She clutched at his clothes, trying to stop him and finding he was shirtless again. She pulled her hands back in, wondering why she was so shaky. She put a hand to her chest and then gritted her teeth against the pain. She leaned back, placing her hand on the wall as her white dress turned red.

"Shower," he murmured again.

Isla couldn't clear her mind. She tried to focus on Gray, but he scared her. The idea that she might be lost in the dark of that night scared her more. She stood slowly, finding it harder than she'd imagined.

Her bloody handprint was surreal against the stark white of the room. "Damn," she muttered, glancing over the white cushions and the lines of blood marking them.

The handprint faded and disappeared. She stepped away from the wall and backed into Gray, who wrapped his arms around her. She cried out. He muttered something, took her hand firmly and pulled her through the bedroom into the bathroom, where he looked more lost than she felt.

"What happened?" he managed as she started to shiver.

"I was remembering."

"Strong memories," he muttered. "I need to get help."

"No, please. I can't explain this. I don't want to spend the rest of the night trying to explain this. There has to be something here." She pulled open the first drawer and rattled through the lotions inside, but nothing seemed to be of any use other than cosmetic. She leaned into the basin, her whole body aching and stinging. It was like one of the worst training sessions of her life, and every time she closed her eyes, she remembered the blades slicing into her.

She groaned out loud before she could stop and turned to the shower. The water would also sting, but it might help. Maybe she had done this to herself with the crazy thoughts. She cried out again as she tried to pull the material from her skin. With a sigh, she looked to the nervous man hovering too close. He nodded once and between them, they pulled the bloody material away from her skin.

She stepped into the shower bay, and the hot water started instantly. She cried out with pain but stayed where she was.

"Do you want...?"

"I don't want you in here, if that's what you're asking." She tried to sound calm, but the blood pooled around her feet. She wanted to wrap herself in a soft white towel, but she couldn't face seeing her own blood on it. Not like this.

"Great," he murmured.

"You don't have to sound so disappointed," she tried to joke.

"It is a weird night."

"What?" She opened the door, the water still running over her.

"Now there are mushrooms growing from the wall."

"Mushrooms?" Isla pushed the door open wider, and the water stopped behind her as she padded wet, red puddles across the floor.

"Red ones," he said, moving to the side and reaching for them.

"Don't!" She put her hand on his arm to stop him. "Extremely poisonous."

"Are they glowing?"

"Find a bowl, wooden if you can."

"A bowl?"

"It's everywhere," she whispered, catching sight of herself in the mirror. The deep, angry red slices across her skin looked familiar. "They were deeper," she said, touching the skin.

Gray stood and stared at her. "Deeper?"

"Through bone and organ," she murmured, running her hand over one across her belly and then another she knew had nearly cut off her left arm. "Bowl?"

He nodded mutely and raced from the room. She re-entered the shower and searched for the air dry, then stood for a moment as the air moved around her, slowly drying her skin. She was thankful for the gentle breeze.

"Isla?"

She opened the door and stepped out, looking longingly at the soft towel and then at the red fungus that was spreading across the wall. She prised the bowl from Gray's fingers.

"You said poisonous."

"Not for me." She sat the bowl on the basin and tried to calm her breathing as she held her hand over the fungus. She heard the exhale of breath and opened her eyes to the soft blue glow, nodded once and collected all she could into the bowl. Then she rested her hand against the wall. "Thank you," she whispered.

Her wounds were still bleeding, although not as they had been; small rivulets of blood trailed down each cut. She held her hand over the bowl and pushed the knuckles of her other hand into the fungi, feeling them squish between her fingers. "Was there a pounding tool or something amongst the utensils?"

When he didn't answer, she looked up into the mirror to find him staring at her. "It doesn't matter," she said.

"I'll look."

He returned quickly, holding out a wooden pestle. She wondered where on this planet the wood had come from—or was it something imported? Something expensive? She worked it through the paste, which was slowly becoming white. She sighed, staggering as she let the bowl go, and Gray caught her too easily.

"Here," he said, pulling up a stool. She sat down, pulling the bowl into her lap and running her fingers through the cool ointment.

She smeared some across the cut at her belly, and the relief was almost instant. She sighed and reached for more. Her fingers brushed over Gray's. He was silent as he wiped over her back, and she tried not to flinch. She shivered as his fingers ran through her hair.

"I found a band," he said. She glanced in the mirror as he bit down on his lip in concentration and loosely tied her hair up off her shoulders. It was messy, but it would do.

"How did you learn that?"

He shrugged. "It isn't very good."

"It works."

"As does your poisonous cream."

She looked down as she smeared more across her arm. The wounds were fresh, clean, and her fingers missed the raised scars she knew better than her own memories as they moved over her body. Maybe she could have healed them before, but she had needed them. Maybe she didn't need them anymore.

"How?"

She gulped down the fear building in her chest. A soft hand rested on her shoulder.

"How did the mushrooms grow?" he asked more gently.

"Rohen. I think."

He looked at the wall, and she missed the heat of his hand against her skin. Then he put his fingers to the wall and removed them almost instantly.

"I said it was everywhere."

"Did you ask?"

She shook her head. In some strange way, it had given her what she needed. The bloody handprint disappearing suddenly made sense. "Do you think it kept me safe?"

"I thought I was doing that," he said, although his words lacked the confidence he'd had earlier as his hand hovered out from the wall.

"That day, when the unit..." She stood up, indicating her body, and he surprised her by blushing and licking his lips before turning away. She turned back to the mirror. The ointment worked quickly, but she could already see that the angry red had reduced greatly. The bleeding had stopped, and the dark scars that had marred her body were fading. She put her hand to her collarbone, feeling for the small dent that was no longer there.

Gray raced from the room and returned with a large t-shirt and a pair of shorts. "I think these were for me, but..." He sat them on the basin and left again.

When she came out of the bathroom, he was already in the bed, his back to the door. She padded back out to the main space, where her handprint was clearly gone. She looked around, wondering when they could leave. The kitchen was a mess of open drawers, with bowls and pots all over the place.

She stood at the bedroom door. The light was dimmed, and although he lay very still, Gray was not asleep. Isla moved softly and slipped into the bed before she could change her mind. He remained still, but she could feel the tension, as though he wasn't sure what she might do.

The bed was huge. Gray was far enough away that she could pretend he wasn't there, but she knew he was. Just being near someone else was enough now to help her sleep, maybe. She closed her eyes and tried to think of nothing but black sky and distant stars.

Twenty-One

I sla dreamt of her life before the day that had changed it all. Of Kalli, mostly. She was reminded of his strong arms, his scent on her skin, sunny mornings wrapped in each other after training. A myriad of images of their time working and training together. How serious he was at times, how tough he made her.

She woke foggy, sure she was still in the dream, her face pressed against his chest, the weight of his arm across her. As the room came into focus and the events from the night returned with full force, she shoved the arm away and leapt from the bed. "What the hell, Gray?"

He grumbled something, sat up, rubbed at his eye and then looked at her as though just realising she was there. He lifted the blanket and looked down at himself, then back to her. "What?" he asked, clearly confused.

A sound in the kitchen brought her back to the present. She inched towards the door as Gray slid from the bed on the other side. A man, dressed in white, stood frozen in the middle of the room.

"Did I wake you, madam?" he asked in a scared tone.

She shook her head. He relaxed somewhat and returned to tidying away the mess Gray had created in the kitchen. Isla turned and entered the bathroom, where the large wooden bowl still sat on the bench. She returned to the kitchen and realised he had delivered breakfast.

"Can you bring me some jars?"

"Jars, madam?"

"I would prefer glass, if possible—tinted, with a secured lid."

"Yes, madam." He didn't look half as confident as he sounded, and he didn't sound very confident at all.

"Lovely." She smiled, and he stepped back. She was somewhat out of practice. "You may leave."

"Leave, madam?"

"Did you want to join us?" she asked, indicating over her shoulder. The man put down the plate in his hand and disappeared through the door. "I didn't realise people could come and go," she muttered. There wasn't the mess she expected in the seated area, no sign of the blood she had been covered in the day before, no sign of the dress either. She returned to the bathroom to find it shredded on the floor.

She jumped as Gray ran a hand over her thigh. "What the hell!"

"You keep saying that," he muttered.

She crossed her arms and gave him her best death stare. He flinched just a little and then grinned. When he said nothing more and her glare wasn't making him back off, she went to ask what he wanted and he pointed at her leg.

Isla looked down and back to Gray, then back to the leg. The dark scar that had run across her thigh was gone. She ran her hand over the smooth skin before inspecting her arm and found that scar gone as well. She pulled at the collar, leaning forward to look in the mirror as she lifted the t-shirt and ran a hand over her smooth stomach. She tried to remember the puckered skin that had been there, that had reminded her of what she was and what she'd lost.

The hot tears surprised her as they dripped down onto her top, and she put her hand to her cheek.

"Do you know what happened?" Gray asked.

She shook her head. "Something—metal, swords. But not why, not who."

"Do you know why this happened?" he asked, indicating her body.

"No," she breathed, taking in the strange sight of smooth skin in the mirror.

"You tried before, didn't you? With the ointment and your mushrooms?"

She pushed past him and out to the table. She didn't owe this man any explanations. He'd just happened to be around, happened to help out. She would have been fine without him; she just would have made a bigger mess.

"Last night," Gray said as he sat down, and she tried to ignore him as she heaped eggs and meat onto her plate. "Last night, the chief said you had done something in this room."

Isla focused on him. "They were watching, listening."

"Who?" he asked, looking around.

She shook her head as she pushed a large forkful of food into her mouth.

"Oric?"

She shrugged.

"Hendra?"

She dropped the fork, and it echoed around the room. "I. Don't. Know!"

"OK," he said, raising his hands. "But the chief knew."

"I don't know what she knows. She is better at keeping things to herself than I first thought."

"She is not what I expected at all," he admitted.

The door opened without a knock of warning, and the older soldier, Hari, stood in the doorway.

Gray stood, but Isla continued eating. She was starving after the work she had done the previous night.

"We've had word the Elite are coming."

Isla continued to eat.

"Calder and his team are working through a routine check of the solar system in their search for outlaws."

"Does he or Hendra claim that you are harbouring outlaws?" Isla asked, sipping at the tea.

"Not in so many words, but we must consider what we do."

"You want to hand us over," Gray said, taking a step towards the man.

"I would, but Ebberah won't. I must do as she directs."

"And what does Ebberah direct?" Isla asked.

"To hide you."

Gray laughed out loud and sat back at the table. Isla watch him warily. "We're dead then," he said, looking at her. "Calder will turn this planet inside out."

"Not if we hide where he can't find us."

"The moon? The Readers?" Gray asked. "They may not take you back."

"Readers?" the soldier asked. "There is nothing on that moon. We tried colonies long ago, but the atmosphere and surface wouldn't support it."

Gray opened his mouth and then closed it. When he looked at Isla, she gave him a subtle shake of her head. There was more to the Readers than she had expected. The name again, clear in her mind, yet she couldn't remember any interaction with them. If they were so secret, why would Gray know so much more?

"We will do as we need to," she said. "Better we don't tell you—if we are caught, you can claim no knowledge."

The man nodded. "Whatever it is, I suggest you do it soon."

She went back to her breakfast as Gray sat at the table and watched. She had no idea where to start, but the rohen had protected her from Calder in the past, in a way. Perhaps it would again. She looked to the wall and sighed; it might be that it could only help her. But as she looked back to Gray, she was sure the wall behind him rippled, and she smiled.

"You know you are infinitely scarier when you smile."

"Good," she said, scooping more eggs onto her plate. "Eat up. You might need your strength."

⬥◯⬥

"Tell me you have a plan," Gray implored, watching Isla scoop the last of the cream into the jars the reluctant servant had delivered. She grinned again, and it made his heart skip for all the wrong reasons. "A plan I will like."

"You might not have the choice," she said, securing the last lid and dropping it into the satchel over her shoulder. She looked him up and down, scowling. "Why aren't you ready?"

"I am ready."

"Like that?"

He looked himself over in the mirror and wondered just what she meant. He too was wearing something that could have been military issue, and he still wasn't sure why the soldier had managed to give it up. The clothes bore no marks to indicate whom they had belonged to, but they looked so much like the chief of Oric's soldiers that it would be hard not to connect them if he and Isla were caught.

"Are you bringing anything with you?"

He held out his hands. Not even a weapon. Concern seemed to cross Isla's face for just a moment, as though she wasn't sure whatever plan she had in her mind would work. Then she took a deep breath, moved back through to the main living room, and surprised Gray by taking his hand and pulling him along after her.

"One night and now we're friends," he scoffed, trying to sound light, but she scowled at him again. He wondered if this woman had a sense of humour at all, or if she only pretended when it worked for her. She was too good a soldier, and he was almost as scared of her now as he was of Calder.

She squeezed his hand tighter and walked towards the wall. He had no idea what she was going to do when the surface before him rippled, silver metal moving across what had been white wall in much the same way as it had across the surface of the ponds in the mine. He was about to ask what the plan was when the wall disappeared and Isla led them into the nothing beyond.

Panic caused his whole body to brace, and his feet refused to move. What if they were surrounded by the stuff? What if he was lost or drowned?

Isla's face softened with understanding. As she gave him a little tug, he stepped forward, trusting that she was what he had hoped. And then they were in the dark. Her grip on his hand grew tighter as her breath hitched in her throat, and then it was as though they were falling. He bit his lip to ensure he didn't call out.

They stopped as suddenly as they had fallen. Gray could hear voices in the dark, and the woman beside him shivered. He wondered if this was her doing and she was wearing herself out as she had before. If he lost her in the dark, he wasn't sure what he could do to find her.

"Come here," he whispered, pulling her closer. She surprised him by holding tight around his waist as he wrapped his arms around her. The voices became clearer. Calder, the chief, maybe the older soldier who was never far from her side.

"I do not like what you are insinuating," the chief cried, her voice too high. "Are you saying that I am hiding fugitives from the Hendra herself?"

"I am not directly saying that," Calder said too loudly. Too close, Gray thought. The woman in his arms had stopped shivering.

"You are definitely implying it."

"We could debate semantics all day," Calder snapped. "Or I could scour your planet and prove your innocence."

"My innocence!" she screeched, her voice raising another octave. "How dare you! Call the Hendra—call a council meeting. I will not have this."

"Your Grace," Calder said more gently.

"I am innocent," she said weakly, and Gray wondered if there were tears shed. "I have nothing to hide; search all you like."

"Finally," the man grumbled, and then there was nothing.

Gray squeezed his eyes closed and his arms tighter around the woman in them, although she mumbled something. How long would Calder search for her, for them? How far would he go?

"Gray!" Isla called. He opened his eyes to subtle green light, then looked around to find they were standing beneath a tree. He let her go and stepped back. She swayed a little, and he reached forward to grab her arms. When she smiled at him, he breathed as though for the first time in hours.

"Are you ok?"

She nodded.

"Did it take much?"

"I didn't do anything," she said, looking around in wonder. "Not a thing."

"You mean the rohen carried us here?"

She nodded slowly, looking around at the trees. He let her go as she stepped forward and ran her hand over the trunk of the nearest one. "They are so different," she said, leaning forward and pressing her nose to the bark.

"If you lick it, I'll be suitably disgusted."

She turned a scowl on him, but she was not nearly as severe as she had been earlier. "I will not lick the tree." She looked at it as though she might consider it.

"So, where is here?" he asked.

"I have no idea," she said, sitting down against the trunk.

"Is it safe?"

"You are an old woman," she said, reaching into her bag and lifting out the jars of cream.

"Do we really need that?"

"Do you see any glowing red mushrooms?"

He looked around and then back to Isla. "No."

"Then we need it. Best batch I've made. You never know when you might need it," she added quietly.

"I hope we don't," he said, sitting down beside her. "Now what?"

"I don't know. If we have been moved to where it is safe, or where they have already looked..." She glanced up into the branches above her and smiled. "We might be safe."

"Might be? And if we aren't?"

"I think someone is looking after us."

"That idea makes me more nervous than I would like."

They sat for a time beneath the large tree, taking in the unfamiliar scent of the trees and grass. Gray had travelled extensively in his time with the enforcers, including most of the planets across the Complex, and yet this was oddly different. "It doesn't smell like the forest on Rennet," he commented after a time, then looked at the woman beside him who was studying him closely. "You don't agree?"

"I do. I'm surprised that you noticed."

He shrugged and stood slowly as a ship passed somewhere above them. They couldn't hide, not in the Complex. But getting beyond it was even crazier than trying to hide in it. There was no way to travel, no ship they could find that the Elite couldn't follow. And despite all his years in space, the one thing Gray was certain of was that there was nothing beyond their solar system. Explorers had disappeared over the centuries trying to find life. It just wasn't out there. He didn't know how far they had travelled, as too many had never returned.

As another ship rumbled above him, one small part of his brain thought perhaps there was something or someone out there who had prevented their return. But he didn't really want to think about it. There was enough diversity amongst the planets within his known realm to keep him occupied, he decided, and no matter the risk of the Elite, he wouldn't be trying to find out if there was something else out there.

He turned one way and then the other to find he was alone in the grove. His heart actually stopped beating. "Isla?" he whispered, too scared there might be someone around who had found her.

He heard her call, a muffled sound, and he walked around the tree. "Isla!" he whispered hoarsely. Again, he heard something, but it appeared to come from the tree. Had it really come from the tree? He stared at it. A hand appeared through the bark and motioned towards him. He stepped back. Isla appeared half out of the trunk, and Gray was sure his legs gave way as she reached out and grabbed him, dragging him towards her.

He was standing in the dark, her hand tight in his. "Are we *in* the tree?"

A finger pressed against his lips. They were standing close, but it wasn't as though they were trapped within the confines of what he knew was inside a tree. "Is the rohen in the tree?" he tried to whisper around the finger, and it was joined by two others pressing more firmly on his lips.

He couldn't hear anything. Couldn't make out anything but the dark. He wondered then, despite the tight hold she had on his hand, why she wasn't as shaky as she usually was in the dark. He had so many questions. Why did she think this was safe? Why was she scared in the first place? Very little scared this woman, and if the dark scared her, he felt as though he too should be worried.

He heard footsteps, loud, crunching through the grass and stepping over twigs. It was almost as though he could see it, sense them. He pulled Isla's hand away from his face, and she rested her head against his shoulder as she drew in a deep breath. Soldiers, Elite—he could see them in his mind's eye. Their uniforms against the green backdrop, their boots moving carefully through the grass. He could hear every blade of grass bend. Their weapons held at the ready to kill before they asked any questions.

One towards the back of the group stopped as they spread out through the trees. Calder. Gray shivered as Isla did. She still had a tight hold of his hand, and he reached out to feel nothing around them. He wasn't sure if that should worry him more. But whether this was the metal or the woman, it was keeping him alive.

"Where are they?" Calder murmured, the feel of his breath moving across Gray's skin as though the man had asked him the question directly.

"Not here, no sign."

Calder stepped up to the tree, and it was almost as though Gray was looking him in the eye. He squatted down and ran his fingers through the grass that grew at the base of the tree. "They were here," he mumbled, straightening up. "Look again."

"Sir," one soldier said, and they moved without question or complaint around the trees. Calder looked up into the branches above him.

"Go up," he instructed.

Gray wondered if the rohen was trying to protect them or move them into the area. Was it testing Calder? Was it working with him? Gray's heart beat too fast. Isla stepped back from him, although she still held his hand. She moved out into the sunlight and, Gray was sure, into the path of the man standing by the tree. He tried to hold her back, but he couldn't.

And then he was back in the room they had been in earlier. He blinked at the unnatural light. As she let go of his hand, he leant back against the wall.

"You have to trust," she said.

"Trust you—or the metal that is moving us around this planet and into the path of the man who wants us dead?"

"Do you really think that is the case?"

"I don't know. I don't get any of this," he said, sliding down the wall to sit on the floor. Too much had happened, and none of it made any sense. "Where is Reilly?"

"I don't know."

"You were with him, on the moon—"

"We both were," she interrupted.

"I was unconscious."

"And he was flying away in my dragonfly."

"Could you see him? Calder? In the trees?"

She nodded but said nothing.

"Are you working with the Elite to capture us?"

She looked truly lost for a moment as she turned to take him in. "What?"

"No 'what the hell, Gray'? No 'they are trying to kill me too'? You're just going to stand there and try to look as though I've lost my mind. I suppose I dreamt all this, the scars"—he indicated her body with a wave of his hand—"the moving walls, the overhearing, all of it."

She stood unmoving, not saying a word; and, as usual unless she wanted him to, he couldn't read her. He had never been able to read her. The idea stung, like her climbing into the bed last night, snuggling against his body, taking his hand. Leading him to Calder.

"Was any of it real?"

"You kept saying that you were saving me," she whispered. For a moment she sounded hurt, but he couldn't trust the act.

"I heard things. I found you by accident. Maybe you started the rumours—maybe you planted the bomb."

Isla's face hardened, and she closed to him completely. The look reminded him of the Elite on the Sparrow when they had been led astray, or at least led in to be patsies. Yet here he was being sacrificed again, thinking he was working to save someone else, help an old friend in some odd way.

"Did you kill Kalli?" he asked, the words harsh and hateful as an anger bubbled in his chest that he hadn't felt in some time. He wasn't sure what to do with it except direct it at the soldier before him.

She turned and ran then, the door opening, and she was gone before he had the chance to take it back. Not that he wanted to—not until the moment she spun, her loose hair catching the light, and he saw the horror on her face. She had been truly scared the night before, with the blood and the new wounds. But the whole series of events only made sense if she was working with Calder, and Gray was sure he had been taken in.

Twenty-Two

Isla stumbled down the hallway, unsure where she was headed or what she could do to make this right. She could hand herself over to Calder, who would likely have her killed before he could claim her for Hendra. She should have died that day, and now she didn't even carry the scars of what she had survived. The only tangible link she'd had to the nightmare that plagued her.

For the first time, she had thought there might be a way through the darkness, that she didn't need to hold on to the scars, that there might be more. But one question had ended that, and she wasn't so sure surviving was what she wanted.

He was just a man, just someone who was sure she needed saving when she very clearly didn't. And yet, Gray's words had hurt. They had cut her more sharply than the metal swords had that night. Deeper than she'd ever thought someone could hurt her again. She shook her head as she bounded along the hallway, bouncing off the walls. When a door slid open, she moved through it with little thought.

He was the first person she had allowed herself to connect too. And she should have known better. She knew perfectly well what happened when she got close to people—they died. This was worse. It was as though he wanted her dead. Gray thought she was still what she had been, but that had stopped that night. It had all stopped.

The room before her came into sharp focus, dragging her back from her thoughts. It was perfectly white, every surface, every fabric. And yet it didn't appear clean. A figure moved by the wall. Isla had to blink to ensure she had seen something, and then they were gone. Or she hadn't seen them. The white hair, the pale skin, the dark eyes.

The door opened behind her, and someone cleared their throat. Isla turned slowly to take in Chief Ebberah of Oric, her hands held together in front of her midsection. She appeared relaxed, yet Isla knew too well that she wasn't.

"I got lost," she muttered.

"I thought you were hiding."

Isla scratched at her head, searching for the words, her hair loose from the braid. She felt a moment of longing for her cream, not that it would have kept her hair neat for long.

"You look different," Ebberah said, stepping closer.

Isla shook her head quickly.

"Your scars."

Isla looked down at herself, completely covered in the black fabric of the soldier's uniform. "You can't see..."

"I see far more than you could imagine. You are limiting my options. Another who has lied to us."

"No," Isla said quickly, feeling her control of the situation slipping away. She had thought the rohen could help, but maybe Gray was right—maybe it wasn't helping her. Maybe it was working against her. The walls seemed to shift around her, and she felt lost. Isla's vision blurred. She staggered, slipping to her knees. A young woman stood over her—the white Isla had been sure she'd seen against the wall—her lank white hair, hanging down as she looked over Isla.

"We will have to give her up," the quiet voice of the child said.

"I thought she could be useful," Ebberah said.

"Only in sending the Elite away, and the attention of the Hendra with them."

Isla wanted to ask more, learn what they were talking about, but her vision faded to black, and she felt as though she was cocooned in a bed of warm rohen. "Do as you will," she whispered, any strength she had slipping away.

All that fighting, all that surviving, had taken its toll. She couldn't do it anymore; she didn't want to do it anymore. She had wasted the last six years trying to outlive what she should have let take her.

As the warm metal slowly enveloped her, clarity came. They hadn't let her die, and she should have. But they had worked against it, against nature, to ensure she was the witness to tell the story. She searched for what had happened in the dark, but she still couldn't find it. The truth was off in the distance; she couldn't reach it.

Distant voices talked over each other, the same words again and again. They were telling her the story of what had happened, showing her the footage, telling her what she had seen, what she had said. But still she couldn't remember what had come before. She learnt the lines, learnt the stories, and they became the memory.

If she asked why, asked what had been the reason behind it all, they only told her the story again, as though she hadn't learnt it. But it wasn't enough—it wouldn't be enough. She sighed into the silver expanse that surrounded her, comforted by the memory as though it was enough to know it had been planted. Even though she would never remember the truth behind it.

A sword flashed in the dark, and she cried out. But someone else was crying out. Through the haze, it was like it had been earlier in the tree, as though she could see the men in the room, their weapons humming through her. The metal pulled away, and she was left on the floor. But it was only momentary before she was lifted, barely conscious of what was happening around her. She searched the room as the metal ran into the walls and the white girl, almost lost against the wall, disappeared with the metal. The group focused on Isla.

"She broke in!" Ebberah screamed. "She has this odd skill. Metal came from nowhere."

Nothing was said. She was just dragged from the room, her feet never coming close to the floor. After a moment of traveling through blank corridors, someone behind her asked, "Sparrow?"

"What?" Isla asked. But there was no response, either about the sparrow or why they had asked. She struggled then to understand the meaning. The word sang to her like a bird singing a familiar song, yet she couldn't understand the words. She laughed and then pulled away, surprised at her own reflexes as one of the men carrying her tried to slap her. The party stopped. Calder came closer, and she would have glared at him if she'd thought it was worth the effort.

"Did you bring the metal with you?"

She couldn't understand what he meant. Didn't he know it was everywhere? Didn't everyone know it was everywhere? "I don't control it," she whispered.

He scoffed then and walked, the small convoy following. "I don't believe you."

"It would have taken me away, if I did."

He slowed but didn't stop, glancing around at her, and then he was nodding to the doorway that led to a lift. She wondered absently if they were going to throw her from the roof or fly away with her.

Isla was surprised to find the lift travelling down. Someone stood in front of the flashing lights to indicate what level they were on, but Isla sensed it as though the metal around the shaft screamed at her to run. She wasn't going to now. It was too late.

An odd sensation covered her skin, and she thought of the child—no, young woman—she had seen in the chief's room. Unwashed, unsure of herself. She had moved the metal. She had been in control within that space. She was a hummer. Isla knew Ebberah would never endanger the young woman, and she wondered what the woman had planned.

The lift stopped, and Isla found herself looking out into a dark hall. Her feet planted themselves into the floor, her legs rigid, and despite the hands on her arms they couldn't move her forward. A boot hit the back of her knee, and she cried out as she fell hard into the floor. She was losing her edge. Gray had done that; Gray had broken far more than she'd thought he had the power to do.

She was dragged out into the hall. The light from the lift shaft lit some way into the space, but not far.

"No," she said simply.

Calder grinned.

"The great war hero is afraid of the dark," one of the others scoffed.

"I'm surprised you survived at all," another remarked.

"Who said I did?" she asked quietly.

Several of them looked between themselves. If nothing else, she had unsettled a few. They didn't know how to take her. They weren't real soldiers, not like they had been trained to be.

Isla was shoved then, hard, and she landed with a groan on her back on the cold floor. Surely, they didn't think they could keep her here. They were quick to rush back into the lift, but something made her sit up as Calder, the last to enter, was silhouetted against the light. A sharp pain drove into her chest.

"Kalli?"

There was the smallest hesitation as he stepped into the lift. Not long enough for anyone else to have realised it had happened—but she knew this man. She had known him better than anyone. Whoever Calder might be, he was once a bear. The Bear.

The door closed before she could say anything else, and the space around her was suddenly completely pitch black. She blinked madly, but it made no difference; her heart rate was too fast. If they reappeared in the space, she would be unable to deal with one of them, let alone all eight.

She sucked in a deep breath, trying to imagine herself somewhere else, but in the dark she could only imagine the field that day, the flash of swords, the screams and cries of those she knew and cared for as family. Kalli wasn't there. In the madness, amidst the burning pain that would not stop, she searched the faces around her but couldn't find him.

She remembered that from her recovery, searching for him, the desperation she'd felt that he wasn't there. They had tried to reassure her, remind her in a way that he was gone. That they were all gone. But it wasn't that he wasn't there with her when she needed him. It was that he hadn't been there with them when the attack had occurred.

Suddenly Gray made sense. The man who had searched her out, the man who had stayed by her to ensure she was safe. The one who just happened to be there when Calder had taken her to the mine. He knew who and what Calder was—what he had always been—and the story he had told her wasn't the truth. Like all the stories she had been told in the last six years, there was something else behind it, the truth lost.

He had found her for Calder, and when she had been lost, he had found her again. Isla lay back on the cool floor, longing for the world to take her away, when she heard footsteps echoing through the darkness.

Either someone was already here, or there was another way to access this space. The footsteps grew closer. It wasn't the bear. She remembered the way he moved, or the way he *had* moved. Far more had changed than his face, or she would have recognised him sooner. She lay still and waited.

The footsteps echoed across the darkness. "We need you," an older voice whispered. "She didn't want to put you in danger, and if she could have kept you hidden, she would have. How did you find the child?"

"She's a hummer," Isla said. Any emotion she had felt, all of them were lost now. As though her body no longer needed them. Like in the days when she had cried herself dry and so no longer needed to cry. Her fingers moved to her cheek, reminded of the previous night, but it had been one moment of weakness.

"How can you be sure?"

"I am." She sat slowly, unsure where he was in the darkness and yet not afraid. "Maybe that is why I found her. But it doesn't matter. I wouldn't tell."

"We need you," he repeated.

"She is your child," Isla whispered as a hand closed around her arm. "You are protecting her."

"It is my job," he said, but there was something there, something behind the bravado that told Isla she was right. This man not only worked for the chief of Oric, he loved her and their child.

"She's different," Isla said.

Silence followed, and then he pulled her to her feet.

"They will know that you have taken me," she said, but he led her away from the lift. A moment of familiar panic filled her chest. And then a soft light glowed along the wall. She watched it, looking for signs of fungi or life. There weren't any, but she sensed the metal. In all she had worked with the master to learn, she hadn't been able to sense the metal. Now that she understood the rohen, it was as though she couldn't get away from it.

"Gray is looking for you," he said.

She stopped. She didn't want to see him. But then they were inside a small space, the pale green light making his features appear unnatural. As the shaft carried them higher, the light became gradually lighter. Was she leaving the dark behind for something better? The door opened into a small, dimly lit space, and then she heard his voice again as they stepped forward. Still not what she remembered. But now that she knew who he was, there was something familiar in it.

The soldier beside her lifted a finger to his lips and then pointed to a space. She nodded her head once and stood on the spot he indicated. The panel closed silently behind her. He walked around the wall before her and disappeared.

"There you are, Hari," Ebberah greeted. "I want you close. They found the girl in my rooms, but they can't find the other one."

"The Sparrow," Calder kindly answered for her.

"How, my lady, did such a thing happen? I'll speak with your guards directly. I was searching further afield, and I have had no reports."

Calder sighed then, and Isla knew that he didn't believe him. "I'm not sure the boy is of much consequence. We know what the Sparrow did, and he might be the only one left." Isla wondered if he knew more of Reilly than she had previously thought. Had he been used by Gray as well, or was he in on the situation? "It is the soldier we need. She is something far more dangerous, and we cannot allow her to run around the Complex unchecked."

"I would certainly prefer if she wasn't running around my part of it." Ebberah cleared her throat. "The Hendra would be terribly upset if it were my fault she was free."

"I don't think..." her guard started.

"You will have much to answer for." Her voice was strained, the unstable leader on show. "I will have all your guards reviewed, all your checkpoints checked." She cleared her throat. "Colonel Calder, I would like to impose upon you, if I could."

"I think I am busy enough, Your Grace," he added, but the words carried little respect.

"You will not leave her here?" The panic was evident in her voice again.

"We will not," he said gravely.

"I am relieved," she sighed. "And when will you take her?"

"We will fly out first thing tomorrow, whether we have found the Sparrow or not. The Hendra herself would oversee this."

"Of course," Ebberah said, and Isla could hear the lush material of her dress rustle as she stood. "You will continue to search for the man in the meantime, won't you? You might not think him a threat, but I can't bear to think of him somewhere loose on my planet."

"Your Grace," he said, and Isla waited as they disappeared from the room. She wondered if Gray would pretend to be taken or play along with their charade. Entering the space, she took in the grandeur of Ebberah's dress.

"Do you have a ball?" she asked before she could stop herself.

Ebberah opened and closed her mouth, clearly frustrated, then looked to the soldier. "Hari, tell her."

"We need you to determine what the Hendra is attempting to achieve."

"How do you propose I do that from a cell?"

"They won't kill you," Ebberah said, turning to the window and looking out across a city that was covered in a dull orange light, the sunset muted by the low-hanging moon. Isla wondered if the Readers would be of any use to her now. "They need a hummer."

"And you would rather they take me."

Ebberah nodded without turning from the view.

"And if I have no interest in surviving?"

Ebberah turned then, confusion filling her face. "Why would you say that?"

Isla shook her head. She didn't want to go through her thought process again, not with this woman. She might finally do some good for the Complex if she tried what she wanted. And if she died in the process, it didn't matter.

"What of Gray?" Hari asked.

"I'm sure he has friends to help," Isla said. She wondered where her satchel was. Lost in the metal, maybe. It had given her the gift to make the ointment and then taken it away. Maybe she no longer needed it. They shared a look she didn't understand. "How will I tell you what I find?"

"You'll work it out," Ebberah said, waving her hand towards the door. "They'll be checking on you soon. I'm afraid you will need to return."

Isla surprised herself with a nod before she walked back to the hidden lift on her own and disappeared inside.

Focus on the mission, she told herself. *All I have to do is focus.* She hoped that would be enough.

Twenty-Three

G ray felt sick at the idea that he could have imagined, for even a moment, that he couldn't trust Isla. All his fears, all his concerns that she was not what he had hoped, vanished too long after she had left the room. The hurt in her eyes had played over and over in his mind, torturing him and reminding him how stupid he was. It was his fault she was in Calder's hands, and he had no idea what he could do to help her this time. They were eight Elite soldiers. He would struggle with a couple—with eight, he didn't stand a chance.

Hari had tried to explain that Isla was safe, that they would want to use her for her skills rather than kill her. He had nodded dumbly. He knew what she had, but who knew what they might do to get her to do what they wanted? He had pushed her away and into their trap, and now it was up to him to get her out.

Neither Hari nor the chief were prepared to step in again, other than to tell him she was being held on the lowest level of the building while the soldiers prepared to leave. Gray helped himself to a duster and a rifle not nearly as nice as the Barilla from the armoury of the chief's guard. He couldn't let her disappear again. He needed to let her know that he trusted her, that he had made a mistake.

Gray was certain there was an easier way to reach where she was without alerting Calder and his men, but that information wasn't forthcoming either. He didn't have the time to work it out. He stepped into the nearest lift and aimed for the lowest level, but when he exited the lift he was still far above the city. It took him too long to jog through the corridors, passing no one, and then he found another lift and headed down again.

The lift opened into a dark space, and he moved quickly out of the light trying to adjust to the dark. If he had been unlucky enough to stumble into Calder's men, he had no doubt they would have fired upon him without hesitation. He crept forward, trying to determine where he was and what these levels were used for. He doubted anyone entered via the street. An idea formed that there might be an unused exit they could take advantage of.

All he had to do was find Isla and not get killed by Calder. How hard could it be? He longed for Isla's gift with the metal and the ability to move through walls, or at least have them open up. He had pushed his hand against a wall at one point and begged. But it must not have heard what he needed like it did for her, because nothing had happened.

He stretched out the weapon in his hand. It banged against something, the sound echoing through the space. He cringed, holstered it and stepped forward, running his hand over the cool wall. Someone thumped a table, and light flickered in the corner of the room.

Gray rested his hand on the duster but realised the scene before him was odd. He wasn't in the room; he was somewhere else, maybe in the wall. It was similar to when they had been in the tree, only Isla wasn't holding his hand and he had no idea where she was. At least the rohen appeared to be helping him in some way. He whispered his thanks.

"This woman is more dangerous than we understand," a soldier said, his voice carrying in the sparsely furnished room. "I think we should ensure she doesn't reach the Hendra."

"And then you can explain why the woman she has asked for is dead." Calder was emotionless. "Although you are likely to be dead before you get the chance."

The man sighed.

"She is one woman, Mal," another said. "There is no way she can escape us."

The other man hummed, as though he didn't quite believe him.

"No harm is to come to her," Calder snapped.

"Sir," they chorused.

"Go and check," Calder said, indicating across the room with his chin.

Mal stood, but Calder stared, and he sat back down. Another soldier stood and headed directly towards Gray.

He needed to get to where she was first. He stumbled backward, finding himself inside another lift. As the door opened, the soldier looked at him with surprise. Gray slammed his hand into the panel as the soldier raised his weapon and fired, and the doors slid shut.

The shot shaved across his shoulder and burnt into the wall behind him.

The lift hummed softly, and the doors slid open to complete darkness. He searched the wall for a switch or a panel. "Come on," he grumbled, then realised the light from the lift behind him would have lit him up. He was rushing, not thinking, and losing his mind. But when no more bolts shot at him, he realised he must have come out on another level. He raised the duster all the same and stepped out.

In the silence, his boots squeaked across the floor. The Elite could be sneaking around him and he would never know. He only hoped Isla wasn't somewhere here in the dark and at risk of getting caught in the crossfire.

"Did he change his mind?" Isla's voice rang out. She sounded odd, different, and although he knew she didn't like the dark, that wasn't it.

"Who?" he called, then ducked as a flash of light from a weapon lit up the space for only an instant. There was a soldier in the space, only Gray had no idea how he had arrived or where he was. Isla had been standing in the middle of the space; she'd looked different in that little flash of light. She'd looked hard.

"Kalli."

"What?" Gray found it harder to hold the duster up as the air left his lungs. Was she working with him? Was he not dead? "What?" he mumbled again, trying to understand what she was saying.

"Gray?" she called, and he dropped to his knees as something hard hit him on the back of the head. Not hard enough to knock him out, but it did the damage it was intended to do.

"Enough!" Calder's voice boomed through the space.

Lights flickered around him. He wasn't sure if they had come on or if his vision was going. Isla was closer than he had thought. She still looked hard, and he thought of how different she had looked the night before when her scars had disappeared. He wanted to reach her, but he couldn't. He had managed to maintain his hold on the duster. His hand was surprisingly shaky when he lifted it up, the gentle hum moving through him as it trained on Calder.

"What did you do to Kalli?" Gray wheezed. Isla took another small step towards him.

"Enough!" he bellowed again, the sound piercing his aching skull. "What do you think this is?"

"Kalli," Isla said, her voice too calm, too cold.

"He is dead, little dragonfly, long dead."

"If he ever existed in the first place."

"What are you talking about?" Mal asked. As he stepped forward, the large colonel held out a hand, and he stopped.

"I've told you," he warned, although he was looking at Isla as he said it. The soldier stepped back.

The duster felt heavy in Gray's hand. He blinked, trying to regain control and maintain consciousness.

"Someone take that," Calder directed, and the duster was ripped from Gray's hand with very little he could do about it. "You aren't doing very well at keeping her safe, are you?"

Gray gulped down whatever words he might have said. He was trying to understand why Isla was talking about Kalli. What did Calder know? The large man shifted from foot to foot.

"I only need one of you," he said.

"Then take him," Isla said, her back straight. She didn't take her eyes from the man before her.

"Somehow I think you would be more compliant if I had him along to threaten you with."

"We aren't friends," she said—too easily, Gray thought. "He is your friend, Kalli."

"Sir?" Mal asked again. Before Gray could fully understand what he had done, Calder raised a duster of his own and the man was gone. Disintegrated in a single blast. A different kind of silence fell on the room.

"You never were a good team player," Isla said, and Gray watched the smile light up her face. "Even when you were *good* with the team, you were never really part of it."

Calder swung the weapon towards her. The anger seethed openly on his face, but his hand never wavered.

"It doesn't frighten me," she said as he stepped a little closer. "I should already be dead. I am, in some ways, fighting my way through a world I'm not meant to be in. Pull the trigger, Kalli—you would be doing me a favour."

"I am not who you think I am," Calder said, his voice level as he lowered the weapon and then holstered it.

"I won't call you Bear," Isla said, crossing her arms, but she smiled as though she were chatting to a friend at a bar. Calder growled something as he stomped towards her, and for the first time Gray understood why they had called him the Bear. Isla raised her chin to him. Her head snapped to the side, and the sound of his fist against her face echoed in the room. But she didn't move. It was as though her feet were glued to the floor. Her body held firm. She scared Gray. She clearly scared the man before her, and that was why he was prepared to destroy what he had already destroyed one of his own men for.

"Get the ship warmed up," he growled. "Cuff them."

Several men ran for the lift. Another moved towards Gray, who didn't have the strength to stop him. He was cuffed with wide plastic ties that were pulled too tight, and he was dragged to his feet. He swayed. The soldier kept him standing by pulling tighter on the plastic ties, which cut into his wrists.

Isla stood with her hands outstretched, an odd smile on her lips. Calder pushed the man who had cuffed her out of the way and stepped up close.

"You don't scare me," he whispered. "Hendra is going to love what you can do."

Isla reached forward and kissed him. He stood too still for too long. As he stepped back, she grinned again, then raised Calder's duster and took out the man beside Gray. He swayed and slipped back to his knees as Calder used his entire body to knock Isla to the ground. The duster skittered across the floor. Gray watched it slide out of reach.

Isla groaned as Calder pressed her head into the ground, his knee on her back.

"Go on," she said, her eyes closed. "You know I want to die. Help me get there, Kalli."

He was off her in a heartbeat, pulling her to her feet and then lifting her up by the ties around her wrists. She winced. Gray knew it was taking all she had not to show him just how much it hurt as the plastic bit into her skin.

"Get him up!" Calder barked. And then they were being shuffled into the lift, squashed between soldiers. Gray wondered whether she could reach the rifle he had strapped to his back if he somehow got her attention and managed to turn in the tight space.

He had thought Isla was somewhat reckless before, and now she didn't care if she died. He looked at the tall man beside her. He might have been the same size, but there was nothing of his old friend there. Nothing that indicated he was the man Gray had followed this woman for.

The bright lights as the lift opened made him squint. He was confused, and his head ached. Hari stepped between the group, moving across the landing bay, and Ebberah as Calder murmured something. Gray thought she had looked happy at seeing them captured, but as he glanced back, she looked somewhat defiant. He wondered just what benefit their capture was to her.

The cool wind blew around them. Gray noticed the loose curls of Isla's red hair moving in an odd slow-motion dance, escaped from the confines of her braid. A large bruise was already forming on the side of her face. They were shuffled inside the ship, strapped in across from each other, and Gray couldn't take his eyes off her.

"Why does she call you Kalli?" one of the soldiers asked as Calder secured the door.

"She's insane," Calder said coldly, double checking that Isla was secured in her seat and heading through to the flight deck. "You know what happened, don't you? Lost her entire unit, and she might think we are it. She'll start calling you by another man's name soon enough."

The soldier mumbled something as he took a seat by the door. Isla raised her green eyes to Gray, for the first time acknowledging he was there. *I'm sorry,* he mouthed. She just barely nodded, and he knew she understood. Or at least she had heard him.

"How did you survive that day?" the soldier beside her asked.

"I didn't."

He seemed a bit confused for a moment, looking to Gray and then back.

"I didn't die," she said with a sigh. "But I didn't survive."

The soldier looked towards Calder, no doubt thinking he was right and the woman was insane. Although if it were Gray, he wouldn't want to be involved in a mission to collect an insane woman with likely more training than he had. Isla closed her eyes and leaned back against the hard wall of the ship. For a moment, Gray thought the wall behind her moved. But he said nothing and gave no indication that he had seen anything. They were watching him just as closely.

"Why?" Gray asked after a time, looking away from Isla when he was sure she wouldn't disappear before him and focusing on

Calder's back. Could he really be the friend Gray had lost so long ago? "You knew who I was on the Sparrow."

"I serve the Hendra, and I will deliver what she commands. Only Hendra," he said.

Gray blinked and refocused on Isla. Sitting too still and silent. The straps around her wrists had already cut through her skin. He wanted to take her hands and assure her that it would work out, but he wasn't sure it would. And despite her strength in the dark, he feared she might have given up the fight.

Epilogue

In the stark white room, Tevia stepped out from the wall. She had heard the ship leaving, felt the loss of the woman as it had lifted from the landing bay, and yet she knew it was where she had to be.

"You are sure?" she asked, running her fingers through her hair to pull it back from her face and then rubbing her oily fingers across her leg. The wall rippled beside her. "I was sure," she said. "I knew she was needed elsewhere." She spoke with confidence, and yet she missed her, missed the connection.

"She doesn't understand what she is," a soft voice whispered across the wall.

"You will help her find out. You will show her what she is."

"If we can, if we must."

The door clicked softly, and she sat on the couch. Her mother's gaze shifted to her as she moved into the room. She could hide from her, but she didn't want to.

"They have gone," she said.

Tevia nodded.

"I'm not sure she can do as I need her to do."

Tevia smiled. There were greater plans for Island Tarle, different plans for the world her mother was so sure she understood yet knew so little of.

"She has skill," her mother continued, looking around the room as though someone else might be there. Hari, perhaps. The girl sighed. Hari would get in the way.

"I helped," she said.

"Of course you did," her mother said sweetly, her focus elsewhere. "We must keep you hidden." Tevia wondered if she really was in any danger. Certainly not nearly the amount that her mother was so sure of. There were other ways she could remain hidden. The Hendra didn't even know of her existence, let alone who she was, who she was connected to.

"Don't do that," her mother said absently, and Tevia lifted her hand from the couch as the silver threads disappeared into the fabric.

If only she could explain that she didn't call to the Rohen—they called to her. All of them. And she would serve them before her mother, before what she thought was best for the Complex.

Hari appeared, and they exchanged a look. She would listen later to what they thought were secrets. What they thought they were doing to win the Complex back from the power of the Hendra. Only she knew that the Hendra didn't have the control she thought she did. Not even close.

Acknowledgements

The team at Deranged Doctor Designs (DDD) for absolutely brilliant cover design work and all the marketing extras. Thank you for your support and clear emails around what was needed from me to make the magic happen.

TWG members for listening and support in all things writing related. Special thanks to Yasmin, for taking the time to read my draft and providing ideas to make the story stronger.

Allison E Wright for wonderful editing work to make my sentences smoother and my intentions clearer.

My parents, Francine and Ken Smith. Amazing, supportive people who I don't thank often enough. Thanks for keeping me grounded and being the best grandparents ever.

As always, Temwa for being my biggest supporter.

About the Author

Georgina Makalani survives life as a servant of the public by hiding in her office at lunch time with dragons, witches, a laptop and a little bit of magic.

For more about Georgina and her books visit her website: www.theflowofink.com